ONE
FOR
SORROW

MARY REED AND ERIC MAYER are a husband and wife team writing under the name M.E. Mayer. Mary was born in Newcastle-on-Tyne and ran the Theology Faculty office at Oxford University before she emigrated to America and met her husband and co-author Eric, who also writes comic books, as well as programming text-based computer games and interactive fiction.

DEATH · IN · BYZANTIUM

ONE FOR SORROW

·

TWO FOR JOY

·

THREE FOR A LETTER

·

FOUR FOR A BOY

·

FIVE FOR SILVER

·

SIX FOR GOLD

·

SEVEN FOR A SECRET

·

EIGHT FOR ETERNITY

·

NINE FOR THE DEVIL

ONE
FOR
SORROW

M.E. MAYER

HEAD
ZEUS

First published in the UK in 2012 by Head of Zeus, Ltd.

9 7 5 3 1 2 4 6 8

A CIP catalogue record for this book is available from
the British Library.

ISBN (HB) 9781781850046
ISBN (TPB) 9781781850053
ISBN (E) 9781908800893

Printed in Germany.

Head of Zeus, Ltd
Clerkenwell House
45-47 Clerkenwell Green
London EC1R 0HT

www.headofzeus.com

Dedicated to Eric's Grammy, who read *The Wind in the Willows* to him, and to all the Reedies

Acknowledgments

Our thanks to the following for their assistance: Sir Rodney Hartwell, Dr. Robert Cleve, Professor Robert Gurval, Dr. Robert Ousterhout, Samuel S. Long II, and to Mike Ashley, who introduced John, The Lord Chamberlain, to the world.

Bosporos

Wall of
Theodosius

Wall of
Constantine

Golden
Horn

Forum
Bovis

Forum
Theodosius

Forum of
Constantine

Mese

Forum
Arkadios

Sea of Marmara

5   4   8

6

2

1   3   Great
Palace

7

1. Hippodrome
2. Church of the Holy Wisdom
3. Baths of Zeuxippos
4. Stylite

5. Isis' House
6. Inn of the centours
7. John's House
8. Cistern of Hermes

Chapter One

On an unnaturally hot and humid spring evening in 535 AD, during the reign of Roman Emperor Justinian, the unruly celebration of the founding of Constantinople had shifted from the city's Hippodrome to its forums, streets, and alleys. In the narrow passages between tenements, revelers drank, sang, and cursed and blundered into fights or liaisons in a miasma formed of sweat, torch smoke, and cheap wine and perfume. Many would wake the next morning with headaches that would have them praying for death. Others would in fact be dead before the coppery sun materialized out of the sea mists. Among them would be one of four friends from the Great Palace.

The tall, lean Greek from the palace strode straight through the crowds. Something in his look and bearing cleared a path before him. As people stepped aside they whispered.

"Isn't that…?"

"Yes. It's the Lord Chamberlain."

"The one called John the Eunuch?"

"Not within his earshot, fool! Quiet!"

If John heard he gave no sign. He spoke quietly but forcefully to the burly, bearded man at his side. "No, Felix. I am sure it was her. Do you think I would forget what she looks like? Fifteen years isn't so long."

Felix served as Captain of the Excubitors, the palace guard. He liked to consider himself a hard-headed man. "It's a long way from where we were sitting to the floor of the Hippodrome. There was the glare from the sunlight, the dust stirred up by the bulls and horses."

"How many bull-leaping troupes do you think there are in the empire today?"

"Until this afternoon, I'd have said none. It's strange."

"I was thinking exactly the same thing when the performers came out onto the track. How strange that I should be seated in the emperor's box, watching a recreation of bull-leaping. When I saw Cornelia for the first time, I was a poor, young mercenary with dust on my boots."

"The girl riding the bull was hardly more than a child, John. She couldn't be the woman you knew."

"I will find her, Felix. Then you'll see."

"You'll have to beat Anatolius to her." Felix referred to their younger friend who had sat with them at the Hippodrome. "He seems to have lost his senses too. It's a good thing Leukos had to leave us to see that so-called soothsayer before the bull-leapers appeared. I'd have to keep all three of you away from each other's throats."

John nodded absently. The memory of the bull-leaper floated before him, obscuring his companion's conversation and the thronged streets.

"I'll wager Anatolius is asking the soothsayer about that girl right now," Felix continued.

"Probably. His appointment was later than Leukos', wasn't it?"

"Yes. The two of us must be the only ones at the palace who haven't had the benefit of the old fraud's wisdom."

"In a month he'll be forgotten, replaced by a new sensation, perhaps the elephant the empress is having sent from India."

"An elephant! There's something much more interesting than any soothsayer. Now let's find a tavern before this mob drinks the city dry."

John regretted having agreed to join Felix after their official duties ended. His body was exhausted, his mind agitated. He wanted only the solitude of his study.

He made his way reluctantly through the swarming streets. Bonfires sent sparks cartwheeling upward toward the thin swatches of night sky visible between the buildings. Men paraded in costume, disguised as demons or wild animals. Others lurched along arm in arm, holding each other upright. Grotesque shadows groped past blank lower story walls toward open windows higher up.

"This will be a long night for the urban watch," muttered Felix. He deftly elbowed aside a staggering duck-headed thing that gave a pitiful cry, collapsed into the gutter, and crawled off. A trio of ruby-lipped women in a doorway laughed shrilly.

The press was thicker in the square opposite the well-known brothel run by Madam Isis. Several men emerged from the building, staggering drunkenly. A corpulent fellow slunk out in their wake, looked around guiltily, and lumbered away as fast he could manage. John thought this was not the evening to stop and talk with his old friend Isis.

"Look," directed Felix, "it's the bear trainer who was entertaining at the Hippodrome."

In the light from the fire in a corner of the square, John saw a bare-chested man in green tights standing in front of a cart which held an iron cage. The bear was a restless shadow behind the bars.

"Who'll be next?" barked the man, brandishing a stout pole at the milling crowd. "Come on! You call yourselves Romans?"

A young man in a brocaded tunic and cloak stumbled forward, pushed by several comrades. One of them flicked a coin at the bear trainer, who followed its flashing arc and plucked it expertly from the air.

The bear trainer held out the pole to the obviously intoxicated young man, who took it gingerly in one hand. He appeared to feel he needed both hands free to remain standing.

"Give 'er a poke, then," ordered the bear trainer.

"You trying to steal Madam's trade?" yelled a wit among the spectators. The young man stood uncertainly, swaying from side to side.

"Go on," repeated the trainer. "Give 'er a poke!"

"Go on, Aoinos!" urged his companions. Their friend took an unsteady step forward and gingerly pushed the pole through the bars.

The bear reacted instantly. With a roar, it caught the pole, wrenching it out of the youngster's hands. The suddenly free end whipped upwards, smashing the would-be tormentor's nose.

The wounded man stumbled backward, turned, swung wildly at his laughing companions, and hit a bystander instead. The stranger pushed the young man down and Aionis' companions took exception.

The bystander had friends too.

Daggers flashed into view.

The surrounding mob surged toward the cart.

Anyone who lived in Constantinople knew that the slightest spark could set off a riot, making a city street more dangerous than a battlefield.

"Quick, let's get away from here," Felix urged.

Before John could react there was a roar, a chilling mixture of shouts and screams, and a mass of humanity crashed into him, like a wave against the seawalls. Caught by surprise he was driven nearly to his knees and propelled across the square. By the time he regained his balance Felix was nowhere to be seen.

The square grew silent. John realized that the crowd had suddenly drawn away from the cart. He pushed through massed bodies until he saw what had caused the flight.

The bear trainer's iron cage had toppled off the cart. Its door was open. Atop the cage an enormous shadow moved.

A woman let out a shriek.

The bear rumbled deep in its throat and jumped to the ground.

John froze. The beast might shamble in any direction.

No longer the tormented, the bear lurched forward. A man in the short, simple tunic of a laborer found himself in the monster's path. His head turned first one way and then the other, but he could not make himself run. His eyes gleamed in the bonfire light. A gurgle of fear escaped his throat and he crumpled to the ground. The bear, heedless, stepped over him.

The beast's head swung from side to side, and then stopped, its bright, hard eyes focusing intently. It turned, advancing purposefully toward Madam Isis' doorway.

That was where the bear trainer cowered.

The man whirled around nimbly, doubtless seeking to escape inside. But the bear was already moving. As the trainer's hand scrabbled at the door, the bear's massive jaws were already tearing out the side of his throat. Blood spilled down the trainer's chest.

While the bear occupied itself, drawn swords and daggers glinted and a few onlookers cautiously moved toward the oblivious animal.

John didn't wait to see what happened. He glanced about for Felix and, failing to see him, moved toward an alleyway as the quickest route of escape.

The alley was little more than a crevice between buildings which leaned toward each other overhead. Away from the fire-lit square, the night was impenetrable. Unseen cobbles were slippery underfoot. John steadied himself by running a hand along the rough side of the wall of the tenement opposite Isis' house. He heard a rat skitter out of his way. The air stunk.

His boot was caught by something soft but bulky and he toppled forward. His knee banged down painfully on the stones.

Darkness shimmered before his eyes, dropping a veil of black silk as he scrambled to hands and knees. At least, he thought, the cobbles here were dry. He was blinking, trying to see what had tripped him, when shutters flew open directly above and closed just as quickly.

In the flash of light from the window John looked down into a pale but familiar face. The eyes were wide open, blue lips drawn back.

John spoke the man's name, but his friend did not answer.

Chapter Two

During the afternoon, when the dead man was still alive, John had sat with him and the others at the Hippodrome. Between the chariot races there had been other entertainment. Acrobats, wild animals. A trained bear.

The bear amused the spectators when it was down on the floor of the Hippodrome and not in their midst. They shouted their approval from the safety of the stands as the animal lashed out futilely at its trainer. Restrained by a chain, the bear could not quite reach the man's wagging buttocks.

Shifting his lean flanks on the hard marble bench, John had sympathized with the wretched bear. This afternoon he felt chained himself. Chained by his high position at the court, weighed down by his richly embroidered ceremonial robes. The sunlight was too fierce for early May. A tepid sea breeze did nothing to relieve his discomfort.

What did the friends beside him make of it, he wondered?

Felix, the excubitor captain, scowling intensely, was probably gauging the trainer's deftness with the trident he was brandishing at the bear.

Anatolius, who wrote poems when he was not serving as imperial secretary, looked as if he were only half-attending to the performance. The handsome and elegantly dressed young man might be composing an ode, but to the bear or to its tormenter?

The Keeper of the Plate, Leukos, was a kind man, a devout Christian. John was not surprised to notice him frown and look away as the trainer darted in at the captive animal, prodded it with the trident, pirouetted, and retreated.

"I suppose our empress is enjoying the entertainment," remarked Anatolius, "considering her father was a bear keeper."

"Indeed." From his seat in the emperor's box, John could see only the backs of the elevated thrones occupied by the emperor and empress. Theodora's father had died when she was a child, leaving her family destitute. The racing partisans known as the Greens had turned them away but the Blues had offered charity. Which was why she had spent the afternoon raucously cheering for the Blue chariot teams with all the exuberance of a fisherman's wife.

As an adult she had turned to acting and caught the eye of Justinian. Otherwise she might have been down in the dust assisting the bear trainer instead of observing from a throne.

The bear was chained to a stake directly in front of the imperial box. The trainer broke into a run, circling the stake with a comical, high-stepping gait. The bear, though encumbered, pursued him, still hopeful of exacting revenge for its injuries. So intent was it on its pursuit that it did not notice that every turn around the stake wound its chain tighter, shortening it inexorably so that suddenly the beast found itself trapped, unable to move.

The bear roared its pain and fury to the unheeding sky as its trainer gave the beast's shaggy back a final vicious dig with his trident.

The crowd responded with coin-throwing enthusiasm as the bear trainer finally departed with his ill-treated charge and slaves, swathed in whirling dust devils, removed the stake and raked the arena's churned floor smooth.

"I wish the only enemies I had to guard against were bears attached to lengths of chains," grumbled Felix.

"Don't worry," offered Anatolius. "You don't have any enemies here. At least not within arm's length. You lost our bet though. The bear didn't draw blood."

Felix grunted. "Maybe next time it will."

"Since our enemies don't have chains, our best defense is to learn which way they are going to jump," remarked Leukos. He ran a thin hand across his gleaming, bald scalp. Behind his back the apprentices said their master's skull so resembled a silver bowl that there must be an imperial seal stamped behind one ear.

Anatolius pushed a few dark curls off his forehead and regarded Leukos with surprise. "Why have you been so gloomy this afternoon? What enemies do you have?"

"We all have enemies. You might want to consult the soothsayer who has recently arrived in the city. Perhaps he can point out a few of yours for you."

"Oh, I've heard about him. Who hasn't? He disemboweled a chicken for a certain office holder we won't name and was able, from its guts, to assure this august personage that he would not end up like the unfortunate chicken, or at least not for a week or two. I'm visiting the soothsayer later."

"He's going to be busy today," Leukos said. "I have an appointment with him at the inn in a short while."

"Do you both think it's wise?" put in John. "It might cause the emperor embarrassment if anyone spots his officials dealing with a charlatan like that."

"Actually, he's very knowledgeable," Leukos replied. "I've already had him cast the augurs for me."

Felix shook his head. "Leukos, you of all officials must be aware that the more plausible the rogue, the tighter you need to hold on to the silver. You can't trust people these days."

Anatolius grinned broadly, an expression which diminished somewhat his resemblance to a classic Greek sculpture. "Are you thinking of these kidnappings and extortion plots we've been plagued with lately, or the street violence, or…" he paused for effect, "…is it that little tart at Madam's?"

Felix's directed a chilly gaze at him. "You're a gossip, Anatolius. If you don't watch your tongue you'll lose it."

Anatolius pretended to look hurt. "That's unfair, Felix. Gossips are the ones who spread tales about the patriarch's tribe of illegitimate children—such slander to cast at a churchman—and swear that the emperor is really a faceless demon in human form. I just pass along the news."

Leukos stood up. "I have to be off to see the soothsayer. I'll be glad to be out of this sun." He fumbled with the leather pouch he carried on his belt, closed it, and wiped the sweat from his broad forehead with the back of his hand. "Do you want to come with me, Anatolius?"

"I can find the Inn of the Centaurs, Leukos. I think I'll stay for the next performance and another race or two. I'm not supposed to call on him until the end of the afternoon."

A moment after Leukos had left the imperial box the massive teak gate at the far end of the chariot track slid open and, as the crowd cheered, a monstrous black bull garlanded in blossoms and ribbons charged out into view. The bull raced around the arena's perimeter, violently tossing gold-tipped horns.

John drew in his breath sharply. The magnificent beast was the perfect incarnation of the sacred animal of the Lord of Light, John's own god.

"Mithra!" he exhaled, forgetting for an instant that he was practically within earshot of the ruler of an officially Christian empire.

A trio of figures followed the bull out of the gate. All were clothed in azure loincloths and beribboned chaplets of flowers. Barefooted, they moved smoothly and swiftly along the track until they stood near the imperial box. John realized, with a shock, that they presented the image of bull-leapers from the ancient days of Crete. He had not seen bull-leapers since….he pushed the memory away, as he always did when it ambushed him.

The bull wheeled around, kicking up clods of earth, and then charged at the trio.

Two of the figures, armed with spears, stepped aside. John saw that the remaining figure, unarmed, was a slim woman. His heart leapt as if he were the one confronting the bull.

The spectators' clamor subsided into a silence like that between breaking waves. In the eerie hush, the beat of the bull's hooves carried clearly up into the stands.

The woman stepped forward, raising delicate arms as if preparing to push the onrushing beast aside.

John tried to pick out details of her features, but shimmering heat waves hid her face.

The bull closed in. It lowered its massive head. Horns flashed in the sunlight. The woman left the earth as easily as a sparrow, grabbed the bull's horns, vaulted over them, and landed lightly on the animal's back.

The crowd's thunderous appreciation echoed around the Hippodrome.

The bull whipped its head back and forth, but the woman already sat securely astride its broad back. The maddened beast raced around the track to the far side. As it completed its circuit and galloped back toward where John and his friends were sitting, John could see the gleam of the approaching beast's wild eyes and the foam flecking its mouth. The rider pulled herself up into a crouch and then executed a back flip, ending in a handstand on the arena's floor directly in front of the imperial box.

She made a low bow, then straightened, raising her arms to the noisy adulation of the crowd and gazed up toward the imperial box.

John stared, transfixed. He did not notice how the spear carriers reappeared to chivvy the animal out of the arena. When the woman looked up John had looked straight down into her dark eyes. Eyes in which he had lost himself, years before.

"Look at her!" Anatolius blurted out. "I have to meet her!"

How many times had John heard the same refrain from his younger friend? But this time Anatolius sounded far away, a voice in a dream. John didn't hear what he said next. He didn't notice the second and third bulls, or the rest of the troupe, enter the arena.

"John? What's the matter? You look as if you've seen a demon."

"I knew that woman," John managed to say, his voice little more than a whisper. "Long ago, in another place, we were lovers."

Chapter Three

As he gazed down at the bull-leaper, death had been as far from John's thoughts as when he was twenty-three and watching Cornelia for the first time.

And now, only hours later, Cornelia's dark eyes were replaced by the sightless eyes of John's friend.

He caught only a fleeting glimpse of the face. The shutters of the window which had briefly illuminated the scene had slammed shut and he was alone with the dead man in Stygian darkness.

"Leukos," John said to himself. "What were you doing here?"

He became aware again of the noise of the mob in the square. The shouts and screams had diminished. He heard the bear roar. It sounded far away.

As he peered toward the dim light at the head of the alley a line of fire shot through the night toward him.

He ducked and felt the heat of a torch fly past his face. The still burning torch clattered to the cobbles, leaving John exposed in a ring of light as heavy footsteps thundered toward him.

The murderer or murderers?

His hand went to the dagger he carried. He leapt up and faced a creature out of a nightmare.

A towering, bullish Persian with a braided beard. As the monster raised its sword the flaring torchlight sparkled off dainty wings sprouting from its wide shoulders.

John recognized Madam Isis' doorkeeper.

"Darius!"

The Persian lowered his weapon.

"Lord Chamberlain. I wasn't attacking you. I thought you might be in trouble but now I see…." His gaze went to the body lying on the ground.

"Leukos, the Keeper of the Plate. A friend of mine."

Darius swore. "Let's get him inside before the vultures strip him."

John agreed. If the mob realized there was a dead man here he and Darius would find themselves fighting to defend the body like a couple of soldiers at the gates of Troy.

It was only as they got hold of their awkward load that John noticed Leukos' killer had left a knife in his victim. Had someone scared the murderer off or had the mild palace administrator put up a fight?

John hope the latter had been the case.

They carted Leukos out of the alley.

"If it weren't for these damnable wings I'd have simply thrown the poor man over my shoulder," Darius complained. "Madam has me dressed as Eros."

Luckily the square had emptied out.

Madam Isis greeted them in her brightly lit doorway. An ample woman, whose actual outlines were disguised by layers of billowing pink silks, her face showed traces of the beauty she had once been. "John, thank the goddess you're safe! I thought I saw you when the riot broke out. Who do you have there?"

John explained.

Isis clucked with distress and ushered them inside into a fog of perfume and incense almost as choking as the poisonous stench in the streets. Several barely clothed young women peered at them with curiosity. They laid Leukos' body on a couch in a side hall and Darius left to return to his post, fussing with his right wing which kept flopping forward.

"What were you doing observing the mob, Isis?" John asked.

"I went to the doorway to see the bear. It got away. Broke loose from the crowd. That's why the square's deserted. Everyone fled. Except the trainer."

"Did you see Leukos in the crowd?"

Isis shook her head.

"Was he in here earlier?"

"No, John. I never saw the man, and you know I never forget a patron's face."

"Or remember a patron's name. Yes, I know. I wouldn't have expected Leukos to come here anyway."

John felt lightheaded. The fever of battle that had gripped him as the mob turned violent was fading away and he was beginning to feel the pain of his loss.

"Did you notice anyone who seemed suspicious, looking for trouble, looking for a victim?"

"No. And I always keep a close watch. I pride myself on running the most civilized house in the city. During the celebrations the wolves come out and my establishment is a good place to find stray lambs."

John knew Isis was right. But why had Leukos strayed into the alley next to her house? Unless he had been on his way to his appointment? "Is the Inn of the Centaurs near here?"

"Oh, yes. Just around the corner." Madam described its location. She further agreed that the alley where Leukos died could have served as a short-cut along his route to the inn.

John would have thought Leukos was too cautious to go down alleys, but he had been excited about going to see the soothsayer.

"I'll question all my girls and my guards as well," Isis told him. "Someone might have seen or heard something. It might be one of them saw your friend. That bald head must have stood out in a crowd like the dome of the Church of the Holy Wisdom."

John stared down at the still figure on the couch. It resembled Leukos yet already death had begun to smooth out the details.

Leukos was gone and what was left was as hollow as a bronze statue. Had he reached wherever it was Christians imagined they went after dying?

"I will need to inform the urban watch, Isis. If it will be a problem…."

She waved a pudgy hand and her numerous rings glittered. "It's no problem. I pay the prefect more than the tax collector."

"Besides which, we're here already," boomed a voice from behind John. Three helmeted men wearing leather cuirasses and armed with spears clattered down the hall in hobnailed boots.

"We put the bear trainer—what pieces we could find—in the kitchen," said the man who had addressed John. "A little more blood in the kitchen won't make any difference. Someone will be round shortly to collect him." The man directed his gaze to Leukos' body. "And now, what have we got here?"

Chapter Four

Returning home in the middle of the night, John heard what sounded like cracked sobbing from behind the iron-studded door. His servant Peter had waited up for him. The mournful noise was Peter's rendition of a Christian hymn written by Justinian. Peter often sang to himself when he thought no one was within earshot.

The dirge stopped at John's first knock. The door creaked open, and Peter's leathery face peered out from dim orange lamplight.

"Trouble, master? I can see from your face it is trouble."

"Yes. Leukos has been killed."

Peter made the Christian sign. "The Keeper of the Plate. You spoke well of him. I'm sorry." His expression darkened. "On every side the wicked prowl, as vileness is exalted. So the psalm says. I wouldn't walk the streets at night. The devil's abroad. It's not like ages past."

John did not believe that past ages had been less evil than the current one, but said nothing. Peter served him well. And he was a free man. John would not have employed a slave. He related what little he knew about Leukos' death.

"That explains the vision I had," Peter said. "When you were so late I suddenly saw you dead in an alley. But it must have been Leukos. My eyes are not what they used to be."

"I would have been back earlier but the urban watch got involved. The prefect's a prickly character. He's kept the dagger that was thrust into Leukos' ribs. I had to mention my official position several times before he agreed to have Leukos' pouch sent to me after the authorities have examined it."

"His family would want that."

"Yes," agreed John. No doubt Leukos had family somewhere, though he never mentioned them. Like so many in the capital, the man who had risen high may have arrived alone from a distant corner of the empire to seek his fortune, or flee his fate, or do both.

They went upstairs. John did not feel ready for sleep. He went into his study and Peter brought him a jug of the harsh Egyptian wine his master favored.

"I will pray for your friend's soul," the servant said as he turned to go.

John sat at his plain wooden desk and poured wine into a clay cup decorated only by a stained crack in its lip. He was troubled by Leukos' murder and haunted by the bull-leaper. The image of the woman's dark eyes shouldn't keep pushing aside the fixed stare of his dead friend.

Mithra, he wondered, is it enough for a man to control his actions, or are you pleased only with those who can control their thoughts as well?

John forced his attention toward Leukos. That was where his duty lay. Soldiers of Mithra were bound to follow duty. They did not allow themselves to give in to personal weakness.

Long ago John had served as an apprentice in the Keeper of the Plate's storerooms. Although John had advanced to high office, the two men continued to work together frequently. On a few occasions Leukos had visited to share a meal. Yet John knew very little about the man he called a friend. Like John, he rarely spoke about his past and then only in generalities. Perhaps that was one reason John had been at ease with him.

One thing he knew was that no man deserved to be murdered in an alley. It was true that death at the hands of a cutthroat was so common as to be almost in the nature of an accident. Every day some of those who lived in city fell prey to its predators. Anonymous murderers were about as likely to be brought to justice as a deadly plague or fire.

But was Leukos' death a random street crime?

Why would a common robber use an ornamental dagger with entwined serpents on the hilt?

He had not mentioned that detail to Peter. The superstitious old man would have doubtless seen in it some dreadful omen.

John refilled his cup more than once and as always, his gaze was drawn finally to the wall mosaic, a bucolic landscape of fields and forests. In daylight elaborate clouds filled the big sky. Now, however, the trembling light of a clay lamp danced across a debauched heaven alive with lusty Roman gods and goddesses. The artist had carefully shaped and colored the glass tesserae and pressed them into the drying plaster in such a way that lamplight revealed scurrilous secrets invisible by the light of the sun.

The tax collector who commissioned the mosaic when he owned the house had possessed different tastes than John.

It was not the rioting gods and goddesses that John's gaze sought. Instead, his attention was drawn to one of the mortals gathered below. A young girl aged perhaps nine or ten stood apart from two boys playing knucklebones. Her eyes were large, almond-shaped, reminding John of the ancient funerary portraits he had seen during his time in Egypt.

There was a touch of naturalism about the girl the other figures lacked. She alone seemed to have been drawn from life. She might have been the artist's daughter, John thought. Though the girl gave no overt sign of noticing the heavens, her mouth was drawn up in a grimace of pain, suggesting knowledge and suffering beyond her years.

For no reason he could name, John thought of her as Zoe. She was, he knew, a stoic. Much like himself. At times, he could feel her presence in the room.

John lifted the cup again. The rough wine burned the back of his throat. He had been known to ask Zoe questions which he always answered himself, but on this night he did not ask what she would make of a friend stabbed in an alley, or a vision of a lost love.

Zoe stared out at him. The flickering light catching the tesserae forming the corners of her lips hinted at movement, but she did not speak.

Chapter Five

Elsewhere in the city, another girl, lips trembling, warily pushed open the heavy, rotting shutter of a second floor tenement room. The air outside was fetid, smoky, sour with the stench from the alley beneath the window, but still more breathable than the air inside, thick with the smell of humanity and cooking. The girl's husband rolled over in his sleep, muttering, disturbed by the creak of the shutter. He flung one heavy arm out, barely missing the pot of night soil the girl had set next to the window. He was big and could almost reach across their space, one of several created by subdividing an already small room with thin, rough boards.

During the day he worked as a laborer at the new church Justinian was building. Or had until his fall.

"The dome will rival the heavens," he had told her.

"Why do the heavens need a rival? Aren't the heavens we already have good enough?"

"They may be but they are hard to appreciate from a miserable city room." He must have regretted his words, seeing her frown, because he continued, "You don't regret leaving the country with me, do you?"

"You're my husband." It was a simple statement, carrying everything within it. "We're not country folk now. This is Constantinople, the greatest city in the world. Our home."

She had made herself smile.

Then one afternoon he had fallen from high up in that great dome. His fall had been partially broken by scaffolding. There was something wrong with his skull, one leg was broken, and a physician could probably have found other injuries, if there was any money for a physician. That he had survived had been a miracle, but perhaps a short-lived one. His fever had returned.

Now she bent to pick up the heavy pot, averting her face. She was exhausted. But then, what a night it had been. The second time she had opened the shutters after her first fright, it had been even worse. What had she seen but a corpse apparently looking straight up at her. And to think she'd had the pot in her hand. It seemed indecent. She had almost dishonored the dead.

She forced herself to peer down into the alley. This third time, at last, it seemed deserted. She emptied the pot, leaning over the sill. Its contents splashed on the cobbles below.

She sank wearily down next to her husband and hoped for dreams of the country.

Though the night was far advanced, the liquid sounds of syrinx and flute filled the perfumed air of a private dining room deep inside the palace. A scantily clad girl danced down the middle of a long table that was covered in purple and gold. Not that she knew how to dance. She simply kept her narrow hips moving suggestively while stepping nimbly over and around plates of pomegranates, figs, and boiled duck. The young men on the couches flanking the table laughed as she went by, trying to look up her short green tunic. They seemed pleased.

She was only a girl, young enough so she could remember when men had not noticed her. This new power she had been given was fascinating. She could sense the men's probing thoughts. Their attention exhilarated and repulsed her at the same time.

One of the diners had grabbed her around the waist and thrust her onto the table. She could smell sour wine on his breath. As he embraced her, his stubble brushed the side of the

breast that her tunic, tied only at one shoulder, had left exposed
in what Madam Isis had explained was the ancient manner.

"What's your name, little one?" the man had demanded.

"They call me Nymph," she had replied, mindful of Madam's
admonition to give only that name and not to reveal her real
name, which was Berta. She was puzzled when the man burst
into laughter.

"Dance for me," he'd commanded, and so Berta danced.

Perhaps she would please this man or another so that he
would bring her to live at the palace. It could happen. Look at
the empress herself. She had once been an actress.

She had been hand-fed a few morsels from the table, a slice
of an unfamiliar fruit more succulent than anything she had
tasted before. All was luxury here. Even her indecently brief
tunic was of silk, smooth against her skin. Her underclothing,
too, the same.

As she danced amid the plates, bare feet still retaining their
instinctive childish agility, she felt the smooth material caress-
ing her thighs.

The flutes played faster, cymbals underscoring their sinuous
rhythm. The girl danced in time, skipping between chalices,
ducking under a huge golden bowl of fruit suspended by chains
from the ceiling. A flush rose on her cheeks. Surely this was
heaven. But then, wasn't the emperor a god?

She caught a glimpse of an unwelcome figure. A garishly
dressed page who leered at her from a corner. Odious little boy.
He'd pawed her on her way to the table.

Distracted, she failed to clear the roast boar.

Berta toppled off the edge of the table into an obviously male
lap. Recovering her senses, she rolled over to look up into the
face of whoever had broken her fall. Perhaps he would take her
to his house tonight.

She assumed her most dazzling, ingratiating smile. And
gasped. Later she insisted to her friends that the face looming
above her was the oldest thing she had ever seen. Older than
the headless eroded statue in the ruins near the city wall, more

ancient and weathered than the mummy exhibited in the forums by the traveler from Egypt. The face was brown and wrinkled as the head of John the Baptist—if that relic truly existed. But when the man's leathery lips parted they revealed surprisingly white teeth.

"I am a soothsayer," said the ancient. "I need no chicken entrails to tell me what a lovely creature you are. Do you want to earn a trinket?"

Chapter Six

A visitor was the last thing John wanted the next morning. Unfortunately, just as the watery sunlight of a new day banished the pagan gods from John's wall mosaic, Peter announced a caller.

The stranger was a powerfully built man with red hair and a wild beard. He sat down stiffly on the stool John indicated and introduced himself as Thomas, a knight of the High King of Bretania.

He spoke the Greek used in the capital passably well but with a heavy accent. John noticed, however, that for knight he employed the Latin *eques*, a class which dated back to the early days of Rome.

"You say you are a knight?"

"The High King has trained a cavalry after the Roman fashion and given us that title. I understand it is a long time since Roman knights rode in battle."

"I have heard of King Arthur. What is your business here?"

"I thought you would be expecting me."

John offered only a questioning look.

"The Keeper of the Plate sent me," Thomas explained. "Two days ago I visited him and he said I should see you, that he would arrange for a meeting this morning."

"I was never told. The Keeper of the Plate is dead. Murdered."

Thomas stiffened and his eyes widened.

Peter padded back into the room to pour ruby Egyptian wine into the silver goblets that displaced John's clay cup when the Lord Chamberlain entertained visitors. John noticed the servant scowling curiously at the so-called knight. The visitor looked the complete barbarian with scuffed leather boots and leggings and a wool tunic stained by travel and weather.

"You are surprised to learn that Leukos was killed last night?"

The question seemed to fluster Thomas. "Why wouldn't I be? I only met him briefly. How——?"

John cut him short. "What is it you have come to see me about?"

"If you would prefer I returned——"

"Leukos wished for me to speak to you, so I will. Briefly."

Thomas took a long drink and stared down at the silver goblet clutched in his large, scarred hand. "I'm seeking a sacred relic."

"I see. Relics aren't hard to find in Constantinople. We have hundreds. The staff of Moses, a fragment or two of the True Cross, bones of almost any saint one could name."

"I'm searching for the Grail."

"The cup from the last meal before the crucifixion."

Thomas turned his goblet around nervously. "Some say it is a platter, such as those from which we eat, or a precious gem."

"An interesting legend, but the Grail is one of the few relics I have never heard rumored to be in the city. If it were it would be in the patriarch's charge."

"I couldn't get an audience with Patriarch Epiphanios. I visited the Keeper of the Plate because I was advised that he is—was—in charge of the emperor's valuables. I thought he might know about something as valuable as the Grail. He said you would give me an introduction to the patriarch."

John got up from his chair and went over to the window. A breeze carried the pungent smell of the Sea of Marmara into the study. A detachment of excubitors emerged from the barracks opposite. John was tempted to dismiss his annoying visitor immediately. But was it a coincidence Leukos had died the day after he had been called upon by Thomas? Or the day after Thomas claimed he called upon him? Had that meeting really taken place?

Leukos hadn't mentioned it to John. Then again, he had seemed oddly distracted for some reason, perhaps something to do with his visits to the soothsayer. Perhaps it had simply slipped his mind.

It was best to humor the man until he could learn more about him.

"Why does your king want the Grail?"

"It's the holiest of all holy objects," Thomas said quickly, then added, "and, like mistletoe in the old religion, it will heal all."

"Is that what they say?"

Thomas rose. "I fear I am intruding, Lord Chamberlain. If you see fit to supply me with an introduction, I am staying at the Inn of the Centaurs."

John remembered Anatolius mentioning the inn during the afternoon at the Hippodrome. It was where he and Leukos were supposed to meet the soothsayer.

As John turned away from the window to reply, Thomas said suddenly, "One for sorrow. Unfortunately, the prediction has already come true."

John looked back outside in the direction of his visitor's gaze. A large dark bird had landed on the roof of the barracks and sat there alone.

"You're referring to the raven. I haven't thought of that old rhyme since I left Bretania."

"You're familiar with my land?"

"I was there as a young man." John didn't add that he been a mercenary. For all he knew he might have been fighting for Thomas' enemies.

"Then you know that to see a raven, a single raven, is to foretell sorrow. But for the fortunate one who sees two, this means joy. Three is for a girl, four for a boy, and so on."

"In the part of the country where I lived the old wise women used to say three was for a letter."

The raven rose silently and soared away. John watched it diminish to a speck and vanish into the cloudless sky above the countless crosses that the pious had raised on the rooftops of tenements and mansions alike.

A fortune-telling bird, and the symbol of a Mithran rank at that, yet perfectly at home in the capital of a Christian Empire. It made John think of how eager Leukos had been, devout though he was, to visit a soothsayer. What had the soothsayer foretold?

He pushed the thoughts aside. They were the result of a sleepless night. He needed to force himself to think clearly.

He wrote an introduction to the patriarch and gave it to Thomas. If the man was telling the truth it was what Leukos had wished. If he was lying….well, John did not believe in Christian relics. Let Epiphanios deal with his fellow believer.

After Thomas left, John sat brooding, staring at the fantastically detailed mosaic and the little girl Zoe. She had listened to their conversation so solemnly and silently.

"What do you think then?" John asked her. "Is this Thomas trustworthy? Is there a connection between Thomas' visit and Leukos' death? Yes, yes, you are right, Zoe. It is my task to find that out."

Chapter Seven

Leukos could never reveal what had been prophesied to him, but Anatolius, who still lived, had also arranged to see the soothsayer. John hoped that his young friend might reveal something about the man he and Leukos had both visited, but Anatolius did not arrive at the Baths of Zeuxippos at his usual hour so John decided to follow the footsteps of his colleagues to the Inn of the Centaurs.

The innkeeper and his wife directed John to the courtyard where the soothsayer was dozing on a bench. As John crossed the bare space the hot blade of the sun lay against the back of his neck. The bench and fountain beside it were shaded by a fig tree.

If he had a choice he would have been at the Hippodrome asking about the bull-leaping troupe, but his duty to Leukos gave him no choice.

As John drew close with the silent tread that came naturally to him, the old man opened his eyes—large eyes, bright and shrewd, under bushy brows. The eyes of a man who had seen a lot and lamented over much of what he had observed. John realized the other had not been asleep, but resting watchfully. Despite the heat, robes the color of age-yellowed bones were drawn closely around the old man's bird-like body.

"I greet you, sir." The soothsayer's voice was surprisingly resonant for one so slight.

John sat down next him. He noticed a striped cat perched on the edge of the fountain basin, engrossed in trying to catch ripples with its paw. To John, the cat seemed to be leaning alarmingly close to the water.

The old man smiled. "I should not worry about the cat. Unlike humans, they have many lives."

"Cats don't like water," replied John. "And some say even humans have lives after this one."

"Perhaps." A smile flashed whitely in the earth-brown face. "But tell me, what is your business here? I doubt you have deserted your duties at this time of day to have your fortune told, not a man of your rank."

"I see the fine weave of my garments gives me away. But you are correct. A man makes his own fortunes. I am here to ask you about the past, not the future."

There was a burst of shouting from the inn. The portly innkeeper John had spoken to on arriving at the inn emerged, half-supporting a man who was red-faced and cursing.

"With the celebrations, some of Master Kaloethes' customers have been making too familiar an acquaintance with the wine jug," observed the soothsayer.

This particular troublesome customer was, by appearance, a charioteer, dressed for the races in his short sleeveless tunic, his crossed leather belts askew. Not that he was in any condition to stand in a chariot, let alone race. His legs kept giving way.

With a grunted apology to the two men sitting on the bench, the innkeeper steered the inebriate to the fountain and, taking a firm grip on one of the unfortunate man's leather belts, dunked the charioteer's head several times in the water.

The cat ran off, its tail arched in terror.

Tepid water splashed the back of John's hand. He shuddered. To him it felt as frigid as the roiling waters of a swollen northern stream. He quickly wiped his hand on his tunic.

The innkeeper shoved the half-drowned charioteer through the archway leading to the street and trod heavily back to where John and the soothsayer were seated. "We pride ourselves on keeping a high class establishment. We would be most honored if you would sample our fine wines after you have completed your business."

When Kaloethes had vanished inside, John turned his attention back to the soothsayer.

"Before you ask," the old man said with a smile. "My name is Ahasuerus. My family was originally of Antioch, but I left ages ago."

"Were you driven from your home by the great earthquake?"

"No, my lord, although I appreciate your concern. I am, in fact, the last of my line. Since I left, I have traveled many roads, casting augurs, offering advice. Yet for all my wanderings, this is the first time I have seen Constantinople. It is certainly a city of splendor."

The man's weathered face might have been a wrinkled map of the countless roads that had brought him to Constantinople.

John inquired what had brought him to the city.

The old man shrugged. "One day I had a feeling that this was where I should be. And so I journeyed here."

John eyed the cat, which had returned and was dabbing a paw at water spilt around the fountain basin, examining it with interest. "I am told you are a soothsayer," he stated. "Do you find trade brisk?"

"I do. Rich and poor alike want to know their futures. The poor wish to learn whether they will ever possess anything, the rich wish to learn whether they are in danger of losing what they have."

Even in the shade of the fig tree it was hot. The fig was Mithra's sacred tree. The thought reminded him that as a pagan he had not been considering the soothsayer from the same perspective as most of the city's population.

"Don't Christians condemn fortune tellers?"

Ahasuerus chuckled. "Good Christians do not come to me for anything beyond entertainment. The ladies of the palace consult me for amusement. I have been invited to many gatherings to amuse the ladies."

"They are amused by the reading of chicken entrails?" John asked, recalling Anatolius' description of the soothsayer's methods.

"For the ladies, I read currents in a bowl of water or wine, or cast pebbles. One lady gave me gems to cast, to impress her guests. Recently, however, a woman not only insisted on a traditional reading in private, but provided a chicken."

"Have you been visited here by many from the court?"

"Certainly. They don't always trust me with their names, let alone their positions, but I can always tell. Their clothes and their manner give them away."

"Do you recall a large man, pale, completely bald?"

Ahasuerus reflected for a few seconds. "I cast pebbles for such a man yesterday. He had concerns about his health. I was able to reassure him that he would be in good health all his life. Also, if I remember rightly, that he might come into sudden wealth."

Ahasuerus' prophecy had been true insofar as Leukos had been in perfect health until someone slid a knife into him. As for wealth, given the brevity of his life following the reading of his fortune, any riches Leukos might have gained had to have appeared very suddenly.

"Was there also another man to see you yesterday? Young, dark haired, handsome?"

Ahasuerus smiled. "I saw many young dandies from the court yesterday. To me they all look young and handsome."

"Anatolius is his name."

"I never inquire about names and as I said, few offer them."

John wondered if Ahasuerus was being evasive or if Anatolius had not appeared.

"I can tell there is something else engaging your mind," the soothsayer said. "There is something, or someone, you seek."

John got up from the bench. He wasn't about to be drawn into the old man's game. "Who isn't seeking something or someone? Thank you for your time, Ahasuerus."

He went out into the clamor of the street. He knew now that Leukos had kept his appointment with the soothsayer. Whether that had any bearing on his death was something he could not say.

Chapter Eight

Sticking his head out the kitchen window to summon Ahasuerus to his meal, Kaloethes had been chagrined to see the obviously high-born visitor leaving. He had hoped to finally sell a bottle of the wine his wife insisted they stock expressly for such visitors. The wine had cost a fortune because it had supposedly been snatched from under the noses of the Goths who were battling Justinian's armies up and down the Italian peninsula.

Unfortunately, the only people from the palace who ever took an interest in the Inn of the Centaurs were tax collectors and building inspectors.

At least the visitor had not appeared to be on official business. He had questioned Kaloethes and his wife only briefly about the soothsayer and his customers. They claimed to know nothing. Then Mistress Kaloethes had gone off to the market, leaving her husband to deal with the cooking.

Now, having filled his guest's plate, Kaloethes lowered his exhausted bulk onto the wooden bench next to the soothsayer to await Mistress Kaloethes' return. He watched the old man worry a chicken bone as if he were a starved cat.

It occurred to Kaloethes that the inn had in fact had visitors from the palace recently, but unfortunately only to have fortunes told, not to drink expensive wine. "If you wanted, you could tell your clients a thing or two that would make them need a bottle of wine right away and never mind the cost. We could split the proceeds."

The soothsayer dropped the cleanly stripped bone onto his plate. "I prefer to have satisfied customers. As it is, the authorities frown on such gifts as mine."

Kaloethes made a rude noise. "So, if you have gifts, what's my future? A place at the palace, do you suppose?"

"It is what your wife desires, is it not?"

"Takes no fortune teller to see that. But will it happen? Is there ever going to be an end to this incessant labor?"

"Sometimes knowing your past is to know your future." The soothsayer finished his bread and studied his plate mournfully.

"Look at you! You clean your plate like an obedient child. I remember my mother insisted I do the same. And what did it make me? Not big and healthy, just fat. The butt of jokes. Now, what about this future of mine?"

The soothsayer said he would need his fortune-telling tools in order to cast augurs. "The pebbles are quicker but a chicken is more certain and more detailed."

"You've got part of a chicken there." Kaloethes nudged the fleshless chicken bone with a pudgy finger. "What can you tell me?"

"It takes back-breaking labor to build a church, but at the end it is filled with song."

Kaloethes stared at the old man's leathery face, trying to fathom what was meant. "I can see where a fool with spare coins might pay you well, you old fraud," he finally admitted with admiration. "Are you sure you can't bring yourself to see a fine bottle of wine in a man's future, or many visits to the Inn of the Centaurs?"

"I would betray my gift if I agreed to do that. If you'll excuse me, I must resume my meditations."

The innkeeper persisted. "How about this? You could serve your clients some of our fine wines. It would make them more comfortable, not to say credulous. I'll give you a break on the price."

The soothsayer bent down to his plate and passed his hand over the chicken bone, then shook his head and said solemnly "I regret that I must inform you that such a plan is not in my future, Master Kaloethes."

"Go back and nap in the shade then. If you have more high flown admirers should I wake you or advise them to come back when you're done meditating? Who was that tall fellow anyway? Let me guess, from the severe look of him, an assistant to a bishop."

"He didn't say who he was. A wealthy and powerful man—"

"If that's the best you can do then you can call me the Oracle at Delphi. Anyone can see that."

"You will find it difficult to cater to such people when you so obviously envy them, Master Kaloethes."

"What I hate is how they always act so clever and self-assured, those men. If only you were half so clever as I, they seem to say without actually saying it, you would not be toiling away your pitiful existence. Ha! What do they know? I'll wager your caller from the palace was born to his rank."

Ahasuerus offered no opinion and returned to the courtyard and the shade of the fig tree.

Kaloethes muttered savagely to himself. "The only shade I'll see is when the wife's looming over me with some complaint. Where's the slim young thing I courted, the girl who told me I was going places?"

He picked up the soothsayer's plate and tossed the chicken-bone out the window to where the striped cat waited. "You'll be disappointed when you see how bare that bone is. Well, life is full of disappointments."

He looked down at the plate. Silver. From their own private table setting. His wife must have taken it out to impress the soothsayer, or more likely his important visitors. The woman's pretensions were intolerable.

But so was her nagging tongue. He had to find a way to appease her. What was that the soothsayer had said about it all ending in song? Not likely.

Chapter Nine

Leaving the Inn of the Centaurs, John stepped into a narrow sun-scorched street that was unusually deserted. Many of those who would normally have been hurrying along the street were likely lying in bed battling the Furies in their heads.

John couldn't help noticing once again the large brass plaque beside the inn's brick archway. The polished sign promised much more than the bare, dusty courtyard and run-down building beyond.

The elaborately engraved beast depicted below the inn's name, half man, half horse, brought to John's mind a vision of the bull-leaper, feet planted so surely on the bull's back that she might have been part of the animal. He stopped, tempted to turn in the direction of the Hippodrome where he could inquire about the whereabouts of the troupe that had performed there.

Instead, as always, he forced his feet to move in the direction where his duty lay, in this instance toward the establishment of Madam Isis. She would have had time by now to question her employees about what they had seen during the afternoon and evening of the day Leukos had died. After that, he would return to the palace and seek out Anatolius. Whether he had kept his appointment with Ahasuerus was probably irrelevant, but John knew that it was not always possible to judge in advance what facts might be important to the solution of a problem.

He had walked only a short distance when he heard raised voices and saw Thomas. The self-styled knight might well have been on his way back to the inn where he was staying. Now he was talking loudly to the charioteer who had been dunked in the fountain.

The charioteer sat on a bench beside a statue of a stern, bearded old man in the classical Greek style. John guessed he had picked the seat because of the sunlight slanting under the colonnade onto it rather than to meditate on philosophy. The charioteer's long hair still hung damply around his face.

As Thomas' tirade continued, the charioteer stood, swaying slightly. A short man although muscular, he made a rude gesture and wobbled away. Thomas looked after him in obvious consternation, his face as red as his hair and beard.

John had not made out anything Thomas had said, beyond cursing, if in fact he had said anything else. As John approached, Thomas spotted him. He looked startled.

"Lord Chamberlain! I was just scolding Gregorius," he explained, without John having asked. "He and the rest of the charioteers kept me awake all night. The inn was in a ferment. The noise went on almost to dawn."

"Was there a reason for the excitement?"

"Aside from the general festivities? Apparently a lot of money has been changing hands this past week and no small fortune is riding on the racing today. Some of the Hippodrome performers are staying there and they tend to be very loud as well."

"Are there any bull-leapers staying there?"

Thomas looked puzzled.

"A youthful looking woman, slim, with dark hair and eyes?"

"The inn's a rough kind of place. The only woman I've seen there, aside from the innkeeper's wife, was a young lady who… well…."

"Who what?"

Felix looked away from John and toward the sculpted philosopher they stood beside. "She's trained chickens to peck grain from her naked body."

John smiled at the big redhead's apparent discomfiture. "That wouldn't be the woman I'm looking for."

"I could hardly believe my eyes, Lord Chamberlain."

"You haven't lived in Constantinople long enough, Thomas."

"I'm not used to this city yet. Would you mind if I came along with you for a while? You could educate me about the ways of Constantinople."

Thomas resembled a big, bewildered, ginger-whiskered child. Was he really so naive or was it a pretense?

"I doubt you will find my destination very edifying, but accompany me if you wish." John continued along the colonnade, Thomas at his side. "Have you visited the patriarch yet?"

"That's where I was coming from. He refused to see me. I was told he was ill, but it looked to me as if other callers were being admitted."

"I'm surprised my introduction wasn't sufficient."

"I suppose there was nothing untoward in it?"

"You didn't read it? You are indeed an honest man, Thomas."

Thomas regarded the ground. "Lord Chamberlain, if there is one thing I guard above all else, it is my dignity. Still, I suppose I should be honest with you. I am unable to read or write. They are not skills I have much use for."

John wasn't surprised. "I shall speak with the patriarch personally and see what can be arranged."

"How can a man bear to live here?" Thomas suddenly burst out. "If I have to bend my knee to one more pasty-faced clerk looking down his nose at me, even though he's barely up to my shoulder....If he were a ruffian blocking the road, I'd clear my path easily enough!"

"You need to learn city ways," John told him. "Take this delicious fish, for instance." He had come to a halt in front of a slovenly fellow tending a brazier. For the price of a copper coin the cook handed John and Thomas each a skewer holding blackened chunks of fish. The cook looked as charred and greasy as his wares.

Thomas eyed the fish warily but John took a hearty bite.

"It's good soldier's fare," John remarked, wiping a spot of grease from the corner of his lips as he strolled away.

Thomas nibbled at his fish and smiled. "Excellent! But this is the last place I would have expected to find you dining, Lord Chamberlain. A man in your position must get used to eating at the emperor's table."

"Only at official banquets. Besides, Justinian doesn't eat meat. But you can thank him for this fish."

Thomas cocked an eyebrow. "How can that be?"

"In order to protect the monopoly of the merchants, Justinian has forbidden fishermen from selling their catch themselves. However, the sale of cooked fish is not prohibited. The fish vendor was a fisherman. You can't find fresher cooked fish than in the street, not even at the palace."

John tossed his empty skewer into the gutter and Thomas' soon followed.

"I am beginning to understand your city. Even what goes on in the streets depends on the emperor. Nothing happens that cannot be traced back to the palace."

John offered his companion a thin-lipped smile. "That might not be strictly true, but for those of us who live here, it is a wise attitude to maintain."

He stopped in a small square. From an open doorway came a tinkling of bells, the sound of lyre and pipe, and the scent of exotic perfume. "We've reached our destination, Thomas."

Chapter Ten

John stepped inside the cool honey-colored building, followed by Thomas. Delicate melodies, mingled with the muted tinkling that John recognized as ankle bells, emerged from behind a curtained archway.

The doorkeeper Darius blocked their path. The huge, long-haired, and highly perfumed Persian was still sporting the tiny wings John had seen him wearing the night of Leukos' death. "I see you are still playing Eros."

Darius gave a disgusted grunt. "Isis has turned the house into a Temple of Venus."

Or, more correctly, John amended mentally, an Egyptian-born madam's idea of how such a temple should appear. "Don't worry. She'll decide on something else before long."

"That's what worries me. The girls have been whispering something about the Temple of the Virgins."

Thomas stared around, wide-eyed.

Reverting to his official role, Darius continued, "I must remind you gentlemen that weapons cannot be carried into the Temple of Venus. Or at least not the sort you might raise in anger."

John surrendered his dagger. Darius added it to the international selection piled in an alcove: a stiletto with an Egyptian motif on its blade, two swords in worked scabbards of Persian origin, and what looked like a palace-issue excubitor's sword.

Darius turned gaze toward Thomas, who handed over his weapon with obvious reluctance.

"You Britons always hesitate," grumbled Darius. "But you wield the iron handily once you set your minds to it, I'm told."

"Darius is an expert on international travelers," John informed his companion. "I'm here to see Madam, Darius."

Darius stepped aside and stood in front of a brass gong on the wall. "She is unoccupied. You know the way." He nodded down the hallway toward a rosewood door carved with doves and myrtle, sacred symbols of the goddess.

Thomas looked hesitant. "Should I wait here, Lord Chamberlain?"

"No one waits at Madam's," said Darius. He picked a mallet up from an ornate table and struck the brass gong behind him.

A girl with blonde hair piled high in the Greek fashion emerged from behind the curtains. She wore a short green tunic and was adorned in barbaric fashion with brass and green-stone necklaces and bracelets. Her cheeks and lips were painted and she carried a timbrel.

"Berta, we have a foreign visitor here, a guest of the Lord Chamberlain, who wishes an introduction to Roman culture." As Darius spoke he relieved a fat newcomer of his dagger.

"Forgotten me already, Berta?" called the fat man as he passed, ducking between the curtains as the music grew louder.

Berta favored her admirer with the same studied lack of attention Empress Theodora might have given a whining cur seen from her carriage. The girl was, John guessed, all of fifteen. When she took Thomas' hand the knight blushed but he also allowed himself to be led away.

John looked thoughtful. "The big fellow who just came in, wasn't that the owner of the Inn of the Centaurs? I'm surprised he dares to stray so close to home."

A thunderous bellow like the scream of the Great Bull when Mithra plunged his dagger into its neck reverberated around Madam Isis' private quarters.

The horrific racket stopped when the plump Isis stepped back from a contraption set between two carved screens next to the window at the back of the room. A dozen gleaming bronze pipes of varied lengths rose from a polished wooden box on legs. There was a keyboard on the front of the box.

"It's a portable organ," Isis explained. "It'll give me something to do now I'm retired, or at least semi-retired. I was playing it this morning to stop brooding over what happened last night."

John realized the instrument was a miniature of the organs sometimes employed ceremonially at processions and in the Hippodrome. They were not permitted in churches. And no wonder.

Isis sat down beside John on a cushioned couch drawn up to a low table burdened with a jug of wine and filigree silver plates of fruit, nuts, and sweetmeats. "I do wish you would visit me more, John. But not under such circumstances."

She was an Alexandrian with eyes as dark as her raven-colored hair. Belying her profession, she eschewed cosmetics. She invariably wore a lapis lazuli fertility amulet suspended from a thick gold necklace, which amused John. Fertility would be the last thing to cultivate in her line of business.

John declined the wine she proffered. Though usually abstemious Isis took a long drink, then occupied herself with a silver fruit knife, cutting a dried apple into neat segments. "Before you ask, I wasn't able to learn anything about your friend Leukos. None of my guards or doorkeepers noticed such a man, and none of my girls tended to him either."

"You must have been busy with the festivities. Would the girls have recalled him?"

"With that bald head? They would have giggled about it for days! They notice much smaller peculiarities than a shiny dome. Anything to relieve the tedium of the job."

"So the closest Leukos got to your house was the alley where he was stabbed to death."

Isis seemed to see the knife in her hand for the first time and set it down with a clink on the platter. She swallowed the apple segment she was chewing and almost choked.

"This murder has me so upset I can't even eat," she said, between coughs. "Wine…." Red, green, and blue fire blazed from elaborately worked rings as her chubby fingers rose through a shaft of dusty light falling across the room. Few but John would have noticed the thin gold marriage band worn in Egyptian fashion on the middle finger of the left hand. Isis had never revealed whether or not she was or had been married.

Isis took a gulp of wine. "That's better. I would hate to be carried off by a piece of apple."

"I appreciate your looking into this, even if there was nothing to learn."

"Oh, but I only said no one had seen Leukos here. I did learn something. Not much, perhaps." Her gaze met John's.

He smiled. "I understand. Yes. What did you find out?"

"I remembered you asking whether the Inn of the Centaurs was nearby. I am guessing Leukos may have been on his way there."

John said nothing.

"Anyway, last night there was a private affair at the palace put on by Theodora. Raising money for that pet project of hers, elevating streetwalkers to polite society. Ironic, isn't it? There aren't enough emperors around to elevate them all, like she was." Isis sniggered quietly, recalling common rumors about the empress' less than respectable past.

"And how do you know this?"

"Some of my girls attended. Berta's been showing off this pendant she was given there. It's got what they call a bloodstone, although actually it's green. She dotes on green, you know. Anyway, she was boasting to the girls it was worth more than all the wealth in the city."

Berta, John recalled, was the little blonde who had led Thomas away.

"I hired them out to dance. In a manner of speaking. And they also carried jugs of wine around," Isis went on. "Supposed to be nymphs, you see. That was just Theodora's unpleasant sense of humor, since for most of the ladies my girls served, they'd already served the husbands—and not just with wine."

"And what is the connection with the Inn of the Centaurs?"

"There was a fortune teller there, some ghastly old man. A foreigner. Justinian will be furious if someone is foolish enough to mention it to him. Not quite the thing, is it, for barbarians to go about telling imperial fortunes? Mind you, it was quite all right in the old days when prophets did so for patriarchs."

John recognized her description as the soothsayer. "He's staying at the Inn of the Centaurs."

Isis' rosebud mouth formed a pout. "You already knew."

"Not exactly. I know of the man but I didn't know he was at the palace last night. Did Berta hear anything he said?"

"It was something about how the empress would shortly hold a great treasure in her hands. Well, even Berta could've predicted that! But then the powerful always hear the fortune they hope to hear, don't they?"

"Yes, even barbarians want to keep their beards as they say, not to mention their heads." John got off the couch.

"I'm sorry if you've had a wasted journey, John."

"Not at all. At this point I know almost nothing about what went on last night. Anything I learn might turn out to be vital."

Isis looked happier. "I always enjoy talking to you. Drop in when you don't have to be here on business and we'll talk about old times in Alexandria."

Isis automatically included John in those bygone days, although they had not actually met in that teeming city.

"Certainly. But now I must continue about my business, and you yours." He clicked a coin onto the table top. Friendship was friendship. Business was business.

Chapter Eleven

As Keeper of the Plate, Leukos had performed his business in a more austere setting than Isis conducted hers. The palace's administrative complex occupied a drab labyrinth of plaster-walled corridors and rooms decorated only with the occasional cross.

John had preferred meeting Leukos outside the keeper's offices and now, as he made his way toward them, it was if he were walking back into his own past. He could hear his boots on the tiles. Footsteps in the halls of bureaucracy echo as hollowly as in a tomb.

The guards at the entrance stepped aside at John's approach. Passing between them he entered a familiar open area scattered with desks and tables. The late afternoon sunlight slanting through barred windows striped the room with shadows as it had years ago. At the back the massive bronze door to the windowless storage vaults stood open. The air smelled of the vinegar that was mixed with clay to remove tarnish from silver. It completed the illusion that he had traveled back in time.

John spotted a round-shouldered, middle-aged man standing by a long table at which boys and young men were polishing wine jugs. Any of the young men might have been himself. The man was checking off items on a tablet. He suddenly whipped his stylus against an apprentice's ear.

"Put some effort into it! Do you think the emperor's putting a roof over your head so you can admire your reflection in his silver?"

The voice brought back more memories. John's lips tightened and he felt heat rise in his face. He had spent his first years in imperial service counting and polishing a vast array of plate. He had polished so many goblets that wine from one always tasted more bitter than wine from a ceramic cup. And he had frequently been mistreated by the man before him.

"Xiphias!" John snapped at the man who had just cuffed another apprentice.

Xiphias turned. His eyes widened. "Lord Chamberlain." He sounded as if he might choke on John's title. His narrow face made him resemble a rat, John thought.

"You will answer some questions," John said. He saw the apprentices sneaking smirks at one another as their obviously flustered master gestured them away.

"Excellency?" Xiphias' voice shook.

John noticed the clerks hunched at their desks raising their heads from their work to glance in his direction.

"We'll speak in the treasury," he told Xiphias and led him back past the bronze door.

There was no one there. The two men were alone with wealth possessed by few but kings and emperors. The shelves were crowded with tableware manufactured of precious metals, much featuring incised designs of religious importance, as well as sacred vessels and other gifts to the emperor from visiting dignitaries—huge meat platters boasting gem-studded covers, silver lamps decorated with engraved scrolls of flowers, gold goblets almost too heavy to lift with one hand.

And there were many other vaults beyond this one.

"How can I help you, excellency?" The corner of Xiphias' mouth twitched uncontrollably. He was only head clerk and John held much higher office. Knowing how he would take revenge had the situations been reversed, Xiphias expected no better from John.

He had been one of John's chief tormenters, ordering him about with blows and sneers of "eunuch!" although never when Leukos was within earshot. His chief ambition, as he often boasted to his fellow clerks, was to become head clerk and, who knew, perhaps Keeper of the Plate and after that Master of the Offices. Now his hair was touched with gray and he had achieved only his first modest goal.

"Coming here brings back memories," John said. "I should return more often. Although since the Keeper of the Plate is gone—"

"A terrible tragedy."

"As a man of such feeling I am surprised you can manage to work today."

"We must keep to our duties, excellency."

John picked up a delicate filigree fruit basket of beaten gold and turned it over in his hands, admiring the workmanship. "Leukos used to say the gold is worth nothing, the craftsman is the treasure."

"Very true, excellency."

"A wise man, was Leukos. And kind. He used to summon me here to speak quite often, as you no doubt recall."

Xiphias' tic was pulling his mouth continually up into what might have passed for a lopsided smile, but he was not smiling.

John reflected that had Leukos been a harsher master he would have had the hasty-tempered young slave John had been in those days flogged four times a week. Leukos had only sighed when another complaint about John fighting with his fellow workers came to his ears.

"John," he had said. "You must control your humors. You are the most intelligent man in my employ and I expect you will go far. Remember that while your body is not your own, your mind and soul remain your possessions. Control your anger, and in due course I shall not be ashamed to say I gave you your opportunity to become something more than one of my assistants."

It was excellent advice. John ultimately saw its wisdom. He was grateful to the Keeper of the Plate for his patience with one who was, after all, merely an imperial possession. When, afterwards, they became friends, John wondered if Leukos' kindly nature was natural to him or sprang from his devout Christianity.

Not every worker in Leukos' employ had been grateful for the master's considerate treatment.

"Xiphias, tell me about the traveler from Bretania who met with Leukos the day before yesterday."

A look of near panic washed over Xiphias' features. "I....I don't remember a visitor...."

"A burly redheaded man. He claims to be a knight."

"I did not see such a man, excellency."

Xiphias' evident terror at not being able to give the desired answer convinced John that the man was telling the truth. Had Thomas lied? Then again, Xiphias might simply have missed seeing Thomas when he arrived to see Leukos.

"Did Leukos mention anything about expecting a visitor?"

"No, excellency."

"Did he seem himself the past few days? Did he appear preoccupied? Worried?"

"Not at all."

"I can see you are not going to be able to help me." Or not willing to help? John asked himself.

He questioned the clerks, but no one had seen Leukos' exotic visitor. They had not necessarily been at their desks or at work at the time he arrived.

Xiphias looked relieved at not being contradicted.

"I will be back," John said. "Continue considering my questions."

Halfway down the corridor, John regretted his final words. He heard Xiphias taking out his chagrin on his workers.

"Thought it humorous, the eunuch's visit, did you? I'll teach you!" His words were accompanied by the thud of heavy blows. John wondered whether they were administered with the aid of Xiphias' favorite weapon, a heavy wine jug presented to the imperial couple by a bishop from Antioch. More than once he had had the task of cleaning it after it had been used to belabor his head. The gems embedded in its sides had hurt.

John paused in mid stride, his anger rising, then hesitated, hearing again Leukos' advice years before.

"Yes, Leukos, you are right," he muttered. "I must not allow losing my temper to distract me from finding your murderer."

Chapter Twelve

The next morning John approached the Baths of Zeuxippos with trepidation. Would Anatolius be absent again? And if so, what might that mean?

Scaffolding obscured the double tiers of enormous arched windows at the semicircular front of the building. The marble cave of the vestibule, empty of ornamentation, rang with the sounds of hammers and chisels wielded by laborers who outnumbered bathers. The baths had been burnt down by the mobs during the riots three years earlier, but several wings had reopened.

By the time John reached the private bath reserved for palace officials he had acquired a fine coating of plaster dust. He undressed in the outer room, shook off his clothes, and stepped into a cloud of steam billowing from an archway.

He was relieved to see Anatolius lounging against the wall of the oval basin, staring dreamily up into the foggy dome overhead.

"I was surprised you weren't here yesterday." John eased himself into the hot water. It took an effort of will. During his time in Bretania he had seen a comrade drown in a swollen stream. Bodies of water still terrified him.

"I was out with Bacchus all night after the official celebrations. I think in the end he beat me around the head with his staff and threw me down a flight of stairs. That's what it felt like when I woke up yesterday afternoon. I didn't emerge from the house all day."

"Then you haven't heard?"

"Heard what, John?"

"Leukos was murdered. Felix and I found him in the alley beside Isis' place. He was stabbed."

Wherever Anatolius had been dreaming when he gazed into the dome, it took him some time to travel from there to the alley where an acquaintance had died. Finally he muttered, "I…I don't know what to say. It's too horrible to be believed. I barely knew Leukos myself, but still…I'm sorry…."

John realized his friend's lack of words evinced his shock better than any flowery phrases could have conveyed. He recounted quickly what he knew about Leukos' death and his investigations of the previous day.

"No," Anatolius replied in answer to John's questions. "I didn't run into him at the Inn of the Centaurs, or on the way there either. Is there any reason to think it was anything other than a robbery?"

"Nothing was taken from him so far as I could tell."

"That is suspicious. And he appeared to be out of sorts at the Hippodrome."

"So you noticed that as well? He seemed to have something on his mind. I thought it might have to do with his visit to the soothsayer."

"And the question is whether the visit to the soothsayer had anything to do with his death?"

"One of the questions."

Gritting his teeth slightly, John slid down until water lapped his chin. Most found the hot baths soporific and pleasant. John wished he could say the same.

"The prefect is sending me Leukos' pouch after he's examined its contents. He didn't want to part with any evidence."

Anatolius raised his eyebrows. "You persuaded him? He usually answers to no one but the emperor."

"I told him that Leukos' family would want its contents, whatever they might be, and that it would be unwise to anger the bereaved family of a high official."

"I don't know anything about Leukos' family."

"Neither do I. The pouch might offer some clues to what was on his mind, where he was going, apart from the Inn of the Centaurs."

Anatolius pushed his dark, dripping hair away from his face. "Perhaps someone saw the attack."

"It's possible, but that person might be anywhere in the city. No one at Isis' house saw anything."

"Unless one of the urban watch happens by at the right time or a mob catches the fellow immediately and tears him to pieces, street crimes are never solved. And it could have been one of us killed in that alley. I passed by there myself."

"Did you happen to spend any time at Isis' last night?"

"No. I was preoccupied. Do you suspect Isis of being involved?" John shook his head.

"But what if her livelihood were threatened?"

"I trust Isis. We've both known her for years. I am more suspicious of the soothsayer."

"You said you spoke with him. What did he say when you told him Leukos had died so soon after his consultation with him?"

"I didn't mention it."

Anatolius looked surprised. "Didn't you ask the soothsayer where he was when Leukos was killed?"

"That would be the prefect's way. I wouldn't expect a murderer to tell me the truth and I don't have a small army to go about the city knocking on doors and verifying stories."

"But you could have observed his reaction when you broke the news."

"A man who can convince most of the imperial court he can divine their futures is too good an actor to be caught out that way. Yet the soothsayer troubles me. Only the gods know our futures."

"That may be," said Anatolius. "On the other hand the gods may communicate with us in whatever way they choose. Even through garrulous old wanderers."

"It sounds as if you are more impressed with him than I am. Did you keep your appointment with him?"

Anatolius' face brightened. "Yes, and I found him to be impressive."

"What did he have to tell you?"

"He immediately augured I was in love."

"A safe wager!"

"Perhaps, but he was quite accurate. He poured some colored pebbles out of a leather pouch and when he read them, he proclaimed I would be lucky in love."

John laughed. "You aren't still thinking of the bull-leaper? She's much too old for you."

"I'm sorry, John. It's clear that even a man as wise as you can be misled by the memories of a pretty face. Last night, after my head stopped throbbing, I started a poem for her. I will be Pindar to her Aristomenes."

"Aristomenes? The wrestler? The bull-leaper didn't strike me as such. And as for Pindar, didn't he remind us that man is merely the creature of a day, the dream of a shadow?"

"Well, if life is only a dream it is very pleasant one right now. According to the soothsayer."

"And how do you know his happy prediction for you will turn out to be true?"

"When we were talking he told me some of the men from the bull-leaping troupe are staying at the Inn of the Centaurs. The rest of the performers are quartered on an Egyptian ship at the docks."

Chapter Thirteen

John stood uneasily at the edge of the dock, dark eyes narrowed against the harsh light, looking down into the debris of the city sloshing at his feet. He felt his stomach tighten.

Anatolius, shading his eyes with his hand, was staring at the horizon where dark clouds lay in a sullen stripe across the sea. "There will be a bad storm soon."

They made their way through the oppressive heat that lay over the raucous harbor, the lines of sweat-streaked slaves burdened with crates and sacks, the dark-sailed merchant ships sweetly redolent of old cargoes of spices rising and falling on the same sparkling swells as many-oared warships.

John should never have come here. He had only seen the woman from a distance, for an instant. In the dim solitude of his study it had seemed possible that he had found his old love again. In the brassy sunlight, it was obvious it had been nothing more than self delusion.

They identified the *Anubis*, the ship named by the soothsayer, by the protective Eye of Horus painted on its prow. It was as silent as the dead its eponymous jackal-headed god conducted to the underworld. A man dozed at the foot of its mast. The gangplank was not in place. Waves sloshed loudly at the bottom of the gap between dock and ship.

"Hey! Watchman! Visitors!" yelled Anatolius. The man continued dozing.

Leaning down, John picked a shard of pottery from the litter strewn about the dock and lobbed it at the boat. Its clatter did not awaken the sleeper, but brought forth from the ship's bowels an angry boy. The Lord Chamberlain had seldom been announced in so undignified a manner.

He soon found himself standing in front of a low-lintelled door. If there were any sounds to be heard from inside, they were masked by the regular fretting of waves against the ship. He raised his hand to knock. His fist was shaking, and not from the proximity of the water.

He paused. Although he had done his best to concentrate on his search for Leukos' murderer, the performer at the Hippodrome had been constantly at the back of his thoughts, drawing him into a past he could never regain. Now there lay between him and the reality of the present only this plank doorway.

"Go on," urged Anatolius.

"Mithra, it's worse than waiting for the cornu to sound the attack," John muttered. He rapped briskly. Light footsteps sounded within. A woman opened the door.

There was a hint of gray in her dark hair. Close up she looked less slender than she had seemed at the Hippodrome, although she was apparently still agile enough to vault and leap over razor-sharp horns.

"Cornelia!"

She stepped forward, pulled him into the cabin, and dealt a stinging slap to his face.

"And they say Cretans are liars! By the goddess, you took long enough! And what do you want after all these years?"

John reached for her hand, half-expecting his fingers to pass through hers as through a mirage, and it was a shock when they were stopped short by the warm solidarity of her flesh.

"How did you know where we were, John? And what do you think you're doing, coming here? And, now I think of it, what are you doing for a living these days?" Her features were white with fury except for an angry spot of red on each cheekbone.

"Still the same Cornelia, all questions and never a pause for breath so I can answer!" John wiped tears from his eyes with a quick swipe of his knuckles.

"The John I knew wouldn't have cried." Her voice cracked.

"The Cornelia I knew was gentler."

She looked him over appraisingly. "You look strange in those fancy clothes. You must have done well for yourself."

"I am not the John that you knew, Cornelia."

There was pain beneath the anger in her eyes. "How I prayed to the goddess for word from you! But it never came. Why didn't you at least tell me you were leaving?"

"I never intended to leave you. I accidentally crossed the border and ran into a band of Persians. I ended up…well, eventually I ended up in Constantinople."

"And I stayed with the troupe. I keep expecting you might show up in every new place we visited."

"When I saw you in the Hippodrome I thought how kind the years had been to you. You looked just as young as when we first met."

Cornelia laughed quietly. "Your tongue is still as smooth as ever, I see. But in fact—"

Anatolius managed to squeeze into the cramped, dim cabin. "I owe you an apology, John. I could have sworn the bull-leaper was little more than a girl."

John introduced him. "My friend Anatolius, secretary to Emperor Justinian."

"Secretary to the emperor? That sounds like a high position." Cornelia looked John up and down again. "And so, what is it you do, John?"

Anatolius broke the ensuing silence. "He is Lord Chamberlain to the emperor."

Before Cornelia could say anything there appeared in the doorway a slim dark-haired girl. "Mother, who are the visitors?"

Shock washed over John in a cold tide. "You have a daughter?" As soon as the words were spoken he regretted them. There was no reason why Cornelia should not have taken a lover in the years since he had been forced to abandon her.

"She's the one you saw bull-leaping. Her name is Europa. She looks a lot like me, doesn't she? Though there are those who say she looks more like her father. Like you."

The ship lurched as an unusually large swell pushed it toward the dock. Anguish washed over John. He closed his eyes, feeling lightheaded, as if he were about to topple into a chasm suddenly opening at his feet. It was not the vertigo which had so recently seized him at the dock, but rather an instinctive reaction to the sudden yawning of unfathomable depths as terrifying as those revealed when the split earth disgorged Hades, intent on abducting Persephone.

Struggling with his emotions, John realized he was not what he thought he was. Half of his being, his identity as a man, had been wrenched away from him and twisted around and then thrust back into his dazed grasp, all in the space of time it took for Cornelia to say two words. "Like you."

Europa was his daughter.

Yet the thought which made him so lightheaded had also loosed a gray miasma of apprehension.

How would his child—he tasted the word—his child react to meeting the father she had never known?

Chapter Fourteen

The lengths one went to for women, thought Felix. He nervously ran his hand through his shaggy beard as he hesitated outside the entrance to Madam Isis' establishment.

The square was deserted. The sun beating down had driven stray dogs into the shadows of doorways and colonnades. There was no sign of the mayhem he had been caught up in two days earlier. No one would have guessed a bear trainer and the Keeper of the Plate had both died here, within a few steps of each other.

"Come in out of the heat, Felix!" boomed a voice from Isis' open doorway. "No reason to stand there shuffling your feet like a schoolboy." Darius, the big Persian, grinned at him.

Felix shambled inside. "I see you're still sporting dainty wings, Darius."

Darius gave a snort, and reached behind his back to snap a finger against one of the wings. "If only these things worked I could fan myself with them. It might almost make up for feeling ridiculous."

"Or you could simply fly away and find a more reasonable employer."

"Sometimes I am tempted. Shall I tell Berta you're here?"

"Not today. I'm here to see Isis."

The doorkeeper led the way to Isis' private quarters. The hallway vibrated with the lugubrious moaning of the organ.

"She's been driving us mad trying to play that accursed instrument," Darius muttered. "I'm surprised the urban watch hasn't complained about the noise. If Justinian spent an evening here they'd be outlawed the next day from one end of the empire to the other."

Before Felix could remark on the unlikelihood of the emperor passing the night in a brothel the groaning ceased and Isis answered Darius' necessarily thunderous knocking.

She directed Felix to a chair and settled herself on the cushioned couch across from him. "My playing has been improving," she said. "Perhaps Euterpe has smiled on me at last. What can I do for you, Felix?"

"I...well...commerce is not something I have a knack for and...."

"Have some wine." She poured out a generous goblet full and handed it to him. He gratefully took several large gulps.

"So you are here on a business matter," Isis prompted.

"Yes. It's about Berta,"

Isis patted Felix' knee with a plump hand. "You want to marry her."

Felix simply stared. Isis laughed. "Many of my girls have loose tongues amongst ourselves. We all know about your intentions. We were beginning to think you'd never get around to asking."

Felix reddened. "We won't have to haggle?"

"No, no, no. I've already made a firm decision about Berta. I don't want to part with her, but I'd be willing to sell her to you, Felix. Fifty nomismata."

Felix choked down his mouthful of wine. "Fifty! I could buy a scribe for that!"

"Whatever would you do with a scribe? You'll get more pleasure from Berta. Why, you've probably spent as much gambling on the races."

"You aren't selling her. You're holding her for ransom."

Isis waved a hand and her rings flashed. "What is such a small sum to the captain of the excubitors? You are a wealthy man. It costs more than fifty nomismata to keep a lady in silks!"

"Yes, I know. It isn't the price, it's the principle."

"What does love have to do with principles? Is it true what they say? That you are having financial difficulties?"

Suddenly, despite her ample form and billowing silks, Isis did not look soft at all. Felix thought of a ripe plum. If you bit into it unwarily you'd break your teeth on the pit.

"There are endless expenses connected with property. It isn't that I am short of money—"

"And gambling can be expensive too. The Hippodrome is enormous. All of Justinian's gold could vanish into it."

"You've been listening to the slanders being spread by my enemies!"

"If what is being said is untrue, the price I am asking should be a pittance. Besides, you don't think I am concerned with the price, do you? I want the best for my girls. I don't want to send Berta out into a disastrous situation."

"I see. Very considerate of you."

"You think you're the only one interested in Berta? There may be a better choice waiting for her."

Felix finished his wine and sat his goblet down on the table between them with a resounding thud.

"I am temporarily pinched, but I will get your price. Rest assured I will give her anything a lady could wish for."

Isis smiled. "I'm glad to hear it, Felix. I'll be happy to see Berta settled. I managed to save up enough to buy my freedom and go into business for myself. But Berta spends everything she earns before the coins are cooled. Where do you think most of that jewelry she wears comes from?"

"I've never asked her." Felix admitted. He did not add that he didn't want to know. "You'll prepare the papers?"

"Certainly. Everything will be properly signed and sealed, and I shall settle the Curse of the 318 Fathers upon the document of sale, just to be safe."

Chapter Fifteen

John walked home from the docks alone, having parted with Anatolius at a tavern.

He wanted time to himself to think.

He had barely spoken to his former lover and his daughter before Cornelia had ordered Anatolius and him off the ship. Had she been angry, confused, overcome by some other emotion? He couldn't tell.

One thing hadn't changed in all the years since he'd been with Cornelia. She was beyond his understanding. At night, when they were together in the darkness of their tent, he imagined she withheld no secrets from him, yet in the light of day, she was often a mystery.

John made his way through the press of laborers in rough tunics, ragged beggars, bent old men in patched robes. He was relieved Cornelia had not wanted to speak with him at length because there were matters she needed to know which he was not ready to tell her.

He thought of the relic that the self-styled knight Thomas claimed to be seeking. The Grail. The "heal-all," as Thomas had also referred to it.

He had heard legends. The world was full of magical potions and charms possessing powers far beyond those of physicians. The Christians claimed their god could not only heal people but bring them back from the dead. Unfortunately, the potions and charms and miracle workers everyone believed in were never to be found.

What if the Grail were really what Thomas claimed, as unlikely as that might be? And what if it actually were to be found in Constantinople?

Could such a wonder exist? At times it had seemed to John that his splendid civilization was but a toy boat floating precariously on a bottomless sea of mystery. And did he take the tales of his own Lord Mithra at face value? If a fig tree had truly fed and clothed Mithra, might this holy relic have power to heal even wounds such as he had suffered?

He had reached the top of the steep incline leading up from the docks. He paused. Looking back he could see across the open market square of the Strategion and over the seawall to the ships resembling toys lining the docks and scattered across the northern harbor. From this distance he could not identify the *Anubis*.

Had Thomas arrived on one of those ships? Was he really what he claimed to be? He said he had spoken to Leukos, but Leukos' head clerk Xiphias denied having seen such a visitor.

John continued on to the circular Forum Constantine with its two-tiered colonnade and turned down the Mese. As he approached the lofty wall of the Hippodrome he recalled seeing Thomas speaking to the charioteer Gregorius outside the Inn of the Centaurs. Thomas had explained that he had been chiding the man over his behavior at the inn. It hadn't looked that way to John.

Perhaps he should speak to the charioteer. He took the street which ran alongside the Hippodrome, descending toward the sea and the southern harbors. He had crossed the narrow peninsula on which the capital was built.

At the sea end of the Hippodrome where the land fell away, a series of huge archways gave access to the substructure beneath the race track. John went through one of the archways, moving from brassy sunlight into the cool dimness of a curved corridor.

It took a moment for his eyes to adjust to the change. The smells of stables and sweating humanity accompanied him as he strode past a series of rooms whose open doors revealed men working on chariots, grooming horses, or clustered at games of knucklebones. Charioteers were an elite fraternity and he did not need to question very many of those he encountered before he ran his quarry to ground. Gregorius was sitting on an upturned bucket and in conversation with another charioteer wearing the colors of the Blue faction.

Gregorius looked around and leapt to his feet as John entered the small room, evidently a storage space where horse feed was kept. "Lord Chamberlain!"

His companion hastily excused himself and hurried away.

"I'm surprised you know me, Gregorius."

"Oh, well....you were at the inn."

"We weren't properly introduced. If I recall, you had your head in the fountain."

Gregorius managed a sickly smile. "Everyone knows the emperor's Lord Chamberlain."

"Your friend Thomas didn't tell you who I was?"

"I wouldn't call him a friend. He's staying at the same place I am. We've talked about the races."

"Do you race for the Blue team? I noticed the man you were speaking to just now was a Blue."

"As a matter of fact, I do. But we charioteers tend to get along, whether we're Blues or Greens. We're all in the same profession. It's the partisan factions who fight."

"Is Thomas a supporter of the Blues?"

"I couldn't say. I've only known him a few days. I came from Antioch last week for the races and he arrived around the same time."

John noted that Gregorius' voice had wavered, a sign of nervousness. "I'm surprised you could talk about racing without discovering where his allegiance lies. Do they race in Bretania?"

"We spoke of other things too, I can't recall exactly what. A few cups of wine, and—"

"What is his business here?"

"Why would he tell me? I barely know the man."

"It would be best for you to tell me the truth." John's tone was soft but unmistakably firm.

"Do you mean his search for that relic? I'm not convinced such a thing exists. However, I understand there are many wonders in this city."

"Do you travel widely, following the races?"

"Yes. After I'm finished here I'm off to Thessalonika." Gregorius shifted his feet and glanced at the doorway, as if looking to escape.

Before he had a chance to make an excuse to leave John continued his questioning. "What do you know of the soothsayer staying at the inn?"

"As little as possible, Lord Chamberlain. He's a clever rogue, taking advantage of ignorant people who believe men can foretell the future. I've avoided him."

"It's been my experience charioteers are superstitious. Racing is dangerous. Don't you own a protective charm or two?"

Gregorius stiffened. "I trust in my skills. And, no, if you were wondering, I would have no interest in this relic Thomas is seeking."

"Now that you mention it, a charioteer might have some use for a heal-all," John observed.

Gregorius' jaw tightened.

John sensed the charioteer wasn't going to say more. If he pressed him further he might very well leave the city immediately, taking with him whatever information he might be holding back.

John left the room. Instead of retracing his steps he wandered through the stables and work spaces beneath the track, thinking, trying to see connections between Leukos' death, Thomas, the charioteer, the soothsayer.

Charioteers traveled widely. They would be in a good position to secretly obtain relics and transport them on their journeys across the empire.

Perhaps Gregorius had not been telling the truth about his lack of interest in the relic Thomas sought.

A snort interrupted his thoughts. He had chanced on the stable being used by Cornelia's troupe.

None of them was around but John spent a long time leaning on the rail, admiring the three magnificent bulls, sacred animal of his god Mithra, and the animal that had carried Cornelia into his life.

Was there a connection between those things?

Chapter Sixteen

John awakened to darkness and the sound of raised voices. He had been dreaming. Not of Cornelia, strangely, nor of his daughter, but of his childhood. He had been running across a summer field. Not pursued and with no destination. Simply running, skimming over the top of the wiry grass. The stones and tussocks, the sun-hardened depressions where cattle hooves had sunk into mud, none of these tripped him. He glided over all of them. Although he was running and not flying, he felt at the crest of every hill that he might take to the sky and soar. He was tireless. His legs did not weaken. His breath did not grow labored. He could run, effortlessly, forever.

Now he was awake, his heart leaping, his breath catching in his throat. The careers of palace officials ended as often with unexpected midnight visits as with presentations of commemorative diptychs before the assembled senate.

John rolled off his bed, hastily donned clothes, and grasped the dagger he kept close to hand. Without lighting a lamp, he moved toward the door of his bedroom.

Voices echoed from the atrium downstairs.

As he trod quietly down the wooden stairs, John saw Peter holding a lamp and looking perturbed. He was blocking the way of a slight figure fantastically dressed in beaded tights and colorful plumes.

It was Hektor, a court page and one of Justinian's decorative boys. John thrust his dagger back into his belt.

Hektor caught sight of John. He feinted to his right, and then darted around Peter's left. The old servant's slow swipe at the agile boy found only the bobbing end of a feather.

"You, John," shrilled Hektor. "Your master wants you!"

"You don't give orders to the Lord Chamberlain," protested Peter.

"I speak for Justinian, old fool."

"Never mind, Peter," John reassured his servant. "Bring my cloak." He turned his attention to Hektor, who was posturing insolently at the foot of the stairs, hands on hips. The boy's reddened lips shone in the flickering light from Peter's lamp. "What does the emperor want in the middle of the night?"

"You'll find out when we get there. Hurry up!"

John pulled on the cloak Peter offered. The old man scowled at Hektor.

To John, the boy's rudeness meant nothing. It was the emperor who concerned him. Few in Constantinople were closer to Justinian than the Lord Chamberlain, but the emperor was no man's confidant. He was a Janus. John had watched the emperor jest affably about favored charioteers with courtiers whose glib tongues and evasive eyes would be sitting at the bottom of a torturer's bucket before the next sunrise.

Outside, the cobbles glistened in the light of the moon, a thin clipping from the edge of a silver coin. Hektor raced ahead. John followed.

As they neared the Octagon, John could see light in its windows. Lights always burned in the emperor's residence. Justinian did not sleep like other men. Perhaps he didn't sleep at all. Perhaps he wasn't a man. It was whispered abroad that he wandered the hallways all night.

"Perhaps the imperial demon will have forgotten to put on his human face at this time of the night," suggested Hektor. "They say he is as unnatural a man as you."

John ignored the impertinent remark. He did not believe such superstitious tales. He understood that the emperor had an abnormal capacity for imperial business. Did part of Justinian's success lie in the fact that his sleeplessness having given him more time to learn, he had already lived—and had time to master the lessons of—a natural life span? It was a trait John might have envied had he allowed himself such weakness.

Having passed numerous guarded doorways John was ushered—thankfully without Hektor—into a small, plain room. Here in the center of his private quarters Justinian had discarded his amethyst-studded collar and brocaded cloak and was dressed in a simple tunic and hose. He had, however, retained his imperial pearl-studded red boots.

"John," he said, turning away from a desk piled with codices and scrolls. "How good of you to arrive so quickly." He assumed the smile John had seen him give to allies and condemned men alike.

John inclined his head. "My good fortune, Caesar." He doubted the emperor had any idea of the late hour. "I see you are busy."

"A new theological treatise. At the Hippodrome celebrations—was it only a day or two ago?—it occurred to me how I might help reconcile some of these quarreling sects who are so troublesome. Have you given much thought to the nature of Christ? How is it possible to intertwine the divine with the human? A tangled knot indeed."

"It is said Alexander took the expedient of cutting the Gordian knot."

"Yes, a simple enough solution for a mere conqueror, but I am an emperor. I will order Anatolius to make a copy of my conclusions for you. I know you study such things."

John bowed his thanks.

Physically Justinian would have been lost in the crush of the rabble which was never allowed to approach closely enough to see his face. He was of average height, his face pudgy and splotched red as if he drank to excess, although in fact he abstained from wine entirely. He was of such unprepossessing appearance that more than one ambitious man had forgotten that the life of every person in the empire hung on the fragile thread of Justinian's whim.

"I am sorry about your friend Leukos," Justinian continued. "Replacing him will be a vexing problem for me. He was a most trustworthy man. Meanwhile, I intend to give you free rein, John, to honor him to the height of your ability, which will be very high honor indeed. But first, there is the question of the manner of his death."

"The prefect informs me that an investigation is under way," John said softly.

"An official investigation, yes."

"It would appear to be nothing more than a common street murder."

Justinian smiled. "Do you believe that, John?"

"I do not yet have enough facts to form any belief, Caesar."

"Then you shall proceed to find out the facts. I wish you to ascertain, in confidence, who was involved in this so-called street crime, and the real reason for it."

John nodded. "I will report to you and no one—"

"I'm sure you need your rest now," Justinian cut in.

Dismissed, John turned to leave, but arrested his step when the emperor added, "About that ill-concealed weapon beneath your cloak, John…."

The guards at the door raised their swords instantly. John's heart seemed to stop. Half asleep, he had neglected to remove the dagger he had thrust into his belt back at the house. He forced his suddenly clumsy tongue to move. "Caesar, in my haste to see you, I must have forgotten…."

Justinian's expression was as smoothly blank as the walls of the room. "If I did not know you so well…." He paused and his full lips tightened slightly, although his eyes betrayed no emotion. "But then, how well can one man know another?"

"I will be more careful."

"We must all be careful, Lord Chamberlain. Especially an emperor."

Chapter Seventeen

John's heart was pounding as he strode hastily down the wide steps outside the Octagon. How could he have been so careless? The emperor could have had him executed on the spot. Then again, he reminded himself, the emperor could have him executed on the spot for no reason at all. The thought gave him little comfort.

Agitated as he was, he had walked halfway home before he realized he was being followed.

Yet another lapse.

At first it was merely the sensation of another presence intruding into his consciousness. Then, alerted, he began to distinguish quiet movements mirroring his own.

Ahead, the path lay dark and deserted. Although the palace grounds were heavily patrolled, he saw no guards, and only a fool would discount the possibility of some cutthroat having managed to slip into its maze of buildings, pathways, and gardens.

He forced himself to continue at an even pace. Listening hard, he thought he could discern only one set of steps behind him. Against one man he would have a chance. Once he had been a trained fighter. However, his follower might be a military man also, one much younger than he and with more recent training.

Why would anyone want to follow him from his meeting with the emperor?

Had Justinian decided to have him killed after all, but on the grounds instead of in his private quarters? John doubted that he would leave such a task to a single guard. The emperor was nothing if not cautious.

He considered his options. If he cried out for help guards would appear almost immediately. They were never far away on the palace grounds. On the other hand, John's pursuer was nearer to him than any guard. Would the man flee when John called for help or try to carry out his mission before help arrived?

If his mission was in fact to kill John.

A low archway punctuated the stucco wall John's path paralleled. He ducked through it into a garden. He considered lying in wait to one side of the archway, but decided any trained man would be alert to such an obvious ploy. He heard the gurgling splash of a fountain. Faint moonlight, falling toward the rooftops of the tenements visible beyond the wall encircling the palace grounds silvered dwellings, water, and the fountain alike. Beyond the garden he had entered, he could distinguish a line of trees, a black mass of branches.

He moved toward them. The footsteps turned after him into the garden as he had expected. The trees appeared to be figs. John waited until he had almost reached them, then broke into a run. He stopped suddenly, turning back toward his pursuer. He could now see a bulky outline, moving forward rapidly. John took a step to the right, then, pretending to be confused, to his left.

With a burst of speed he knew his legs would regret later, he raced around to the other side of the line of trees, then doubled back. But they were too widely spaced to conceal him. He would be visible to the man chasing him, and, what was more, by detouring around the trees he had lost valuable time, time he might have used to escape.

John's pursuer, seeing his chance, took the direct route, straight through the row of trees.

There was a resounding splash and the clatter of a metal blade on marble.

"God's blood!"

John recognized the voice of Thomas.

The burly redhead had emerged from the sunken pool when John reached it. Thomas was still spluttering, cursing, and shaking water out of his ginger mustache.

"Thomas, I see you have discovered one of the emperor's little jests. It was especially designed to catch trespassers. Though usually they creep in here to steal, not to pursue Lord Chamberlains."

"I wasn't pursuing you. I was out walking and saw you. I didn't want to be shouting about in the middle of the night, and you walk faster than a Pict in full retreat."

Several guards, attracted by the noise, arrived at a run. John dismissed them without explanation. No doubt they would soon be weaving lurid tales in their barracks about his strange assignations with foreigners in garden pools in the middle of the night.

"Why were you walking about the palace grounds at this time?" John asked, wondering exactly how Thomas had managed to get inside the walls at such an hour. "I thought you were staying at the inn."

"Who can sleep in this city, with all those barking dogs and people shouting and such?"

"You have refined sensibilities for a soldier. And why was your sword drawn? In greeting?"

Thomas looked at the sword in his hand, as if just realizing it was there. He snorted and resheathed it. "It came out when I fell into the water. But you are right, it wasn't the noise of this damnable city that kept me awake. In truth, John, it was that girl. Berta. The one I, uh, saw at the house you took me to. My mind's been troubled since then."

"The soldier's simple life has been changed then?"

Thomas said nothing, but looked abashed. He ran his fingers through his dripping hair, squeezing out rivulets of water.

"Come back to my house and get dry," John offered. "You can return to your inn in the morning. You're likely to get arrested, wandering about at this hour of the night."

Chapter Eighteen

The flame of the lamp in the niche beside the house door had become dim before Peter heard John's familiar rap. "Thanks to the Lord," he murmured, hurrying to admit his master. It had been too long a night for him.

It worried Peter that John was a pagan. He feared that one day Justinian would find out and have John hauled away to the dungeons, or perhaps the emperor already knew and was merely biding his time.

Peter fretted not only about his master's bodily welfare but about his immortal soul. Though, the old man sometimes told himself, his master's god was so like his own true Lord in so many ways that John was perhaps guilty only of getting the name wrong. Still and all, he had been terrified when John was suddenly summoned to the emperor's presence.

Once John and that disgusting boy had gone out into the darkness, as he sometimes did when he was alone in the house, Peter had stolen up to the master's lavatory. Through the slit of a window there, it was possible to see the lighthouse. It was the only vantage point in the house from which it could be glimpsed.

Leaning against a wall, Peter had looked at its light, a golden carpet across the surface of the sea. At times, it reminded him of his Lord, who was mankind's beacon. At other times it brought to his mind more earthly visions of those distant places that lay beyond the sea, places that he had never seen, and so barbaric by all he heard he devoutly wished he never would.

He had been thus occupied when the prefect's messenger arrived and pounded at the front door. It had given him a terrible fright. He had known at once, from the manner of the summons, that it was not John.

Now, at the familiar knock, he opened the door to see not only John but also a sodden and disheveled figure.

The shiftless character who had visited John the day before.

"I prayed for your safe return the whole time you were gone," Peter informed his master while directing a glare toward Thomas, whose wet clothing was making puddles on the tiles.

It was only after he'd been dismissed and was climbing the narrow stairs to his tiny room on the third floor that Peter remembered he'd forgotten to tell his master about the visit from the prefect's messenger.

John showed Thomas into his study where Peter had started a fire in the brazier. Thomas had squeezed into one of John's tunics, and now the two men sat drinking wine under the riot of the fantastic mosaic.

"Ah, this warms where it's needed most," remarked Thomas.

John refilled their cups. "Granted, the streets of Constantinople must be confusing to one who is not a native, but I can't see how you could have wandered onto the palace grounds since the gates are shut at night."

Thomas gave John an embarrassed smile. "I admit I was out walking long before dark. I anticipated I would not be able to sleep if I stayed at the inn and I recalled the pleasant gardens I had passed through on my way to our first meeting. Once in the gardens, I became lost."

John sipped his wine. It struck him as an unlikely story. But anyone foolish enough to invent such a feeble excuse might be foolish enough to actually have acted as Thomas claimed to have done. Was he dealing with a man who was exceptionally naive or exceptionally cunning?

But why should this barbarian knight be such a mystery to him? John was familiar with judging the characters of powerful men at court every day.

He realized he was not thinking clearly. He had already had too much wine. His potentially fatal mistake in meeting Justinian while armed, his encounter with Thomas, and, yes, he had to admit, his reunion with Cornelia, had unnerved him to the point where he had quickly and unthinkingly consumed—how many cups of wine?

He did not usually drink so much.

Thomas shook his head. "Women are troubling."

"You are thinking of Berta?"

"Yes. A little beauty, but she insisted on talking. Talk, talk, talk! She went on and on about her friends and her clothes and her jewelry and this talisman she had, and finally persuaded me to try it on my leg. I have an old wound there. It stiffens up on me at times and she noticed that when I tried to….well…anyway, it didn't do it much good. Where do they get these ideas?"

"You don't think there's anything in the idea of healing talismans?"

"What? Oh!" Thomas frowned. "You're thinking of the Grail's heal-all aspect. But that would be for the good of all. To save the kingdom. It would never be used to cure one man. That's blasphemous!"

"I see."

"And even if the Grail can heal physical ills, can it heal the troubles caused by women? It is not a soldierly thing to be so troubled." Thomas slurred. "Yet it is a manly thing, and to be a soldier one must be a man."

John tapped the big ceramic jug on his desk. "Perhaps this contains the answer to the riddle of women. Men have searched many other jugs for the answer, and yet not found it."

"The greatest men are troubled in this manner," mused Thomas. "There is, for example, your great general Belisarius. They say his wife Antonina rules him by magick."

"The magic she uses she keeps beneath her clothing."

"Even so. But you…dare I say it, John, as a friend? You have the advantage on ordinary men."

"Why do you say that?"

Thomas suddenly looked abashed. "I…I…well, people refer to you as John the Eunuch and…."

"You have been asking about me?"

"No. But people talk and—

"So you imagine I cannot be swayed by feminine magick?"

"Nor…uh…persuaded to swerve from the path of righteousness," Thomas replied. "Who was it said there are those who make themselves eunuchs to better serve heaven?"

John filled his cup again. "One doesn't serve by refraining from that which he cannot attempt. My condition is not of choice, I can assure you."

"It wouldn't be. But how was…no, I apologize. I have had far too much of this excellent wine."

John realized that Thomas wasn't alone in having had far too much to drink. He couldn't remember when he had last been so intoxicated. Not since he had begun his ascent at court. Possibly not since he had been a young man. The little girl in the mosaic looked out at him, reproach in the glass facets of her eyes. He knew he should not say more. Nonetheless he spoke.

"You want to know how I came by my nickname, do you Thomas? Since we are such great friends, as you seem to think, the two of us having met three times, I shall tell you."

"It isn't necessary. Forgive my impertinence."

"No, I will tell you, Thomas. My lover and I were with a troupe of bull-leapers. We traveled endlessly. They entertained, I was one of their guards. The roads are dangerous. We were very much in love. Odd to think of it now, is it not? I wanted the best for her. It was her birthday. I was young. I was impatient. I made inquiries, and heard of a man who sold silk. Illegally, of course. But I wanted my Cornelia to have silk. I bragged to my friends in the troupe that if all those high-born ladies could have it, then so would my Cornelia.

"I had been drinking that night too, and the idea suddenly seized me that I must obtain silk before the sun rose again. So I went. The roads in the area were little more than ruts. Amid the defiles and brush, in the darkness, I took a wrong turning.

"The man I sought was encamped at a crossroads at the base of a prominent hill, or so I had been told. All the hills looked prominent and none of the roads I took crossed others. Still, I convinced myself I was moving in the right direction. I went on and on. I have learned since that it is better to turn back sooner rather than later.

"I crossed into Persian territory. We've been at war with the Persians a long time. I was caught. I wish I could say I killed at least one of them. In my time, I have killed men. But I was taken by surprise, knocked to the ground, a boy manhandled by his older brothers."

Thomas grunted uneasily. He looked ill. "There's no need to...."

"I insist, my friend. You wanted to know. I will spare you the details of my captivity. I was not enslaved alone. After some time we became a burden. We were to be killed. It was Fortuna that brought traders, because to them we were of some value, provided we were properly prepared. Eunuchs are considered by many to be more dependable in certain roles than other men, unburdened as they are by family loyalties or normal appetites.

"You are aware how such a condition is accomplished. When you are young you feel invulnerable. You think you are not like the others. Others may die, but not you. You cannot imagine being shorn of what makes you a man so easily? Are you familiar with the weapon employed by the Persian soldier?"

"I must leave!" Thomas staggered to his feet, knocking his stool over, stumbling into John's desk, sending the jug onto its side.

John heard Peter's door bang open and the servant's steps coming downstairs. He closed his eyes, trying to clear his head. The room was circling. Why had he been telling this stranger the story he never related to anyone?

"But how can one live through such an ordeal?" Thomas whispered thickly.

"We live or we die. It is not our choice." John turned away from the big knight and toward Zoe. "And now," he told the mosaic girl, "I can give Cornelia as much silk as she could ever desire."

Chapter Nineteen

John winced at the sunlight that shouted through the kitchen window. His head pounded and he could feel a vein in his temple squirming. Nevertheless he couldn't stomach Peter's proffered cure which sat untouched in a large goblet on the scarred wooden table in front of him.

Anatolius, newly arrived, gave John a concerned look and inquired about his health.

"Too much wine," John groaned, and proceeded to describe his evening, including a description of Thomas and his supposed mission. "I'm afraid I had very loose lips last night. A dangerous practice for a Lord Chamberlain."

"You had a shock yesterday, John. Meeting Cornelia again after so long. Not to mention Leukos' death and this peculiar foreigner showing up."

"I should know how to control myself."

"You're only human, even if you sometimes pretend otherwise." Anatolius glanced at the goblet on the table. "What's that odd concoction?"

"Owls' eggs and wine, the traditional cure for over-indulgence of the grape, as Peter put it. I'm not sure which is more unpleasant, that mixture or the look of disapproval Peter had when he put it down in front of me."

Anatolius smiled. "Perhaps he intends it as your punishment. You should carry an amethyst. It's said they're a marvelous antidote to intoxication."

"Do you carry one?"

"I tried but it didn't help. You know the way it is with these cures, they always work, but only for someone else."

"True enough."

"And what about this scoundrel Thomas?"

"Peter saw him out. Unceremoniously, I gather. Peter has taken a dislike to him."

"I'm not surprised. Some barbarian trying to pass himself off as a knight from Bretania in search of a holy relic. You can't believe a tale like that! I wonder what he's really up to?"

"I don't know what to believe when it comes to Thomas. He presents a problem."

"And to think he's staying where Leukos and I visited the soothsayer. I never knew the Inn of the Centaurs was such a popular place. You should have told me about him yesterday."

"I would have, but when you told me about Cornelia...."

"Yes, I would have forgotten everything else myself." He reached out and tapped the leather pouch lying on the table. "Is this Leukos' pouch, the one you told me about?"

"Yes. A messenger from the prefect delivered it last night, but Peter only told me this morning. I was waiting for my head to stop throbbing before examining it. No point in putting it off longer, I suppose. But I must request that you tell no one I have it." As he spoke, John picked up the pouch, loosened its drawstring, and poured the contents out into the painfully bright sunlight lying across the table.

Something rolled across the table top, fell over the edge, and ticked down on the tiled floor. Anatolius retrieved a tiny, polished green stone. John frowned, puzzled.

"I have one like that," Anatolius offered. "The soothsayer gave it to me after he told my future. It was one of the pebbles he used to do it. He said I should keep it for good fortune."

John could hardly believe his own good fortune. "So we've learned something already! Leukos must have kept his appointment with the soothsayer. The old man said he had, but objects are not so prone to lie as people."

The other contents of the pouch were more commonplace. There were four coins, three of silver and one gold, the gold coin having been clipped, which John theorized might indicate that Leukos had made a purchase on the last afternoon or evening of his life. But on the other hand, it might also indicate that he, or the coin's previous owner, had purchased something earlier.

"Nothing to be learned from the coins, then?" queried Anatolius.

"Actually they tell us quite a bit. For one thing, it confirms what we had already surmised from the fact that Leukos still had the pouch. It wasn't robbery."

"You mean because they weren't taken? Perhaps the thieves stole something Leukos had just purchased. Perhaps they were scared away as they were in the process of robbing him. That could have happened if they were interrupted by a passerby. Someone might even have come out of Isis' house and disturbed them."

"Yes, something like that could easily have happened but I don't think it's what occurred. We must look for some other motive for Leukos' murder."

The other contents of Leukos' pouch were less instructive. What could be made of a square of linen embroidered with the palace mark and a silver necklace?

"What do you suppose Leukos used this for?" Anatolius said, picking up the cloth. "Surely he wasn't raiding the imperial storerooms?"

"Hardly." John's tone quelled the young man, who had the grace to look ashamed at making such a remark so soon after the man's death.

"He was such a perfectionist perhaps he used it to wipe stray spots off the silver?" Anatolius mumbled lamely.

John said nothing, but picked up the necklace. It was heavy. At the end of its thick silver chain hung two intertwined fish.

Both men knew that the fish was a Christian symbol, and that Leukos had been a Christian.

"A trinket for a lady friend?" suggested Anatolius. "Surely it is for a woman?"

"Not necessarily. And do you ever recall seeing him with a lady friend?"

Anatolius shook his head. "No, now that you mention it."

"Don't forget Leukos and I were always interested in finding accomplished craftsmen to carry out palace commissions," said John. "We often collected samples of their creations. I'd have assumed it was something like that, but consider the workmanship. Crude, don't you think? I would have said it isn't anything that would normally have attracted Leukos' attention."

"You think too hard, John. Even with wine-hags in your head, you're concocting explanations just so you can demolish them. And most of them are ideas that would never occur to anyone else."

John agreed it was possible.

"I'm sure there is a simple solution," Anatolius offered.

"Probably, probably."

John carefully replaced the objects in the pouch. Had it really been a bungled attempt at robbery which had ended in murder? People died on the streets every day. People who had taken a wrong turn at the wrong hour. One moment on their way home to their families, looking forward to all the joys and trials of the years ahead. The next, dead. And for no reason. It was nothing to do with them or the lives they had led, except that a cutthroat thought they might be carrying something valuable. But strangers died for no reason. Not friends, and certainly not John's friend Leukos.

"I don't know," John worried away at it. "Something's wrong. It doesn't make sense."

"Does it have to?"

"Yes," John snapped, regretting his tone even as he spoke. "Yes, it does."

Chapter Twenty

It was almost noon when Xiphias, his head throbbing from the previous night's over-indulgence, arrived at the offices of the Keeper of the Plate.

The past two evenings he had left work and plunged immediately into the well of forgetfulness offered by wine. What he was trying to forget was the visit from the Lord Chamberlain, that wretched apprentice who had by some grotesque aberration of fate managed to ingratiate himself with the emperor.

He also wanted to forget the way he had taunted that apprentice. The times he had lied to Leukos, claiming John was lazy and incompetent. How he had surreptitiously scratched vessels John had been detailed to polish. The occasions he and his friends had ambushed the young newcomer in the dormitories and beaten him.

Xiphias had much to forget. But what he could not forget, what pursued him like an army of Furies, was his awareness of the retribution he would take were their places reversed, and he was now a high official who had been persecuted.

His revenge might be as nothing as compared to what a treacherous, inhuman eunuch could invent.

Still, it had been two days since the Lord Chamberlain's visit and Xiphias had heard nothing more. His terror had almost burnt itself out. Perhaps he was to be spared. For now.

Or could it be that the Lord Chamberlain realized Xiphias was likely to be elevated to the position held by Leukos and thus no longer a person to be trifled with easily?

The day might come when Xiphias, Keeper of the Plate, would not suffer nightmares every time he chanced to glimpse his former victim in the hallways of the palace.

He forced himself to straighten his slumping shoulders and put on a sour smile before he entered the workroom. He listened for the sound of scurrying feet as the feckless apprentices hastened to appear busy when he stamped in the door.

There was a curious silence.

For a heartbeat his panic returned. Had they all been removed for questioning in the matter of Leukos' death? He knew the persuasive methods of certain of Justinian's servants.

And if they revealed what they knew—as undoubtedly they would sooner or later—might they also speak at length on certain matters of no great concern to them as slaves but of great import to him personally?

He entered the open space with its barred windows letting in bright sunlight that made him wince and rub his forehead. The apprentices were there, silent, but conspicuously not at work.

"What's this?" he shouted. "Why are you not at work? You'll suffer for this! You!" he addressed a short, thin slave. "Explain. Has the emperor declared a holiday? Have you all been freed?"

The boy shook his head. "No...master..." The way he pronounced the title was an insult, and Xiphias advanced upon him with his fist raised.

To his surprise, the boy stood his ground.

Xiphias halted, puzzled. An expectant hush had settled over the room.

"You tell him, Beppolenus," someone called out.

The boy licked his lips. "We have decided that we should inform the Lord Chamberlain about your visitor. The one he was asking about."

"Oh, indeed," Xiphias roared, wincing as the thunderbolts of Zeus exploded in his head. "Eavesdropping, were you? I never saw the man! He was never here! One more word and I'll have the lot of you flogged! In fact, I'll set an example with you right away—"

"It is wise not to be subject to rumors," the boy pointed out with a crooked smile. "A person being flogged may say the most unlikely things, but such statements go round the court like lightning. Who knows whose ears they will reach and how they will be used? And even if nothing is done, still, there is always a lingering suspicion, a closer watch on the people concerned. Who knows what watchers might see?"

"A regular little orator, aren't you!" Xiphias blustered. He sat down, trembling, and gaped at the insolent child.

Defied by slaves! They chuckled and nodded to each other. It was intolerable.

But what could he do? What Beppolenus had said was true. Xiphias couldn't afford to attract attention or have his affairs examined too closely, and especially by the keen-eyed Lord Chamberlain. A man who not only had a keen eye but also a sharp grudge.

"Very well." Xiphias drew the words out, trying to sound menacing. "I shall remember what you said. And now, back to work."

There was a long pause and then the apprentices followed his instructions.

Xiphias went into what had been Leukos' but was now his private office, shut the door, and sat with his pounding head in his hands. How could it be that he had suddenly become a man at the mercy of his underlings? Now he dare not strike any of them for fear of consequences.

Was it the Lord Chamberlain's doing? Had he spoken with the apprentices? Was he playing some cruel game?

Xiphias sprang from his seat, grabbed a pitcher, and threw it against the wall.

He wouldn't allow himself to be destroyed by a former apprentice, a slave, a eunuch.

Chapter Twenty-one

Leukos' funeral was a simple affair. The Keeper of the Plate had no known family, a thing not unusual in Constantinople where the ambitious, not to mention the desperate, arrived alone from all corners of the empire, intent on making new lives for themselves. His servants had prepared his body for burial. Now Leukos lay on the couch in a room off his atrium for the short time it took for his few acquaintances to pay their last respects. Light from the lamps illuminating the shuttered room danced across the dead man's rigid features.

John was grateful that none of the mourners engaged in commonplace histrionics. There was no hair-pulling or breast-beating. Christians, John understood, did not favor crass emotional displays. He credited them for that. Waiting in the hall, he found the incense infusing the air with the promise of Paradise made his eyes and the back of his throat burn.

The puzzle of his friend's death would not leave John's thoughts. The prefect seemingly had dismissed the murder as a common street killing, unlikely to be solved. Though he knew it was irrational, John could not bring himself to accept that. So, while feeling it might be seen as disrespectful under the circumstances, he nevertheless sought out the young woman who had been in charge of Leukos' handful of servants.

Euphemia, barefoot and dressed in a short tunic, looked up at John with fear in her large brown eyes when he requested her to accompany him to another room.

"I washed him with water mixed with spices," she told John anxiously. "And then we anointed him with perfumes. Poor master, he never wore perfume when he was alive."

The Lord Chamberlain, realizing that even in one of his less opulent robes he would be an impressive and awe-inspiring sight to a servant, tried to reassure her. "I'm certain you've done everything correctly. I only want to ask you some questions."

He motioned her to a stool. He noticed that the water clock sitting in the wall niche had run dry. Euphemia must have followed his glance.

"Sir, I'm sorry, I forgot to fill it." Her voice trembled. "We didn't need them in the country. We had the sun there. Not so many walls pressing in on us."

"You are from Caria?" John had recognized her accent. The girl nodded. There was an unhealthy pallor to her face. "And what will you do now that your master is dead? Return?"

"Oh yes, sir, as soon as I can go without disrespect to the master. Constantinople isn't for me. So big and dirty, if you'll excuse my saying so, sir."

"I am from the country myself."

"But you have achieved great office, just like the master."

From the atrium came the sound of hushed voices, and a faint odor of perfume. Euphemia looked down at her clasped hands.

"Tell me, now. Did you see anything unusual recently? Did your master say anything to you?"

She shook her head. "It isn't for a master to confide in his servants, is it?"

"They occasionally do."

"Oh, no, sir, not my master."

"Do you think he had something to confide?"

She looked at him questioningly. Again, anxiety shadowed her eyes.

"I just wondered why you mentioned confiding," John said.

"No, there was nothing. We were not…friends."

"I didn't mean that. Did he seem agitated at all recently? Was there anything odd about his actions?"

She shook her head.

"Did Leukos have visitors?"

"No, sir. Never. Sometimes he went out in the evening." Agitated, the girl rose and went to the window, open to a garden where a few spring flowers were beginning to bloom. She turned her face toward their scent and breathed deeply.

"Do you know where he went?"

The girl shook her head again.

"Might he have been going to the baths?"

"Well, I could tell when he'd visited the baths." John looked at the girl quizzically. "He always used the gymnasium too. He was so pale," she explained, "and when he got back he was still flushed, right up to the top of his head."

John considered this insight into his friend's life. Leukos had never mentioned any evening activities to him. Of course, there was no reason why he should. But one would have expected, at least on occasion, to be regaled with a description of a visit to the theater or of a particularly lively dinner party. There again, Leukos had been unmarried and his destinations may have been the sort a scrupulous man does not reveal. There was nothing wrong with that.

"And you are sure he had no visitors?"

"Yes Except…" Euphemia turned from the window. "Well, it wasn't like real visitors, but a few times a man would come to the door."

"Did you see this man?"

"I don't mean any particular man. Different men. They seemed soldierly somehow, but not dressed that way, exactly. It was something about the way they moved. You have something of that yourself, sir, if I may say so."

"They did not stay?"

"No. They just brought him things. A bag, or a scroll, or whatever it might be."

John thought of the charioteer Gregorius, who habitually wore the dress of his profession, either from habit or boastfulness. "You said these visitors reminded you of soldiers, but they weren't dressed in a military fashion. Were they dressed like charioteers?"

Euphemia screwed up her face in concentration, or was it distress? A tear ran from one eye and she put a fist up to her mouth.

"Oh, I don't know, sir. I can't remember."

"Did he go out on those nights?" John said gently.

"Sometimes." The girl folded her face into a frown. Her hands, held at her sides, balled into fists. "It's all so complicated in this dirty city," she finally blurted out. "All comings and goings in the night and nobody saying what they mean and dark alleyways and who knows what hiding in them. It isn't what I thought. I thought it would be so grand and all. And mice. There are so many nasty mice." She shuddered.

"But surely there are mice in the country?" John's voice was gentle.

"Oh, but sir, they're country mice."

Chapter Twenty-two

Leukos' coffin was borne up the Mese on a donkey cart. The small procession accompanying him on his last journey followed on foot, winding through the crowded streets until finally turning past the Wall of Constantine into an area in the shadow of an aqueduct. Here the landscape was dotted with unkempt patches of cultivation, cemeteries, and several of the cisterns that kept the city supplied with water.

It was hot. The cemetery in which Leukos was to be interred smelled of spring vegetation and freshly turned earth. Birds sang unheedingly as Anatolius gracefully delivered the oration. John disliked public speaking, and avoided it wherever possible.

As John listened to his friend's artful phrases he remembered the times he had accompanied Leukos around the city. They had never traveled to its outskirts. Generally they had visited workshops, to keep abreast of the efforts of Constantinople's artisans so that they would know where to turn should Justinian suddenly demand regalia for an office-holder or Theodora evince a desire for a new diadem.

Now Leukos was gone, all his knowledge of the minutest details of every sort of imperial goods vanished. A man is more perishable than a silver chalice or a pair of golden earrings.

John looked at Euphemia across the dirt mounded above Leukos. She stood, head bowed, holding her processional lamp. In the sunlight she looked less pale, less fearful.

"Did I render him due honor, do you think?" Anatolius wondered, as they left. "He was, after all, a Christian. I'm not sure I understand their beliefs."

"I don't think they do either. Or at least they seem unable to agree on what it is they believe if you must listen to what Justinian has to say about the various controversies."

"You should try transcribing his attempts to bring about theological unity, John."

They lingered, enjoying the sun and the birdsong amid the plaster covered vaults of the graveyard.

Anatolius bent to pick a delicate yellow flower.

"Europa would enjoy a bunch of these." He stopped short, frowning. "I'm sorry. I shouldn't be thinking of such things here."

"Don't apologize. Europa and her mother have been in my thoughts too."

"We take all our joys within sight of death, don't we?"

"A poetical way to put it but true enough."

Anatolius let petals fall. "I wonder what flower that is?"

"Leukos could have told you."

"Leukos? I thought the Keeper of the Plate was an expert on man-made treasures."

"He was that but he used to name for me all the exotic blooms Justinian has imported for the palace gardens. We often discussed delicate business in the gardens, safely away from prying ears."

Anatolius wondered where Leukos could have come by such knowledge. John shook his head.

"He never said."

"Reticent, for a friend."

"No more than myself."

"I wouldn't call you reticent. You've told me all about your past."

"You think so?"

They had come to one of the towering arches of the aqueduct. The shade beneath was almost chilly. "I know my friendship with Leukos puzzles you, Anatolius. Remember, when I arrived in this city I was a slave as well as a eunuch. Leukos was the first to treat me with respect."

"I can see you would be grateful."

John let his gaze wander out of the shadow aqueduct and into the dazzling sunlight beyond. There was a period of his life into which his memory rarely ventured, years when he was no longer what he had been but had not yet become what he would be. He had managed to forget most of that time.

"Did you know Leukos was a student of the Christian philosopher Augustine?"

"An ascetic sort, wasn't he? The keeper of the emperor's treasures would seem an unlikely disciple."

"I take it Augustine was no more ascetic than a strictly observant Mithran. Leukos used to compare the philosophies."

"Perhaps he hoped to convert you."

"Indeed, he often told me how Augustine had come to his faith later in life."

"But is knowing a man's philosophy the same as knowing the man?"

"It depends upon the man, does it not?"

Something black moved in the weeds amidst the plaster-coated vault roofs. A single raven, thought John.

One for sorrow.

Then the black shape leapt up on a fresh mound and John saw that it was a large mangy cat with a sore on its belly. It made him think of Euphemia's horror of city mice. Which was worse, the vermin or the hunter?

Chapter Twenty-three

"Five!"
"Six!"

Felix swore across the table at the young charioteer who had opened his fist to display four fingers. Added to the two gnarled fingers raised by Felix, that made six. The other man's quick hand closed over the last few coins on the table.

"You're too quick for an old soldier, Gregorius. I don't know if it's your eye or your tongue," Felix grumbled.

"It's strategy." Gregorius dropped the coins into his pouch.

"Another try?"

Gregorius shook his head. "Don't worry, Felix. I'll win the money back for you at my next race if you place your wager on me. But I must be off. I still have that appointment to keep."

"Very well." Felix affixed his official seal to the parchment the young man had come to his office to request. "If anyone stops you, show them this. It's a pass."

"I can read, you know."

"You'd be surprised how many can't."

A third voice broke into the conversation. "Ironic, isn't it? Some possess the keys to the palace, but not to knowledge. Which do you think would be preferable?"

It was Anatolius, accompanied by John.

"Lord Chamberlain," Gregorius muttered. "I'm on my way to an urgent appointment, otherwise…." He slid around the two visitors and was out the doorway and off down the hall before John had a chance to speak.

"John!" greeted Felix. "And Anatolius. Since you ask, I'd say anyone who has keys either to knowledge or to the palace can't complain, since few have access to either. Anyway, a sword always knows more than a pen when you come down to it."

"Very sensible viewpoint," Anatolius put in blandly.

"Do you know that young charioteer who just left, Felix?" John asked.

"Gregorius? Not very well. Only that he races for the Blues."

"Needless to say you keep track of all the charioteers," Anatolius said.

"If you mean I follow the racing, who doesn't? Except, perhaps, for poets?" Felix pushed his seat back and walked round the table to stand in front of the room's one window, which gave a narrow view of a courtyard and dry fountain. On the fountain there perched a single raven.

"What can I do for you, John? Is it official or…" his gaze moved in the direction of Anatolius "…about the matter of the ceremony?"

John raised a tanned hand to halt Felix. "No, I expect we'll see you there later. Nothing has changed. We've come back from Leukos' funeral. Since your office is on our way I stopped to ask about someone you may have seen the day before Leukos' death."

"Who is that?"

"A traveler called Thomas."

"Yes, I did see the man that morning. He came looking for a pass to see Leukos."

"You granted him access?"

"Well, yes."

"And what did you make of Thomas?"

"Seemed genuine enough. He had a soldier's bearing. Honest and straightforward."

"The sort you'd trust to play at micatio in the dark?" suggested Anatolius.

Felix scowled, unhappy to be reminded of his very recent losses at that game.

"With my luck, I might as well play it in the dark," he muttered. "Here, John. Give it a try." He offered a closed fist. "Ready? On three."

John shook his own fist twice, then held up three slender fingers.

His softly spoken "Four" was almost drowned by Felix's booming "Six!" But Felix had raised only his first finger, which made him lose yet again.

"Once is mostly luck," John soothed the soldier's ruffled pride. "The strategy only applies if you play long enough. Show me your right hand, Felix."

Mystified, Felix displayed his gnarled hand. The fingers were strong and stubby. A livid scar ran along the knuckles and the third finger was hump-backed as the result of an old injury.

"I'll wager you have a little less movement in that third finger, my friend?" John remarked.

"Nothing to complain about."

"But if you can't straighten it quite as readily as the others, you see, you might just be inclined, without thinking, to show one or two fingers more often than three or four."

Felix considered the suggestion. "I never thought of that."

"I wouldn't be at all surprised to learn some of your opponents had come to the same conclusion. It tips the odds in their favor, does it not?"

"Now don't race off to test this theory," cautioned Anatolius. "At least not until you've been paid! Besides, you know you should be saving up to see that little blonde at Isis' place again, shouldn't you?"

"Berta?"

"The same. One can't help hearing tales."

"You mean you can't help hearing tales," sneered Felix. "And, as a matter of fact, I haven't caught a glimpse of her since that affair at the palace the night of the celebrations."

"You were invited to the empress' gathering?" John was surprised Felix hadn't mentioned it to him before.

"Of course not! I meant I was there in my official capacity. And I thank Mithra that it was only in my official capacity, because I can tell you that I didn't like what I saw. Especially the way they had Berta done up, and wriggling about on the table. Everyone was pawing her. She ended up in the lap of some filthy old man who plied her with…well, I don't know what it was, but she was enjoying it. I had to remain at my post, of course, and lucky for him, the dirty old bastard!"

"We all have to do what's expected of us, despite our personal feelings," sympathized John. "You must have seen the sun up?"

"It was a long night. At least Berta stayed where I could keep an eye on her, unlike some of the other girls."

"Let me know if you hear anything, will you? I rely on your discretion."

"Of course." Felix flexed his big hand. He noticed, again, the deformed finger John had brought to his attention. "You might be right," he said, changing the subject. "Perhaps that's why I always lose the game."

John wished he could see the cause of Leukos' death as easily.

Chapter Twenty-four

The sight of a raven feasting on a discarded fish head in the street delighted Berta.

"Look, Darius." She tugged at the sleeve of the Persian's tunic, pulling his attention away from the fish vendor's stall. "Isn't he wonderful? His wings are all shiny, just like a new coin. We had lots of ravens in the country when I was growing up. They used to call from the pines at sunrise."

"You can't get better fish than this!" interrupted the vendor. "Buy my freshly landed fish, and feast better than Justinian!"

"They look old to me," Darius told him.

The raven took wing, apparently disturbed by a scrap of a woman who seemed to be scanning the ground for something lost. Berta watched as the bird rose above the crosses on the rooftops with a few beats of its powerful wings, fish head clutched securely in its talons.

Then she looked back at the vendor waving away the droning flies settling on his wares. "Fresh as country ladies, these fish are!" he protested. "Cheap at half the price."

Shoppers near his stall had begun to move away.

"You, girl!" the vendor barked, addressing the thin, raggedly dressed woman. "How'd you like a free fish or two? You won't find the likes of these fine wares laying about on the cobbles."

"Sir?" The ragged woman sounded bewildered at her sudden good fortune. She was clutching some soiled crusts of bread.

"Yes, you," the man said gruffly. "Being as there's some think my fish is no good, I'd prefer to give it away to some poor soul who deserved it than offend their dainty nostrils. Here, take this."

To the watching Berta's amazement, the vendor handed the woman one of his larger fish, waving away her tearful gratitude. She was even more amazed when, seemingly impressed by the generous gesture, several hitherto reluctant customers suddenly decided to buy his wares, pressing coins into the kind vendor's grasp.

Darius put his big hand on Berta's shoulder, urging her to follow. As she started to turn away she heard the vendor's low growling, "You!" He spoke to the ragged woman. The last satisfied customer had moved well away out of earshot. "I'll have that back or the urban watch will hear about it!" the vendor threatened.

Berta looked on in distress as the woman surrendered the fish. Weeping as she walked away aimlessly, she bumped into Berta.

Berta directed language at the vendor which was as ripe as his fish.

The man laughed. "So now I should be taking advice from a little whore? You've no right to talk! I'll come over tonight and see if you'll accept some of these coins I've earned!"

"Don't mind him, lady. How can there be such coarse people in a Christian city?" The woman's voice shook. Her clothing made a stark contrast to Berta's fine green tunic. "A lady like you shouldn't be walking about in this part of the city, even if you have brought your servant." She put her hands up to her face and began to sob.

Berta put her arm around the woman's shoulder, feeling how thin she was. "You can't let bastards like that see you weep. It just makes them all the happier. Why are you scavenging for food anyway? Don't you have a friend, a lover?"

"I have a husband, lady."

"But where is he? Doesn't he work?"

"Of course he works! He works very hard, only a few days ago he was injured and now — well — I have prayed to our Lord day and night, yet they say my Sabas might not live."

"Sabas? That is your husband's name? And what's yours?"

"Maera."

"I am Berta. And so, Maera, you have no money and now you must beg? I can find you work."

"Work? For you, lady?"

"Well, actually I am not exactly a lady," Berta admitted, somewhat reluctantly, "At least not the sort you seem to mean. And this work, it would be the same sort that I do."

"I am not afraid of any work the Lord might send, however hard it is."

Berta giggled, her spirits restored by the prospect of helping the woman. "Oh, it isn't really hard work at all. And you get to meet some really nice people, people from the palace even. Some of the tales they tell would make a monkey laugh."

"This work you speak of, what exactly is it?"

Berta detected the note of caution in the woman's voice. "It's very respectable, despite what some people say. Nothing to be ashamed of. I've been assured as much by men who work for the emperor himself."

Maera looked at her in sudden horror. "The man was telling the truth, wasn't he? You work in one of those houses!"

"I work at Madam's, yes, just as I have since I came to the city. And a good life it's been, too."

"But have you no family?"

Berta paused. Hadn't she asked this poor woman the same question? "The girls I work with are my family," she finally said. "I know that it seems unthinkable right now but I could introduce you to Madam, and perhaps she would offer you work."

Maera shrugged off the comforting hand on her shoulder. "Never! I would as soon be dead!"

"We all say that but in the end we would rather live. It's not so bad, really. An occasional rough visitor, of course, but we have nothing to worry about. There are guards, we are safe. It's not like being on the street, at the mercy of any passerby. Why don't you at least come along with me and meet Madam, see what you think when you have spoken to her? She's a real lady. You'd be a pretty thing with a little makeup. You'd do well, I'm sure."

Maera shook her head vehemently and stepped away.

"And what of your husband? My family was starving too, but my father was able to buy oxen with the money he got for me and—"

"Oxen? Your father sold his child for oxen?"

"Well, you can always make more children but you can't make an ox, just like Madam says."

Maera whirled around and began walking away.

Berta darted after her. "Think about it, my friend. We come to the market often, Darius and I. You can find us here most mornings if you change your mind. At least take these." She pressed a few coins into a reluctant hand. "It will get you through a day or two."

"No, I can't."

"You must, for Sabas' sake."

Maera trembled but her fingers closed over the coins.

Maera stood and watched Darius and Berta move off along the row of stalls. The coins clutched in her hand burned like glowing embers.

The fish vendor, who had been looking on with great interest, called over to her. "Buy my fish, lady? Good for your husband, especially if he is not well. Why, I'll even toss in an extra couple of small ones, just as a thank you for your help."

Maera glared at him. Though without words to express what she felt, her expression was eloquent enough. It seemed to sting the vendor more than Berta's coarse diatribe.

"Yes, well, my fine lady, it won't be too long before you're serving yourself up at some house or other," he jeered, "and then we'll see how fine you stay. I'll be looking for you, and then you'll be singing a different sort of tune. Now take your miserable face away before you scare my customers off."

Gathering her dignity about her, Maera walked slowly away past stalls offering vegetables, barrels of olives, piping hot loaves, poultry of all sorts. With the coins in her hand, on this one morning she could buy whatever she and Sabas wanted. Then she thought of how they had been earned. Were they a gift from the Lord, or a temptation sent by Satan?

"Oh, God," she prayed as she picked her way across the refuse-strewn cobbles, "show us a way to get out of this terrible place, where nobody cares for anything but money and people have no shame about selling themselves to strangers." She did not add, "and where whores have more charity than their betters," although, when she thought it, she supposed God must have heard that part anyway.

She was still aware of the weight of the coins in her hand as she passed the last stall in the market and noticed a beggar sitting hunched over at the mouth of an alleyway. At least that was how she characterized the emaciated, ill-clothed man, though he was no thinner or more ragged than she was herself.

She stopped in front of him and his bony hand moved slightly, automatically opening in supplication.

"I could never accept these if I had got them the way they were earned," Maera said, as much to herself as to the beggar, "but I came by them honestly and so do you." She stooped slightly to place a coin or two into his leathery hand.

Without looking up, the man rasped something. It could have been thanks or a curse.

Maera walked away, lighter in spirit, thanking her inscrutable God for giving her the opportunity to help another unfortunate.

Chapter Twenty-five

More than a century had passed since Emperor Theodosius had banished all gods but the Christians' heavenly father. Gods, however, are not so easily killed off as political foes and a few pagans, among them worshippers of Mithra, still held to their beliefs even at Justinian's court. However, since Mithra's ever shrinking army was now so outnumbered the mithraeum was safely hidden from prying official eyes at the back of the network of underground imperial storerooms.

So Anatolius descended through the tunnels beneath the palace grounds as he made his way to the ceremony at which he would ascend another rung of his religion's ladder. As elaborately wrought bronze doors gave way to simpler doors of polished wood and finally to crude stone arches, the emperor's secretary felt himself slipping free of the bonds of palace life. The cuirass he wore concealed beneath his brocaded cloak no longer bowed his shoulders with its unfamiliar weight, and he had almost convinced himself he might come to prefer the uncomplicated blade of the sword to the subtler reed kalamos that he was accustomed to wielding in his official duties.

He was late. However, he was expected to be late. The others, perhaps fifty in number and all that the mithraeum could hold, were waiting for him. He heard the faint murmur of their voices as he turned the last corner of the final damp, stone-floored, and poorly lit subterranean corridor.

Two of Felix's excubitors were stationed at a nondescript wooden door. Anatolius handed his cloak to one of the guards. Suddenly, he felt awkward, a fraud, a soft thing in the cuirass he had borrowed from Felix.

The other guard rapped on the door and swung it open, allowing Anatolius to enter another world. Stone steps led down to a nave flanked by pillars, around and between which fantastic figures moved. Strange creatures with the heads of birds and beasts. The assembly was masked.

The mithraeum fell silent. Anatolius could hear the hiss and pop of the torches which threw distorted shadows onto the rough hewn walls and the embedded pottery shards that turned the ceiling into the simulation of a cave's roof.

At the far end of the mithraeum a sacred flame on the altar cast light over a bas-relief mounted on the back wall. It showed the powerful and familiar image of Mithra clothed in a tunic and Phrygian cap. He was in the act of slaying the Great Bull, dagger raised to administer the fatal wound.

Anatolius marched up the nave toward the white-robed priest who waited beside the altar. He could feel the buckles of the overly large cuirass digging into him with each step. He had wanted to savor this ceremony, to burn every detail into his memory. But, as often happened when he tried to grasp time, it slid away faster than usual. Before he realized it, he was at the altar and the Father was extending a sword from which hung a narrow gold circlet, offering it to Anatolius.

Following the ancient rite, Anatolius raised one hand and pushed the sword away. A thread of blood ran down his palm.

"Only my god will be my crown," he declared firmly.

The Father poured water over Anatolius' head, sealing his entrance into the new degree. Now a hymn to Mithra rose to mingle with the smoke.

Mithra, Lord of Light,
May this new Soldier be worthy of Thee;

Mithra, Lord of Battle,
Give him strength and loyalty;
Mithra, Lord of Heaven,
Guide our feet upon the Ladder;
Lord of all, we worship Thee.

Anatolius turned to face the masked celebrants. He knew he had friends present. John, for one. But he saw only ravens, lions, a Persian: all Mithraic ranks.

The emperor's secretary was not a man who thought often of religion, but as he awaited the second stage of the ceremony, the taurobolium, Anatolius felt himself being drawn toward belief. Turning, he faced the image of Mithra. It seemed to move in the wavering light. The god had grasped the bull by its nostrils and was pulling back its massive head for the fatal cut. Anatolius' nostrils flared, burning in the acrid miasma of the cavernous room. A scorpion was shown at the bull's genitals. It symbolized evil, seeking to destroy life at its very source. But the ears of grain which sprang from the doomed bull's tail foretold the victory of good over evil.

Yes, clearly, man inhabited a world where the only constant was the endless struggle between good and evil. At this instant Anatolius knew without doubt that this was true, realized it in a way he had, somehow, not grasped before. The scene blurred as his eyes filled. It was the smoke—or perhaps it was the water the Father had poured over him.

Even then, caught up as he was in this delirious conviction, Anatolius could not help seeing astride the bull not the god Mithra, but a young bull-leaper. The tortured screech of rusty iron on stone shocked this blasphemous image from his mind. He recognized Felix by the beard spilling from under his mask as the captain slid aside the massive grate set in the floor in front of the altar.

A pair of acolytes helped Anatolius disrobe. The heavy cuirass was lifted over his head and his tunic followed. Cold drafts he had not noticed earlier played over his skin.

In the floor, where the grate had been, yawned an oblong of blackness, a pit like a grave. He stepped forward, placing a bare foot into its dark maw, feeling for the narrow steps he had been told he would find there. Colder air rose around his calves and thighs as he stepped firmly down into the waiting pit.

At the bottom, his feet found icy water. The pit was deeper than a man's height. He looked up as the iron grate slid back into place.

Anatolius could not see the bull being led into the mithraeum through a side door, but he could hear the beat of its hooves and the grunts of its handlers and then a resounding crash announced that the bull had been thrown on its side atop the grate.

Looking up past the great shadow on the grate Anatolius caught a glimpse of the white-robed Father, gleaming dagger in his hand. The dagger flashed downward, like the fiery star Anatolius had seen as a child, blazing over the Sea of Marmara.

The bull screamed and Anatolius was bathed in the fire of its sacred blood.

He heard the words of the Father. "Accept this sacrifice to your glory, and accept your humble follower Anatolius to serve Thee in the degree of Soldier."

Then strong hands grasped him and pulled him up out of the pit.

He found himself smiling.

Standing beside a pillar, John smiled as well. He had ascended to the degree of Runner of the Sun, one rank below that of Father. He recalled his own mixed feelings when he had undergone the rite: elation, joy, pride, and perhaps a dash of terror. It had reminded him of the last hour before battle in the days when he had been a soldier both by occupation and by Mithraic degree. How long ago it seemed. It had been another world, another time.

But for now he rejoiced with the others as the scarlet-bedaubed Anatolius, the new Soldier, was pulled from the pit. Bright red rivulets ran down the young man's body and legs, pooling at his feet. A wide, almost insane, bloody grin had transformed Anatolius' gentle face into one which would have given even a hardened battle veteran pause.

Perhaps Anatolius had found the warrior in himself at last.

"It is always moving, isn't it?" came a voice at John's side. "Whether here or in Bretania."

He turned and found himself facing Thomas, who had pulled aside his mask. Before John could reply, Thomas walked away.

John was about to follow him when Felix blocked his path. "It's good to see Anatolius advance," Felix boomed. "Maybe the poet will make a soldier yet!"

"Anatolius will be a better Soldier than some might imagine." John looked over the excubitor captain's broad shoulder. Thomas had vanished into the crowd of worshippers.

"He had a keen eye just now. Blood will bring it out." Felix lowered his voice. "John, I'm going around to Isis' house, and I'd like you to accompany me. I'm buying Berta."

Berta? She was the little blonde at Isis' establishment, John recalled. The girl in whom Thomas had taken an interest. "You should take a lawyer, Felix."

Felix shook his shaggy head vehemently. "Men who fight with words, they're worse than poets."

"Isis drives a hard bargain and I hear Berta is quite popular...."

"It's been arranged. I want you to look at the contract. If it's ever questioned I am sure the word of the Lord Chamberlain will weigh more than the opinion of any lawyer."

"You don't have to worry about Isis trying to cheat you."

"No? I haven't mentioned her price."

"You can find a servant at a better price elsewhere."

Felix looked flustered. "I'm not looking for a servant, John. I intend to marry Berta. We're both from Germania."

Chapter Twenty-six

Berta smoothed the last of the kohl into her eyebrows, pursed the full lips she had reddened with wine dregs—the customers enjoyed that—and evaluated her efforts in her hand mirror. Yes, it was a passable job even if the chalk on her cheeks was a little uneven. She was almost ready for the first of the night's visitors.

She glanced at the small urn sitting unobtrusively in the corner. It was a water clock. She smiled when she recollected that according to Madam it had once graced a Roman court of law, ensuring that representatives for both sides were given an equal but reasonable length of time for their orations. At least Berta, unlike lawyers, could guarantee her clients satisfaction by the time the water ran out.

Berta plaited her hair, thinking how much she enjoyed her life in the city. Perhaps after all her father had been correct when he had told her, as she clung sobbing to him before he left her at Madam's house, that she would enjoy her new life.

Her thoughts turned to the raggedly dressed woman she had met in the market place. The woman was a fool to turn down the chance to save herself and her husband by working at such a fine house as Madam's.

The whole world passed through Madam's house. The men she met had been everywhere. Such tales they told. And the gifts they brought. Cosmetics, perfumes. Wonderful jewelry, as beautiful as anything worn by all those fine ladies she had entertained the other night.

Remembering, she reached into the inconspicuous tear in her mattress and pulled out the pendant the old man at the palace had given her. Its fine gold chain flashed enticingly in the orange lamplight. Dimmer points of light flickered within its flecked central stone like stars on a winter's night.

She smiled as she recalled the palace celebration, how she'd danced, so gracefully, across the table. The handsome young men had all desired her—and the not so handsome old men as well. She liked being desired. It had given her an easier life than having to toil in rocky fields, or chase goats up and down the hillside, or clean out the pens of the swine, just as her father had said. Not but what she still sometimes dealt with swine.

But, as she had recently realized, the career he had chosen for her was a short one. Applying liberal dabs of perfume to her wrists, she weighed the recent offers she had received from some of her regular clients. One or two were rich men. But not young men. Still, a rich lady such as she would soon become could still enjoy her slim, young men as well as her husband, or so the other girls at Madam's house had told her.

She put the bauble back into its hiding place. A determined look crossed her face. When the time came, she would be the one to choose her husband, not Madam.

She glanced around. All was in order. Soon she would be free of this place, she resolved, arranging cushions. But she would not make a hasty decision. It was too important. She certainly would not leave to live with Felix, even though he'd been cajoling her to marry him for weeks. She had been as plain with him about that as she could be without actually discouraging him from returning. He was too old for her.

Yes, when she married, she intended to marry into a noble family. And a wealthy one. Then she would live in a fine house in the city, and spend the hottest summer days at a beautiful villa in the countryside. Her houses would have marble floors and colorful wall mosaics and statues. There would be well tended gardens, with shady trees and flowers and many pools. She would spend her days being waited on hand and foot, with nothing to do but wear lovely clothes and jewelry. Yes, she decided, I shall wear emeralds every day. And all the rich ladies at the palace who think they are better than me will want to come to the wonderful dinners I shall give. They'll envy me, because of my youth and my beauty.

She smiled to herself. I will never have to entertain men again, well, not unless I want to, and then they'll be young men, muscular, smooth faced, clean. Yet still, she found herself thinking again about Felix. The big bearded captain made her smile. He was nice enough. Nicer than the fat man who had been around too often recently. Perhaps the one who called himself a knight would return. He had certainly lived up to the promise of his fiery red hair. A barbarian, to be sure. Not as cultured or, by the look of his clothes, as rich as some of her other clients, yet there was something very attractive about him

Footsteps in the hallway interrupted her musings. There was a soft knock at her door.

She filled the water clock in the corner from a jug. The liquid, less than an hour's worth, began to drip steadily from the spout in the bottom of the urn into the holding bowl.

"Come in, my dear," she said softly, opening the door.

Isis tied up the parchment scroll and affixed a wax seal. The bill of sale having been completed, she asked to speak to Felix in private. "I must take the part of Berta's mother. The legal necessities are over but there are other things I expect of the husbands of my girls."

John left the room. He found Darius sitting on a bench in the entrance hall. When John sat next to him, he felt dwarfed.

"Tell me, Darius, have you remembered hearing anything unusual or strange the night Leukos was found in the alley?"

"More than the usual odd noises, you mean?" Darius smiled at his feeble jest. He looked tired. "To tell you the truth, John, with Madam torturing that infernal organ night and day you can't hear a thing. We had a party of charioteers last night. Rowdy bunch. I had to subdue a couple of them after they made disparaging remarks about my appearance. But no, as I told Madam, I heard nothing unusual."

"And you're sure you didn't see Leukos here before he was found dead in the alley?"

"I'm certain. I would have—" Darius' reply was interrupted by a shriek from upstairs. He leapt up, an erupting volcano. "Someone's hurting one of the girls!"

He pounded for the stairs but had barely set sandal to step when a terrified, half-dressed girl flung herself downstairs into his arms. She clung to him, sobbing.

"There now, Helena." His voice was surprisingly tender. "Show him to me and I'll…. "

"No," wailed the girl louder. "It's not me. It's Berta!"

When John reached the second floor cubicle that reeked of perfume, he saw Berta reclining languidly on her bed, her short tunic hiked up teasingly. Half leaning against the wall, she stared wide eyed, as if surprised by the girls who crowded around her doorway, whimpering and exclaiming over the discovery.

Berta could no longer be anyone's wife.

She was dead.

John pushed through the girls in the doorway. He could see the mark of a powerful hand on Berta's slim neck.

"Strangled," he muttered to Darius.

Darius began to snarl a string of oaths, biting them back as Isis arrived from downstairs.

"Who would do this to one of my girls?" the madam wailed.

The room contained little, John thought as he glanced around. Little except perhaps the dreams any young girl might spin. There was a bed, its coverings rumpled. Berta had been a slight girl, obviously unable to put up much of a struggle against her attacker. On a table nearby, the wine and sweetmeats awaiting visitors were undisturbed beside a few pots of makeup and a jar of perfume. The water clock in the corner, John noted, was still nearly full. Had she filled it in anticipation of a client?

"Felix! Stay back!" Darius warned a newcomer.

The excubitor captain pushed past to stoop over the girl's body. He was silent but tears streamed down his bearded face. He was familiar with the death of fighting men on the field of battle, but this was a much more terrible scene to contemplate.

"Mithra," he entreated his god softly, "so you send a stealthy murderer to my lover? I wonder, would the Christian's god be so cruel?"

"Zurvan!" Darius swore with belated caution. "Who's guarding the front door?"

John heard him pound away, but did not follow.

There was something unnatural in Felix's strangely calm tone, as if his lips were forming words of their own volition while his brain ignored their content.

Then he howled. It was a wolf's howl, a battle cry, a sound of pain and fury. The girls clustered in the doorway began to scream. Some fled hysterically down the hall to their rooms.

Felix stopped, turned away from the bed, and left the room in grim-faced silence, having paused just long enough to adjust Berta's displaced tunic to cover her decently.

Chapter Twenty-seven

Excited shouts greeted Cornelia as she and Europa walked into the courtyard of the Inn of the Centaurs. Unlike at the Hippodrome, the shouts were not directed at Europa. The crowd was clustered around a circle inscribed in the dirt.

"My money's on my plump friend!" cried a rotund man Cornelia guessed was the innkeeper Kaloethes from descriptions she'd been given by members of the troupe. He clutched a quail.

The man the innkeeper addressed resembled a quail himself. He was short and soft looking and wore a dalmatic covered with feathers.

Cornelia halted. "Let's see what this game is about. It might be useful to the troupe."

"That bird's better fit for the table than winning you gold," jeered a young man dressed as a charioteer. He was as short as the feathered man but more muscular.

"We'll let the Master Quail Filliper decide that," Kaloethes replied. He bent over with a grunt and placed his bird on a board in the center of the ring. It stood there blinking stupidly.

The filliper made a show of shaking his hands as if to limber them, sending a few pinfeathers flying off his peculiar garment. He bent forward with an expression of keen concentration and snapped a finger sharply against the quail's head.

The quail instantly fluttered out of the circle and wobbled over toward the women. Europa giggled and scooped the disoriented creature up. "What a silly game!"

"Lost again, Kaloethes," said the charioteer. "Tomorrow I'll bring my bird. It's so well-trained it sits on the board as if it was nailed there!"

"Hand over the bet," the filliper ordered.

The innkeeper glared as coins changed hands. "One more wager! I have another quail and I'll wager both birds it won't stir if you kick it in the beak."

"You're a man who never learns from experience. I'll double your wager."

"Done!" Kaloethes went to the door of the inn and Cornelia and Europa followed. Europa handed him the still groggy bird. "Here's your quail back. Better luck next time."

"He's lucky I don't feel like plucking him or he'd go into the stew pot within the hour," Kaloethes growled.

"We've come to talk to the bull-leaping troupe staying here," Cornelia said.

"Oh, that bunch? They're somewhere about the city." He vanished inside and emerged with a new quail, noticeably less plump then the first. He frowned at Cornelia. "Still here? I haven't seen those rascals. What's your business with them?"

"That's for their ears."

"Ah, that kind of business is it? They have the first room on the second floor."

Without waiting for a response Kaloethes strode back to the ring in the dirt, brandishing his new avian champion. "He can't wait to pluck your coins," he told the filliper, as he sat the quail on the board. He grinned. "Try to beat that, my friend."

The filliper went through his routine of waggling his hands and shedding feathers. He bent, snapped his finger against the quail's head.

The quail fell over on its side.

"Still in the circle," crowed Kaloethes. "I win!"

The filliper reddened with rage. "It's dead!"

"Nothing in the rules about the bird having to be alive." Kaloethes extended his hand for his winnings.

The filliper leapt forward and grasped him by the throat.

The charioteer took a step toward the fighters as if ready to break them apart, but he was saved the effort.

Cornelia, standing near the inn door, was almost knocked over by the cursing Fury that burst forth.

"You fool! You've been losing wagers again!" screamed the innkeeper's wife. "You ought to be a magician! You can make coins disappear faster than anyone I know!"

She belabored both men with her fists. They retreated into the circle with the dead quail.

"Excuse me. If it's magick you want, I can show you an excellent example." The voice was quiet yet somehow, like magick, it cut through the hubbub. The speaker, a wizened ancient, got up from the bench beside the fountain.

Hadn't Cornelia noticed the bench when she and Europa arrived? Why hadn't she seen the old man sitting there?

Mistress Kaloethes turned her attention from the cowed men. "No! We'll have no more trouble today, Ahasuerus. Off with the lot of you!"

She made shushing motions and the crowd began to disperse, grumbling.

"Come on," Cornelia told Europa. They went into the inn and up to the second floor. There was no one in the troupe's room. She rifled through satchels. "Not here!"

"What are you searching for?" It was Kaloethes, suspicious and out of breath, after running upstairs.

"Our costumes. We thought our colleagues had inadvertently packed them with their clothes," Cornelia said.

When she and Europa went downstairs they found Mistress Kaloethes seated at the table with the man she had called Ahasuerus.

"Where did you get that egg?" Mistress Kaloethes was demanding of him.

"From the kitchen this morning," Ahasuerus replied.

"What? If my husband doesn't wager this place away you'll steal it!"

Ahasuerus placed the egg in her hand and commanded her to question it about her future.

Europa stifled a laugh as the woman swallowed her anger and addressed the egg as requested. Ahasuerus put the egg on the table and, waving his hands in mystical gestures, mumbled what sounded very much like nonsense over it. Finally he said "Move that plate nearer. I am going to break this egg open. If the contents are red it means a happy future. If they're black…well…."

As he spoke he tapped the egg on the edge of the plate.

Red-tinted contents oozed forth.

Mistress Kaloethes clapped her hands. "Ah, happiness is in store!" she cooed, by all appearances instantly mollified. "Perhaps I was too hard on my poor husband. I should let him know the good news." She got up and climbed the stairs to find Kaloethes.

Cornelia smiled at Ahasuerus and complimented him on his showmanship. "That was well-done. I saw you exchange the eggs, but then I knew what to look for."

"You have sharp eyes, lady," he returned. "And so do I. Few have the skill to see the future."

"It takes a fair amount of skill to extract the innards of an egg, color them with wine, and get them back in the shell without breaking it."

"You need a steady hand," Ahasuerus acknowledged. "The worst part is repairing the small hole in the egg afterwards, especially if you've been sampling the wine beforehand. I usually carry a couple of prepared eggs with me when I go out and about in case I meet a possible client. In her case I thought it better not to give her the egg filled with soot. It always means trouble ahead, or so I tell my clients. But how did you know how the trick's accomplished?"

"There's a magician in our troupe. He showed me once. Unfortunately he does not always accomplish the effect he intends," Cornelia replied. "One of his most spectacular failures was when he set fire to a house with his flying Hecate trick. We left in great haste."

Ahasuerus smiled. "One of the tricks to being a magician is knowing when to leave in great haste."

Europa laid her hand on Cornelia's arm. "But do you think he could tell us our futures, mother?" she whispered.

Europa knew very well that the troupe's own magician was nothing but a clever charlatan, Cornelia thought. Strange how people were more willing to respect the skills of strangers than of those they knew. "I doubt it." Cornelia smiled at Ahasuerus to soften her words.

"Oh, but you are wrong, my dear. The future is all around us. It's in the shape of the clouds we see through that door. In the wine stains on this table. In the sound of the wind in the fig tree by the fountain. The future can be foretold by anyone who has the knowledge to interpret the signs and the wit to use their eyes and ears."

An orator as well as a charlatan, Cornelia thought as she escorted Europa away beyond the reach of the ancient's persuasive tongue.

Halfway across the courtyard they were approached by one of the men who had been watching the quail filliping. "Pardon me, ladies. My name is Gregorius. I heard you inquire about the troupe staying here. Can I be of assistance?"

Cornelia noticed Gregorius glancing at Europa. It wasn't uncommon. She was an attractive young woman, but perhaps too inclined to encourage such attentions. "We don't need any help, thank you. We'll come back later."

"My apologies. I meant no offense. You're not the first to be interested in Kaloethes' guests. Why, the Lord Chamberlain himself questioned me about them."

"Indeed?"

"Yes. I shall not soon forget it. It isn't every day one is interrogated by John the Eunuch."

The statement hit Cornelia like a hammer blow. Surely she must have misheard. "What did you call him?" Her words emerged faintly.

"John the Eunuch. It's what everyone calls him."

She felt Europa's hand clasp her arm. "People will have their coarse jests about high officials."

Gregorius looked confused. "It isn't a joke. It's just what he is. His kind are underfoot all over the palace. Lord Chamberlains are always eunuchs. Since they can't have any heirs, they aren't as likely to have designs on the empire."

"I see."

Cornelia allowed Europa to tug her in the direction of the street. The courtyard, the archway they passed under, seemed to have no substance. She was dreaming. She had been dreaming since the instant she had opened the door of the ship's cabin and seen John.

Yet it had seemed real.

Perhaps that had been real, and this was a dream. A nightmare. Cornelia willed herself to wake up, tried to push sleep away, but the dream continued to press down on her with all the infinite, crushing weight of reality.

Chapter Twenty-eight

Two deaths in four days.

In overcrowded Constantinople, it was not unusual for death to brush past. But two murders, both involving Isis' house—one in the alley outside, the other inside—could there be some connection?

The Lord Chamberlain's study was lit by wavering lamplight but when a brighter light flickered across its walls, John turned toward the open window, half expecting to see the unsteady glow from one of the fires that so often raged in Constantinople. He was relieved to see a flash of distant lightning.

He drank more wine from his cracked cup. The girl in the mosaic seemed to be looking at him with reproach in her big eyes.

"No, my child, I haven't forgotten you now that I have a real daughter," he muttered. Zoe seemed unappeased. If he were unable to deal with a child of glass and imagination how could he deal with one of flesh and blood?

"Perhaps it isn't that," John continued to think aloud. "Do you imagine I have spent too much time thinking about Cornelia and Europa and too little unraveling Leukos' death? I assure you, I have explored many possibilities."

Why then was he no nearer to his destination, his solution?

"And now there has been another murder. But you wouldn't understand," John told the girl. "You are only a child."

He recalled his dream of running tirelessly across fields, from which he had been awakened by the emperor's messenger, young Hektor. Was the dream perhaps prophetic, or merely wishful thinking?

Surely not. It could be more readily explained as an imbalance in the humors or a reflection of his waking experiences. Seeing Cornelia and her—their—daughter in the Hippodrome had brought back to him the feelings of his youth.

The cup rose to his lips again and John was surprised to find it empty.

As empty as his thoughts.

A well-dressed palace official unadvisedly turns down a dark alley during a celebration and is stabbed to death. A young prostitute is strangled.

These were not unusual occurrences. Perhaps he was trying to find some meaning in them that simply was not there.

And what about Thomas? He claimed to have visited Leukos.

Could a man who claimed to be a knight from Bretania questing after a holy relic be trusted, thought John, a man who had, moreover, surreptitiously followed him through the palace grounds in the middle of the night?

John had begun to find Thomas' behavior suspicious. What was he to think now that Thomas had revealed himself to be a fellow Mithran?

Thunder rumbled over the walls of the city as the storm moved inland. John rose abruptly from his seat.

"Peter," he called. "I'm going out."

After he had secured the house door behind his master, Peter returned to the study. Keeping his watery eyes averted from the blasphemous mosaic, he retrieved John's cracked cup. Why did the Lord Chamberlain insist upon using a thing so time worn? Sometimes it seemed to Peter that John was like one of those holy hermits who denounce every worldly pleasure. Except, of course, that John was a pagan.

More puzzling yet to the old servant was why his master sometimes spoke to the wall of his study. Not that Peter eavesdropped, but in the course of his duties he often passed the room and had observed John gazing at the mosaic as he spoke. That had frightened Peter. Holy men often went mad, it was true. But surely the Lord Chamberlain was a man of this world?

On impulse, Peter sat down on John's chair. His heart raced, although there was no reason he should not rest his old bones. Certainly his master would not object. He forced his gaze toward the mosaic, to see what John would see. He found himself looking into the dark eyes of a young girl. Eyes of glass that appeared to stare back at him. That would in an instant, blink. He was certain of it.

Peter jumped up and was out of the room droning a familiar hymn as he hurried down the hall.

He had not looked at the mosaic again because he knew the girl's expression had changed, and that was a vision he did not dare to look upon.

John veered off the wide, torch-lit Mese into the darker streets and alleys that snaked up to the palace walls, twisting and turning as if looking for a way in, but being continually forced back on themselves. A fitful wind snapped his cloak and whipped drops of rain into his face.

From his swift, purposeful stride, his unhesitating turns into obscure byways, an observer would have supposed the Lord Chamberlain was hurrying to some important destination. In fact, John's movements were unplanned, his speed merely a reflection of the frantic pace of his thoughts. Although his mercenary days were long past, when some knotty problem arose to snare him in its serpent's coils there always came a time when John's body insisted on action. Since he was no longer soldiering and since battling with a blade would not in any case pierce the demons of the mind, at such times he invariably walked, hoping his feet would carry him to a solution.

Noticing a tradesman, an idea occurred to him. The vendor was on his knees in front of a cramped niche, mending the rickety wooden table on which he displayed his wares during the day. The man, a ragged, furtive creature, looked up, startled, at the sound of John's approach.

"Do you have any fruit? Vegetables?" John asked.

The shopkeeper eyed John's expensive garments and boots warily and scrambled to his feet. The lamp by which he had been working projected John's shadow, supernaturally large, against the blank wall of the tenement on the other side of the narrow street. "None that one of your position would find suitable, great one."

"Anything you have would be acceptable. I shall also need a basket."

The man's gaze darted back and forth in the lamplight, his mind alert for a trap. "I could sell you a basket, but the fruit's sat in the heat all day."

"I assure you it will be satisfactory." A coin flashed in the dim light.

"The fruit out here's probably spoiled, like I said, but I might be able to find some that'd be edible."

"I don't need anything fit for the emperor's table." John turned his hand slightly so light caught the coin again. The shopkeeper's eyes gleamed as brightly as the currency.

Rummaging noisily through the baskets and boxes in his niche, the fellow sounded relieved as he replied. "Well, then, I can certainly provide something that will suit you. Nothing here would be fit for the emperor."

John traded the nominal weight of the coin for the considerably heavier basket of fruit and continued on toward the square at the end of the street. The wind howling through narrow spaces between the buildings on each side pushed at his back as if attempting to thrust him bodily out into the open. When it stopped abruptly, he heard raindrops splattering against the overhanging balconies which almost met above him. Suddenly their staccato beat was engulfed in a formless roar as the storm arrived in all its fury.

Under the balconies it had been relatively sheltered, but when John stepped out into the square he was soaked as immediately as if he had plunged fully dressed into a pool at the baths. He paused, wiping water out of his eyes.

At the other side of the square, a column rose into the night to a height just above the two-story buildings all around. John hurried forward.

Reaching the column, he leaned his head back, hand protecting his eyes, trying to look upward through the rain. A lightning flash illuminated a low railing there and a motionless figure.

"I am here to pay you a visit, my friend," John called up. "I have brought some fruit. I mean you no harm."

The figure, which might have been a statue since it did not move, refused to reply. Another flash of lightning illuminated a wooden ladder. John reached up to grasp a greasy rung. Thunder shook the column as John began to haul himself upwards.

It was a relatively short journey, but not an easy one. The ladder was slippery, the rising wind yanked at his water-sodden cloak, and the downpour beat on his shoulders.

Truth to Mithra, John thought, he was not afraid of Zeus' thunderbolts. It was not that the Lord Chamberlain had more courage, or was more foolhardy, than most. He firmly believed that the Lord of Light he followed would not allow him to perish at the hands of a weaker god.

When he reached the top John remained leaning on the ladder, clinging with one hand to the iron railing that ringed the column's tiny platform. He had no wish to step out onto it. There was, he judged, not enough room for him and the stylite unless the man were to move to one side, and John suspected that the stylite's legs had, long since, become locked in their habitual position. It was well known that these Christian ascetics often lived atop their columns for years or decades, never descending to the earth or taking shelter, whatever the season or the weather.

In some strange way this self torture was supposed to glorify their mysterious god.

"There is fruit in this basket," he informed the stylite, carefully setting it down near what intermittent lightning flashes revealed to be sticks of legs. Mithra, how the man stank.

"The Lord in His wisdom announces thunder with the lightning bolt," intoned the holy man in a surprisingly firm voice, without looking at John. "Bless you, my son," he added.

"I have a question."

The stylite nodded, ropy-veined neck moving, while from his shoulders down his body remained motionless. The matted hair hanging past his shoulders and the beard dangling nearly to his waist were dripping in the deluge. "The fire," he muttered. "God's house is consumed. The evils of mankind will be turned to ashes."

John looked past the stylite toward where Justinian's new church was rising. It was certainly a different sort of tribute to God than the one offered up by this holy man. Was the stylite remembering the fire which had destroyed the old Church of the Holy Wisdom?

"There was a man, a friend of mine, murdered not far from here," John said. From his precarious vantage point John looked out over the city. Here and there a few smoldering torches not yet doused by the torrent shone dimly, like spent charcoal in the bottom of a brazier. Crosses rose starkly from the roofs of many houses. Some crosses were wooden, others more elaborate, alerting both God and men to the faith of those who slept beneath them.

"There," John pointed, trying to direct the stylite's gaze. "In that alley. That is where it happened. Did you chance to see anything?"

The holy man chuckled softly. For a terrible instant, a lightning bolt linked the city to the heavens. It was followed by a wave of thunder. John could feel its vibration. Some building close by had surely been struck.

The stylite began to laugh. "Can that be the finger of God seeking out a sinner?"

John felt a sudden wave of anger. "You must have seen something from up here! You have nothing to do but look down into the streets. Consider my question. I'm seeking one who is guilty of murder."

The stylite laughed again. "No man is guilty but one who sets down his cross."

John began to ask the stylite about the guilt of a man who would plunge a dagger into another's ribs but stopped himself. There was no point. The stylite was obviously mad.

He scanned the scene below. The alley he had tried to bring to the stylite's attention ran between a tall tenement and Isis' house, where Berta had died. Further on lay the inn in which he had interviewed Ahasuerus and where Thomas was staying. The narrow alley continued on toward the Mese and the Church of the Holy Wisdom with patriarchal and imperial palaces close by. The city pressed in all around, a jumble of houses and humanity.

He suddenly realized that his climb had not been wasted after all. Looking down from the stylite's column, John was reminded of what he knew so well as to take for granted, that the city, for all its winding alleys and assorted squares and forums, its magnificent architecture and obscene hovels, was a small place. Though the world of the palace might seem far removed from Isis' house and the alley where Leukos had died, it was not, and although the murderer might be lost among the crowd, if he was still in the city, he was not far away.

The stylite was still laughing. John, growing even angrier, demanded to know the reason.

The holy man stopped abruptly. "Is it not comical?" he asked. "Even the holders of the highest offices have sinned, and all of them are but wayward children before the Lord. Even you. Even the emperor himself."

"Mithra!"

A sudden gust of wind caught John unprepared. For a shocking instant, he felt himself swaying backwards, his grip on the railing gone. There was a lightness in his chest, as if he were flying. Then his other hand tightened its hold on the side of the ladder.

The shifting wind slapped a sheet of rain across his face. He climbed back down to the street, ears ringing with the stylite's laughter.

Chapter Twenty-nine

Elsewhere in the storm-shrouded city others had gathered to consult a different sort of oracle.

The cramped palace room was as gloomy as the night outside, one of the indistinct figures squatting in the semi-darkness tended to a partially covered lantern. Acrid smoke from the almost extinguished flame filled the air. The feeble light died at the edges of the darkness in the corners, glimmered on the white of an eye, a moist lip, and cast a sheen on the water in a large bowl.

Justinian's young page Hektor sat beside the brimming bowl, a frown on his powdered face.

"Why didn't you get a chicken? Too scared in case it pecked you?" one of the boys jeered.

"A cook caught me trying to steal one," Hektor replied. "Slapped me too, but he'll regret it."

"What did you do? Spit in his soup pot?"

"Better than that. I went back when he wasn't looking and stuck a dead mouse in the pan of lentils he was cooking. A word in the right ear—and I'm the one to do it—and Justinian will hear about it and the cook will find himself without a head. We all know how much the imperial pair are terrified of being poisoned, and who's to say the mouse was not poisoned first and kept handy until needed?"

The story was met by laughter from the assembled pages.

"Does a cook with its head cut off run around like a chicken with its head cut off?" someone wondered.

Clucking noises emanated from the semi-darkness.

"Shhhh," Hektor cautioned. "Is there anyone in the hall?"

He listened until the rushing of blood in his ears seemed loud enough to drown out any other sound.

"What's the water for?" asked Hektor's interrogator, in a whisper this time. "Going to wash your feet? Smells like they need it!"

"It's to tell your future, Tarquin."

"Without a chicken to sacrifice?"

"Forget about chickens! Now, sit in front of the bowl. You have to stir it with your finger, and then I'll interpret what the currents say. But you have to keep absolutely still or it won't work. The rest of you, hold Tarquin tight and don't let go until I say you can." He paused and glanced around the ring of shadowed faces. "Otherwise demons will appear and carry you all off!"

The pages huddled around Tarquin. They were still in the heavy make-up they wore while gracing the court, but aside from that they were entirely naked. It was obvious they were no more than children.

Hektor snickered, a sound that caused more than one boy to flinch. They had all suffered at one time or another in Hektor's hands. None of them would have changed places with Tarquin.

"Stir the water," Hektor ordered. "What are you waiting for?"

"You're jealous because the Master of the Offices prefers me," Tarquin riposted. His kohl-outlined eyes glittered. "Anyhow, it's not the right way to read fortunes. You have to have chicken guts. Everybody knows that!"

"Oh? You heard about the fortune-teller reading them for the empress at her celebration? Well, I was there, and it didn't impress me," Hektor sneered. "This way is much more accurate."

"What did he tell the empress, if you really were there?"

"Tell us, Hektor," another boy piped up.

"I don't dare repeat it. It's too horrible. A terrible fate. Stop wasting time, Tarquin. Stir the water. Or are you scared?"

Tarquin stared down into the bowl. "You're not going to tell my future. You're only going to make up a lie."

"Swear on the True Cross, I'd never do such a thing." Hektor made the Christian sign. He wished he'd managed to steal the chicken. Crucifying it might be an enlightening experience.

Tarquin must have seen the wild look that crept into Hektor's eyes because he emitted a whimper and lowered his hand toward the bowl.

"Hold him tight," Hektor said.

Tarquin stirred the water with a grubby forefinger.

"Ah, my pretty boy," Hektor leered in what was supposed to be a basso profundo as he looked into the bowl. "Do you see that?"

"What? Where?"

"Here, you fool!" Hektor grabbed Tarquin by the back of the neck and pushed his face into the bowl. "Keep hold of him, or you'll get the same!" he ordered the others. One boy sobbed.

"You baby!" Hektor said, pushing the struggling Tarquin's face deeper into the water.

"You'll drown him!"

"He won't be much loss, and in that case his future was certainly shown in the water!" Hektor laughed and yanked Tarquin's head up out of the bowl. "A little more fortune telling, Tarquin?"

Before his dazed victim could splutter in reply Hektor pushed his head back under the water.

One of the boys jumped up, preparing to run. "Stay there," Hektor commanded. "Don't alert the guards."

The boy dropped back down, leaned over, and vomited where he sat.

Tarquin was allowed to emerge into air again.

"And now for your future," Hektor intoned. "By Jupiter and Cybele and the Emperor of the Toads. By the left arm of John the Baptist and the talisman of all healing, in the names of Justinian and Our Lord Jesus Christ, show us what fate waits for the boy Tarquin!"

Hektor stared into the slowly settling water.

He suddenly felt lightheaded. The floor appeared to be tilting. Perhaps there was something in this soothsaying business, he thought in horror. Perhaps one of those fearsome entities he'd invoked had actually heard him and responded. His heart leapt in sudden panic.

The naked boys looked afraid, startled eyes wide in their garishly rouged faces.

"More light!" Hektor demanded of the lantern tender.

He peered down at the bowl. The eddies squirmed like living things. Surely it must be an effect of the smoke-induced tears welling in his eyes?

"What do you see?"

"Go on, you can't see nothing in a bowl of water!"

"Be quiet!" Hektor' voice quavered. "It's like listening to thunder to tell the future. Look there, see, waves."

He became aware of a powerful presence. Someone or something was looking down at him from a great height. He hadn't meant any harm. It had all been a joke. He hadn't even remembered exactly what the old soothsayer had chanted. Or had he? The uneasy feeling that he was being watched grew stronger. The currents in the water formed shapes. There, a face...a familiar face...it was...no...it couldn't be...and yet...it was....

"Hektor!"

He leapt up wildly at the sound of his name. Startled boys scattered, screaming.

A hand grabbed Hektor's bare shoulder and spun him around.

Hektor gasped. He was looking up into the scowling face of the Lord Chamberlain who, without benefit of chicken entrails or thunder, well knew the destiny of pretty powdered boys who grew into manhood, but was too kind to reveal it.

Chapter Thirty

By the time Hektor had dressed his fright had apparently faded. He slumped on a couch in the nearby room to which he had been led and regarded the Lord Chamberlain with sullen contempt.

His look reminded John that while most court pages left imperial service upon attaining manhood, a number stayed on in other employment at the palace. He wondered briefly if Hektor might take that path, and possible future ramifications if he had already made a bitter enemy of him. Such calculations were never far from the minds of those who wished to survive at Justinian's court.

"What do you want with me?" the boy snarled. "I know it's not the usual reason. Not you!"

John shut the door. The room was simply furnished with the couch, a stool, a low table on which a lamp burned, and a wooden cross on one wall. There were no windows. John pulled the stool to the couch and sat down.

"Were you at the empress' gathering the other night, Hektor?"

"Most of us were. I'll tell Theodora you've been asking about her."

"I'm sure you will." John ignored the boy's insolence. "What went on that night?"

Hektor shrugged. "Nothing much. The usual things."

"Dining, entertainment?"

"Are you sure I can't do something for you, Lord Chamberlain? I'm very obliging. Is there anything anyone can do for someone like you?" Hektor reached out and stroked John's knee.

John brushed the boy's hand aside angrily. Hektor smirked.

"I've been told there was a soothsayer there," John continued, keeping his voice even. "Is that true?"

"Perhaps. I don't remember."

"You will remember to whom you are speaking, Hektor. No doubt there are powerful men at court who would protect you to conceal their secrets. Unless, of course, you are merely silenced, for a dead tongue can tell no tales. But I advise Justinian, who has condemned the sort of services you provide, and I am afraid your friends, if that is what you call them, won't dare to defy their emperor if he decides to grant me your pretty little head on a stake."

Hektor' fists clenched but he said nothing.

"Now," John continued, "tell me about the soothsayer."

Hektor glared, but answered immediately. "The charlatan? For one thing, the smelly old goat had his wrinkled paws all over one of the whores there."

"You mean he didn't prefer little boys? What about his readings? Did he tell anyone's future?"

"Theodora wanted her fortune told."

"Using a chicken's entrails?"

Hektor nodded. John wondered if the woman for whom Ahasuerus had mentioned providing such a reading had been the empress herself. He would have to speak to the soothsayer again. He asked Hektor about the chicken used for the empress' reading.

"Theodora sent one of the guards to the kitchens for it. The knife must have been quite blunt, since the chicken squawked a lot." Hektor smiled.

"I presume the reading was conducted in a more decorous manner than your own?"

"If you mean were Theodora and her guests naked…."

John's warning look stopped Hektor in mid-sentence.

"Do you remember what the soothsayer said?"

"The old goat told her she would be rich. An easy prediction, her being the empress."

John's attention was drawn to the door. There was muted shuffling outside; the other pages were probably taking turns to eavesdrop.

"Did you see the captain of the excubitors?"

"Yes. He and his guards were ogling the women. I could have strangled the empress myself for all the guarding they were doing."

"Who else?"

Hektor shrugged again. "Your usual prissy courtiers and puffed-up officials. And a flock of whores. Some of them dressed like virgins!"

"What about the entertainment?"

"Jugglers, mimes, some poor whiny poet, dwarves. The usual rubbish. Then there were two women, acrobats."

"Acrobats?"

"They were doing handstands and cartwheels, things like that."

John frowned. "Two women, you say."

"I guess you would call one a girl. The other was an older woman. I heard someone say they were performing with a traveling troupe."

Then Cornelia and Europa had attended Theodora's gathering. John felt cold. Perhaps it was just the soaked clothing that clung uncomfortably to his back and shoulders.

Lounging even lower on the couch, Hektor was beginning to regain his courage. "Why don't you get out of those wet clothes, Lord Chamberlain, " he suggested sweetly.

John got to his feet, pushing the stool away more violently than he had intended. It crashed against the wall. The wooden cross, jarred loose, fell. Hektor clamped his hand over his mouth to hide his smile.

John walked out quickly, ignoring the cluster of pages gathered across the corridor in an all-too-obviously innocent game of knucklebones. He hoped the rain was still pouring down. He needed cleansing.

Chapter Thirty-one

In the first light of morning, the Inn of the Centaurs lay quiet save for a repetitive dripping, a reminder of the previous night's storms and the roof's woeful lack of repair. So it was that Mistress Kaloethes, prodding the embers in the kitchen brazier, was immediately alerted by the creak of leather and heavy footsteps to the passing of someone down the hallway. She looked out.

"Thomas!"

Caught at the door of the inn, he turned with apparent reluctance, his face growing as red as his hair.

"Mistress Kaloethes! I thought everyone would be sleeping this early. I was trying to leave quietly. Not permanently, of course," he added, flustered. "You can see I haven't got my baggage. I'll pay you in advance." He fumbled at the pouch on his belt.

The innkeeper's wife emitted a piercing laugh. Her chubby face was as red as Thomas' beard. Her bright color stemmed not from embarrassment but from her customary liberal application of rouge.

"Your word is good here, Thomas. It's a pleasure to have a guest of your quality. An emissary from a king's court. Some of our other guests, well, they're not the sort I prefer. But I hope you can draw your sword more quickly than coins from your pouch!" She gave another loud laugh.

"I hope so, for I am trained in war, not commerce, lady."

"Lady? Well, well, you are a silver-tongued rogue!"

"My apologies, but I really must be on my way."

"Always out and about, aren't you?"

"Constantinople is a most interesting city."

"Have you seen the old soothsayer in your travels?"

"Ahasuerus? Not this morning. Is he causing you trouble?"

Mistress Kaloethes waggled a fat finger in Thomas' face. "I'm not the sort who would disparage my guests, Thomas, but let's just say he eats like a winning horse at the Hippodrome but pays like a loser."

"He's an old man. Just forgetful. If I see him I'll remind him about his debts." Thomas backed out the door. Mistress Kaloethes watched him make his way hastily across the gleaming puddles in the courtyard.

He exchanged greetings with the innkeeper who was staggering in, burdened with a large sack.

As soon as Kaloethes was indoors, his wife fell into his wake, a plump dolphin pacing a trireme. She did not, however, emulate the dolphin's traditional bestowal of good fortune.

"How did it go? A good night?"

Master Kaloethes dropped his sack on the kitchen table.

"Well?" His wife persisted shrilly. "I expect that swindler of a tax collector will be back with his hand out again today."

"People have been celebrating. They've spent a lot. They don't have much left." The innkeeper wiped away the sweat on his forehead with his meaty hand. New beads popped out immediately. His sack, which had not lightened during his rounds, was exceedingly heavy, stuffed with everything from saints' bones to kitchen utensils.

"So? You spoke to a lot of people?"

"People are tired after the celebrations. They have headaches, bellyaches. Give me some wine."

She ignored his request. "They were interested in your wares, though?"

"No," he snapped, wearily sitting down to engulf a stool beside the kitchen's open window.

"You fool, you missed your chance!"

"People say a lot of things, but when it comes to parting with good money, that's a different matter."

"I hope those ruffians you pay to help out have better luck selling to the gullible, otherwise you can have the pleasure of talking to the tax collector."

Kaloethes picked up one of the polishing rags his wife had been using and wiped his forehead. "Sometimes I wish I'd never got mixed up with that bunch. Who knows what they're up to? Look, this collector's new to this quarter, isn't he? Do you think he'd accept a gift?"

"He might. On the other hand, he might tell the prefect."

The ensuing silence was filled by the sound of the water that dripped steadily from a spot near the middle of the ceiling.

"The place is falling to ruin," wailed Mistress Kaloethes. "And now we have guests who don't pay. I don't know what you expect me to do."

"Keep fewer silks in your chest, for a start."

Mistress Kaloethes' porcine eyes glared. "Those are necessary. If you aspire to deal with the better classes you must dress to their standards."

"It's all very well to aspire to standards but I still say we should keep a few girls upstairs. There's always a market for the natural pleasures."

"I wouldn't call what some of them get up to natural! I'd never stoop to that kind of business anyway."

"Naturally I wouldn't expect it of you personally."

"I should think not! I left the theater a long time ago. And besides, how do you think you'd compete with the Whore of Babylon next door?"

"She isn't next door."

"Well, she's near enough so I can hear that dreadful contraption of hers moaning whenever I set foot in the courtyard."

"I've been exploring possibilities with some of her girls."

"Exploring possibilities? A nice phrase to use to your wife. You ought to plead in the courts of law. I suppose you think I don't know you've been over there?"

"As I just told you, I've been talking to several of the girls about moving here."

"How dare you insult me by even considering bringing those disgusting whores to live under our roof! You'll ruin what little reputation I have left, you bastard!"

Mistress Kaloethes grabbed a plate and her husband raised his hands to fend off flying tableware.

Chapter Thirty-two

The gold and silver tableware being arranged under John's supervision on the main table in the Hall of the Nineteen Couches was worth the price of any number of inns equal to the Kaloethes' establishment, which explained why a small army of guards was posted inside and outside the elongated, two-story high building where the most important imperial banquets were held. John only wished he could explain why Justinian had ordered him to oversee a task his assistants could carry out by themselves when John had more pressing matters to pursue.

He was contemplating the placement of a gold platter big enough to hold an entire pig, a platter Leukos had once confided had cost the imperial treasury 1,440 nomismata, when a series of piercing screams echoed through the long room.

Most high officials would have looked around for their personal bodyguards, but John, still ingrained with the habits of his military days, ran immediately toward the commotion.

Near the entrance two guards were struggling to hold a skinny child who was thrashing around like an eel.

John demanded an explanation.

"This little slave seems to think he has an audience with the Lord Chamberlain," replied one the guards.

"He's done well to get inside the hall. Sometimes initiative is rewarded. Let the boy go."

The guards released the boy, who seemed suddenly overcome by awe.

"S-S-Sir…I…I…"

"What is your name, boy?"

"B-B-Beppolenus, sir."

His tunic was bloody and there were bruises and blood on his face.

"Who beat you?" John glared at the guards, who muttered their innocence.

The boy wiped his face and rubbed his hand on his tunic, leaving red streaks. "X-Xiphias, sir."

"You've come to tell me your master beats you?"

"No, sir. I'm to say…I'm here to tell you….the visitor you asked Xiphias about. He did come to speak with the Keeper of the Plate. Xiphias was lying. And…and the man spoke to Xiphias."

"Indeed?"

Tears welled up and the boy wiped his eyes, smearing blood across his face. "Xiphias doesn't know I'm here."

"From your appearance I see he still clings to his old habits," John said. "I shall accompany you back."

As the boy turned to go, his swollen lips formed a smile of satisfaction.

John could not be certain Beppolenus was telling the truth. On their way to the workshop he couldn't extract any coherent details from the boy. On the other hand, John knew from his own experience that Xiphias was a violent liar.

There was the time Xiphias, in one of his daily rages, smacked John across the face with a candlestick. Then Xiphias hauled him in front of Leukos, blood gushing from John's nose, and claimed John had hurt himself when he and another young man had decided to engage in a sword fight with candlesticks.

The accusation that the twenty-five year-old John would have stooped to such childish stupidity hurt more than his smashed nose. It was particularly ridiculous because John, a man who had fought as a mercenary, could have easily killed any of the palace-raised apprentices had he decided to attack one.

John felt long-smoldering fury over that and other incidents as he strode into the Keeper of the Plate's office. Perhaps it was time for Xiphias to suffer for his misdeeds. John prided himself on being a fair man, and he had not taken revenge on Xiphias now that he had power to do so. However, lying to the Lord Chamberlain, who was investigating a murder....that was a serious offense.

However, Xiphias was not there.

"He ran away like a scared dog," one of the older apprentices told John, not trying to conceal his smirk of satisfaction. "As soon as Beppolenus went to tell you, right after Xiphias finished beating him."

"This is true, Beppolenus?"

Beppolenus chewed his lip nervously. "Well, yes, sir. It was time. I mean, I was too scared before but after he hurt me I got angry."

Leukos and John had from time to time talked about Xiphias and so it was that John knew the man, a bachelor, lived in rooms on the edge of the Copper Quarter. The neighborhood took its name from the metal-working establishments clustered there and John had grown familiar with it during his apprenticeship, when he had often visited workshops to deliver orders from the palace.

Xiphias' building was a four-story structure of smoke blackened brick. John was greeted in the vestibule by a withered woman, dressed in soot colored robes, who gave the impression of having been smoked herself.

"Xiphias?" she wheezed. "You must have come for the rest of his things. I hope you brought a cart."

"Is Xiphias here?"

"If he was here, you wouldn't be moving his things, would you?" She looked at John through clouded eyes that apparently could not discern that he was not dressed like a laborer.

"He's gone?"

The landlady coughed, then spat on the floor. "And good riddance. After all these years, this morning he says he's leaving. Immediately! Well, he paid me what was due, so you can get on with it."

"I'm here to speak with Xiphias, not to move his possessions. Where has he gone?"

"Did he tell me? Of course not, the ingrate. Didn't I put up with his friends, in and out at all hours? Not that he didn't make it worth my while."

"He had a busy social life?" John couldn't imagine that. It had always struck him that Xiphias hated humanity in general. Then again, he probably didn't consider slaves and eunuchs and underlings quite human.

"Well, he was a single man, you know," the landlady observed.

Apparently Xiphias had not only fled his workplace but also his residence as soon as Beppolenus ran off to see the Lord Chamberlain. Perhaps John had been wrong to doubt the boy's story.

"Show me Xiphias' rooms."

The landlady cackled. "I don't know how you're going to move anything without seeing them. You're a slow one, aren't you? But I don't suppose they employ you for your brains."

The rooms were on the first floor and looked out onto a walled garden behind the building. They were well furnished. If much had already been moved out the place must have been extremely cluttered. John questioned the woman further.

A couple of men had loaded up a donkey cart.

"When was this?"

"Right before you arrived. I don't know how you didn't see them. You must be blind."

"Mithra!" John muttered under his breath.

He raced outside. There were the usual crowds beneath the colonnades, some hurrying, others loitering in front of shops. The air was heavy with smoke and the sounds of the city.

There was little chance of catching up with Xiphias. Nevertheless, John started down the street, moving away from the palace on the theory that a fleeing man's first inclination would be to put as much distance as possible between himself and what he feared.

John's boots slapped loudly against the cobbles as he dodged wagons and horses. It was easier to navigate around the congested and slow-moving traffic than through the crush of pedestrians.

He overtook a covered litter borne by four hulking slaves. As he went by he caught a glimpse of the curtain opening a crack to allow a heavily powdered and rouged face to gape in amazement at what must have appeared to be a wealthy aristocrat gone mad.

He had spotted a high-sided donkey cart swerve abruptly into an alley, the driver applying the whip.

Was it Xiphias? Had he spotted John coming after him?

John managed a burst of speed and as the cart completed the turn and began to accelerate, he caught up, gained a handhold, and pulled himself on to the cart.

As he crashed down, toppling crates, he realized instantly that his pursuit had been in vain. This wasn't the cart carrying Xiphias' belongings.

Brushing feathers off his garments, he cursed, his oaths drowned by a cacophonous cackling.

He was certain that whatever Xiphias kept in his rooms it had not been chickens.

Chapter Thirty-three

Anatolius gave no thought to Leukos' murder or John's investigation as he strolled with Europa.

He had gathered his courage and called on her at the *Anubis*. As soon as she agreed to accompany him on a tour of the city the unpleasant musings which had been competing for his attention the past few days were temporarily banished.

They had already visited the Church of the Holy Wisdom and the enormous bronze gate leading into the palace grounds, and now they had come to an obelisk at whose base sat a crone surrounded by birds in wicker cages.

She plucked boldly at Anatolius' cloak. "Buy one of my pretties for your lady?"

Europa glanced at the bedraggled birds. Her mouth set firmly in a thin line. Anatolius noticed with a shock how she favored her father in mannerisms as well as in looks. He picked up a cage. "A partridge. Some keep them as house pets."

"It's a pity to see a free creature caged," Europa said.

"Shall I buy one for you?"

"Only if you let it go!" came a voice from behind them. It was a large, redheaded man Anatolius did not recognize. "You must be the Lord Chamberlain's friend Anatolius," continued the stranger. "I've seen you at the palace. I am Thomas."

Anatolius set the birdcage down. "Oh yes, the emissary from Bretania. John mentioned speaking with you." He concealed his annoyance. "May I introduce you to Europa? She is one of the bull-leapers currently performing at the Hippodrome. I am showing her the sights of Constantinople."

Thomas made a slight bow. "I am glad to make your acquaintance. I regret I cannot show you my native land, Europa. This poor uncivilized city suffers by comparison."

Anatolius glowered at the interloper.

Thomas grinned and clapped a beefy hand on Anatolius' shoulder. "You must take the humor of us barbarians with a grain of salt, lad."

Anatolius shrugged away from the man's hand. "Being a visitor, you may not realize that over familiarity is not encouraged here."

Turning back to the bird seller, he dropped several coins into her dirty palm. "How many of your poor captives will this ransom?"

The old woman gazed at the coins in amazement. "These would free every partridge in Constantinople."

"Be quick about it then."

She began opening the doors of the cages. The dispirited birds seemed not to notice their chance for freedom, remaining perched or huddled where they were.

Europa brushed past Anatolius and removed one of the partridges. Cradling it in her hands she drew it up to her face. "Have you forgotten the sky?"

She tossed the bird high into the air. For an instant the poor creature seemed about to fall back to the ground, but its wings flapped weakly, then picked up a stronger beat. And suddenly it had cleared the top of the obelisk.

Its escape seemed to rouse its former companions. The air was alive, then only a few floating feathers remained as partridges scattered up into the sky above glittering domes and roofs.

"Shall we walk down the Mese, or perhaps you would like to see a collection of statues in a forum not far from here?"

"I'd much rather walk and see the sights and the people than look at a collection of old statues," the girl replied, still looking toward the sky. She glanced at Thomas. "But since Anatolius is showing me around," she said to him, "why don't you accompany us?"

Her invitation struck Anatolius as much too eagerly offered. "John tells me you are on an important mission of state, Thomas. I'm sure you have no time for sightseeing."

"There is always time for beauty," the other replied.

Anatolius noted that Thomas' gaze was not directed at the busy street. It was with a heavy heart that he led his two guests away, across the Forum of Constantine and on up the Mese toward the Forum Theodosius.

As they neared it, Europa stopped to stare raptly at a bronze pyramid. "What is this?"

Grateful for a chance to display his knowledge, Anatolius pointed out the various animals, plants, and birds decorating the monument. "The ornaments symbolize spring," he lectured. "It was erected by the order of Theodosius, the second emperor of that name that is, and it seems some of the figures came from a pagan shrine."

Thomas leaned back, hair cascading past the nape of his neck, and squinted up at the female figure pivoting back and forth atop the pyramid. "The wind's moving the woman to and fro. Do the people here believe a woman is so fickle as to change direction with every breeze?"

"Not at all. The decorations represent spring, when all the world renews itself. The female, then, must be the Mother of All."

"I see. Well, still, it is true that there are many women who are fickle. I remember one time when I was in Crete—"

"You know Crete?" Europa looked up at Thomas' ruddy features with the exile's hungering gaze. "You have been there recently?"

"Only a few months ago, after I left Cyrenaica and before I journeyed to Syria."

Anatolius sensed the redheaded foreigner was bent upon passing him in the race for Europa's interest, akin to a charioteer wielding his whip on the final circuit of the Hippodrome. "I hear Crete is a lovely island and has produced many things of great beauty. Let's continue. There is something I think will particularly interest you, Europa."

They had not gone far when three men embroiled in a noisy argument erupted from an alley. Two of the brawlers were squat men wearing the flour-bedaubed tunics of bakers. The third was dressed in the rough garments of a laborer.

Anatolius stopped short, preparing to call for assistance. The urban watch were never far off. Thomas' beefy hand went to his sword hilt. Europa, however, simply skipped nimbly around the melee, hardly glancing at the three combatants.

It was apparent that the trio were a danger only to themselves, but, as he carefully sidestepped them, Anatolius felt renewed admiration for the self-possessed young woman. He shouldn't have been surprised, he reminded himself. Someone who dealt with charging bulls would not likely be intimidated by an acrimonious public discussion.

"Europa," he said. "We are almost there. If you will cover your eyes?"

The girl obliged, giving Anatolius an excuse to take her by the arm. Trailed by Thomas, he steered her under an arch and into the Forum Bovis, where he led her to the foot of an enormous bronze.

"Now you can look," he instructed, hand lingering on her arm.

She opened her eyes. They widened. A broad smile settled on her face as her gaze wandered over the huge bull's head which gave the forum its name.

"How beautiful! You must bring mother to see this too!"

"A beautiful beast," said Thomas, in what sounded like sincere admiration.

Anatolius glanced at him with interest. When had Thomas seen him at the palace? Was this meeting a coincidence or could Thomas be following him for some reason? Surely not.

He turned his attention back to the young and attractive bull-leaper.

Chapter Thirty-four

John waited for Cornelia in the cramped cabin of the *Anubis*. It was growing late. Following his misadventure with the cart of chickens he had returned home, changed clothes, and spent the rest of the day overseeing banquet preparations.

He pondered the mysteries confronting him: Xiphias' flight, Leukos' death, the self-styled knight from Bretania, the emperor's insistence on burdening him personally with banquet details any of John's assistants would normally have handled. Was the Armenian Ambassador in whose honor the banquet would be held such an important personage?

He had worried ever since learning from Hektor that Cornelia and Europa had been at the same private gathering attended by Berta. The young prostitute was dead. Might Cornelia and Europa be in danger too?

John had no reason to think so, but it struck him as prudent to speak with them about that night.

He waited for a long time and when he finally went onto the deck for a breath of air, he found that Europa had already returned. Instead of going inside, she was sitting on the rail of the bow looking out over the darkening harbor where the wavering reflections of countless ship-borne torches formed unfamiliar constellations on the water. He walked over to her and placed his hand on the smooth rail.

"Lord Chamberlain." The girl swiveled effortlessly to face him.

Her formal mode of address sounded wrong to John, but then "father" would have sounded just as strange.

"Europa, you're here…I hoped to talk to Cornelia."

"Mother's probably with the troupe. I'm not certain. I just returned myself."

"I trust you didn't ventured into the city on your own?"

"I'm old enough to take care of myself. But, as it happens, Anatolius showed me around. We met a knight. A fascinating man."

Staring out at the scattered lights in the harbor, John was brushed by a touch of vertigo. It was as if the dome of heaven had been inverted and the *Anubis* was bobbing upon its endless depths. His hand tightened on the rail.

"Isn't that a dangerous perch?" he asked Europa.

"Not compared to the back of a bull," she replied. "Besides, there's water below to catch me, not hard earth." Torchlight glinted in her dark eyes as the ship moved on a swell. She seemed to be studying John. "You're afraid of the water, aren't you?"

John ignored her comment, but it made him uneasy. He was accustomed to reading others, not to being read himself. In the dusk Europa had a remarkable resemblance to the woman he had fallen in love with so long ago.

"What did you want with my mother?"

"I have questions concerning Theodora's celebration and some of the other guests."

"It's about the murder of that friend of yours, isn't it? Anatolius told me all about it."

"Anatolius has a bad habit of talking about matters that are dangerous for him to reveal, and just as dangerous for others to hear."

"I am sorry about Leukos. Was he a good friend?"

"A very good friend, Europa."

"Did he have a wife, a family?"

"None that I know of. He never talked about his family."

"Where was he from?"

"I do not know."

The girl was silent. John could hear the wash of waves against the dock. "A strange friend, one you know nothing about," she finally said.

"That is the way it is at the palace."

"I don't think I would like the palace, if it is truly a place where your friends are strangers. And what about daughters? Are they usually strangers too?"

"Europa, I had no idea I was a father until—"

"Father? You aren't my father. You've killed him." The girl swung gracefully down from the rail. "My father was a soldier. My mother used to tell me about him. A good man. Brave. Something terrible must have happened to him, she always said. He must have been carried down to the underworld, because nothing in this world would have kept him from returning to her. To us. And now, here you are. A rich man, who didn't care!"

For a heartbeat, in the dim, dancing reflections of torch lit water she was her mother's daughter, with Cornelia's pride and fierce temper. Then tears began to flow, and the woman's face dissolved into that of a child.

John stepped forward, reaching out awkwardly to draw her toward him. She shrugged away.

There was the sound of movement behind them, sufficiently different from the random sounds caused by the gentle motion of the ship on the water to be noticeable.

John whirled. Saw nothing. Yet he had heard a footstep. "Europa," he whispered, "is there a watchman on this ship?"

"Watchman?" Europa quickly collected her thoughts. "There should be, but the crew's an idle lot. He's probably asleep."

John scanned the ship. Did a shadow move in the doorway of the cabin he had vacated?

He drew his dagger.

"Mother must have got back."

"No. Someone was trying to make as little noise as possible."

"Oh, I'll just go and—"

John blocked her with his arm. "You may be in danger," he whispered to Europa. "Stay here."

He could see her eyes glittering and she began to open her mouth to protest.

"Quiet! If need be, get ashore and run."

John crouched low and moved away to investigate. The deck shifted under his boots, each movement bringing a different patchwork of shadow and reflected light. But there now seemed no sign of the intruder.

As he reached the cabin's dark doorway, the vessel dipped in a sudden plunge. Caught off balance, he reflexively grabbed the doorframe to keep his footing.

He steadied himself, and putting his back against the cabin wall he peered at an angle through the doorway. The darkness inside was impenetrable. He was certain he could hear ragged breathing.

The intruder must have heard him when he stumbled. There was enough light outside to make him a clear target if he charged blindly into the cabin.

Where was the watchman?

Should he order the trespasser to show himself?

He heard the gangplank creak.

Footsteps approached rapidly.

"John! What are you doing here?"

Cornelia had returned. She came toward the cabin.

A figure burst out of it with a roar and was past John before he could react. Cornelia dodged to one side to avoid being knocked over and John, leaping after the intruder pulled up short to avoid crashing into her.

There came the thud of heavy running steps pounding across the gangplank and boyish cries as the watchman finally awoke.

There was no use in pursuing the man. Once on the docks he could go in any direction and there were endless hiding places.

Chapter Thirty-five

Peter had not been able to disguise his displeasure the previous night when John brought Cornelia and Europa back from the *Anubis*. John had introduced the women and explained they would be staying at the house for their safety.

"But if any wag-tongues at the market should ask, Cornelia is assisting with the cooking and Europa is here as a housekeeper."

Perhaps he could have thought of a better story to save the old man's pride. Some day the strong-willed servant really would need help with his duties. For all his diplomatic skills, the Lord Chamberlain was not looking forward to dealing with him when the time came.

John heard voices in the hallway. Anatolius came in, accompanied by the women.

"It's lucky I happened to drop by this morning, John. The hand of fate must have guided me here."

"You said you needed information on the Armenian Ambassador to write introductory remarks for the banquet."

"Well, it was fate I needed that information the very morning after these ladies arrived."

"Speaking of which, Peter has showed us around the house and we admire your spartan accommodations," Europa observed with a slight smile.

Cornelia chuckled. "John was never one with a taste for luxury," she said, then added quietly, "For himself, at least."

John noticed her gaze flickered to the elaborate wall mosaic which appeared, fortunately, sedate in the light of day. "The previous owner's," he told her.

There were chairs for Cornelia and Europa but John and Anatolius had to settle for stools. Anatolius poured wine Peter brought, and added a large portion of water in deference to the early hour.

"Despite the lack of furnishings, I'm sure you won't have to sleep on the floor," Anatolius smiled at Europa.

John saw the girl's dark eyes were both watchful and serene. Had this curious combination had been born of bull-leaping? She might be a difficult person to take by surprise, a good thing in this complex and dangerous city.

Cornelia sat as watchfully still as her daughter, her gaze locked on John's face. Seeing her after so many years, and in his own house, made his breath catch in his throat.

"I'm glad you brought the ladies here, John," Anatolius said. "They'll be safely out of sight."

John shrugged. "Probably by now most of the palace gossips know that two women are visiting me."

"I know you can rely on Peter to say nothing," Anatolius observed.

"Yes, he can be trusted completely."

"And the excubitors are within earshot if there's any trouble. You'll alert Felix, won't you?"

"I think not. He's distraught about Berta."

Cornelia frowned. "Why do you imagine the intruder on the *Anubis* was looking for Europa and me? The city must be filled with common thieves."

John raised his cup to his lips to disguise his long pause. "Two people have died and one has vanished. There may be connections. As I told you last night when I explained the situation, the girl who died entertained at the same party as you did."

"We've performed at countless private parties over the years, John. There was nothing remarkable about it, except it happened to be arranged by the empress and the surroundings were particularly luxurious."

"Theodora much preferred the lewd contortions of those clumsy dwarves," noted Europa.

"A soothsayer also entertained," John said. "And the day Leukos died, he visited that very person at the inn where he lodged. The same inn where Thomas, our mysterious knight is staying, where his acquaintance Gregorius the charioteer is staying, as well as members of your troupe, Cornelia. There must be a connection."

"But if so, why isn't it apparent? You've talked to all of them."

"And no one has told me the truth."

"If only you could be one of the flies on the inn wall," Anatolius put in.

"Unfortunately the proprietors would recognize me now."

"And myself as well, since I visited the soothsayer. Otherwise I would be happy to serve as your spy. But why so suspicious of the soothsayer?" Anatolius said. "He impressed me. I was pleased by the prophecy he gave me."

He looked at Europa, but she failed to ask what the soothsayer had predicted. "There is so much darkness in this bright city," she said. "It almost makes me wish for the true brightness of Crete."

Anatolius lifted his eyebrows in inquiry. "Almost?"

The girl colored and looked down at her sandals.

John, watching this exchange, was set adrift on a sea of emotions. Cornelia, peering sideways at her daughter, wore a slight smile. The curve of her cheek against the colorful riot of mosaic behind her was uncomplicated, clean. John, suddenly weary, longed for sun washed walls, blue vaulted skies, open fields. His life then had been new and uncomplicated. Now it was anything but and he had no idea what to expect next.

Chapter Thirty-six

Alerted by a shrill squeal, John looked away from the Armenian ambassador, straight into the eyes of a wild boar.

The sharp tusks of the charging beast were not far from John's face, the animal's eyes glazed with death.

It was an expression John had seen before.

"There's another who aspired to sit at the emperor's table but now regrets it." John remarked.

The ambassador, a plump partridge of a man on the verge of old age, laughed too heartily.

John forced himself to smile. He should have spent the day out in the city searching for Leukos' murderer instead of confined to the Hall of the Nineteen Couches fretting over this infernal banquet, thanks to a direct order from Justinian.

Banquets in the hall were a nightmare of protocol. In addition to the main table in the center, windowed alcoves along both sides of the large space housed their own tables. How did the emperor expect him to find a murderer while checking seating arrangements?

He shifted uncomfortably on his couch, an anachronism now except at banquets. Anatolius, reclining to right, had his face in his wine goblet, while the ambassador, to his left, chattered on.

"Lord Chamberlain, please excuse the ignorance of a foreigner, but in Armenia we associate with your title one named

Narses, a native son. Indeed, we have heard he assisted in putting down those unfortunate riots in Constantinople a few years back."

"Yes, Narses is well known outside the city. But the organization of the palace is complex. Theodora has her own Lord Chamberlain, for example. Has his name reached Armenia?"

Before the ambassador could question John further, the pulley arrangement at the end of the long table squealed again and the immense silver platter on which the artfully posed boar lay inched forward toward the carver stationed at the end of the table beside the emperor and empress.

Now the ambassador was exclaiming over the glimpse he had had of the boar's belly, which, cut open and facing upwards, presented a display of roast ducks swimming in a sharp-scented, spiced sauce. "And aren't those fried eels floating just below the surface?"

Anatolius lifted his face from his goblet. "A remarkable landscape of dead flesh to set beneath the nose of an emperor who won't eat meat. Perhaps Theodora ordered the display as a little jest at Justinian's expense."

The Armenian ambassador laughed loudly and John shot Anatolius a warning look.

John glanced around. Several couches away the patriarch was dining frugally on bread and red wine. The Mithran in the Lord Chamberlain would have admired a man whose religious sensibilities did not allow him to indulge in the pleasures of the world even an arm's length from the emperor. Then again, the old cleric's lack of appetite here might be common sense, for at court even members of the church were not immune from political machinations and assassination attempts.

The patriarch looked pale and gaunt. John wondered whether the old man's professional interest in eternal salvation was becoming a matter of personal concern.

His gaze moved to Theodora, who was now busily spearing slices of roast duck with her knife while her husband occupied himself with a bowl of what might as well have been weeds so far as John could tell. Would the empress be an attractive woman without the rouge and powder and luxurious robes? Justinian, he noticed, regarded her with an expression of fond indulgence even as she bit daintily into her duck with her small carnivore's teeth.

After the dining finally ended and Patriarch Epiphanios had muttered the closing grace and departed, the shrilling of flutes announced the start of the entertainment.

John hardly noticed the mimes or the dwarves. When a dancing girl clad in white from shoulder to thigh, her scanty clothing shimmering in the lamplight, leapt onto the table, she merely served to remind John of Berta, with whom Felix and Thomas had been so taken.

The dancing girl glanced down at Anatolius, lost her balance, and fell off the table just as two miniature chariots pulled by small, briskly trotting, long-haired dogs and driven by hirsute brown charioteers burst into the hall.

"Monkeys!" cried the ambassador.

Tiny bells on the dogs' polished leather harnesses jingled merrily as the diminutive charioteers commenced to chase each other around the hall, chattering, displaying their teeth, and waving miniature spears at each other.

The diners roared with laughter.

"The poor dancer must not like monkeys," said Anatolius, scrambling off his couch to help the girl up.

John swiveled around to watch the charioteers, who had made a circuit of the table and were returning.

One of the drivers clutched a bunch of grapes he had snatched from the table.

The other hurled his spear in John's direction.

John heard the tiny projectile hiss past his ear, then the weapon embedded itself in the shoulder of the senator across the table.

As the wounded man looked in stupefaction at the blood blossoming on his garments diners fell utterly silent.

Except for Theodora's cawing laugh.

◇◇◇

When the banquet was over John made his way to the foyer where the emperor and empress were receiving selected guests. He was still pondering the charioteers. Surely the spear could not have been intended for him? A monkey couldn't possibly be trained to select a target, could it? His close call had been nothing more than chance.

Justinian greeted him with his usual bland geniality. "All was perfect, as usual, Lord Chamberlain."

"Thank you, Caesar." John bowed.

Justinian waved a beringed hand. "And that reminds me. I have not thanked you for your efforts concerning the death of the Keeper of the Plate. Do not trouble yourself further with the matter."

John's stomach knotted. "Caesar, if I may ask—"

"You may not."

Justinian turned away with an abruptness that would have been characterized as rude in anyone other than the emperor.

John had been dismissed and dared say nothing further. He was suddenly aware of the empress standing beside him.

"Lord Chamberlain, my husband is too kind. I am not always so pleased with your efforts. You might, in the future, keep that in mind."

"I never forget it, Highness," John replied truthfully.

Theodora's heavily painted features betrayed no emotion. It was commonly said she had not been a very good actress in her youth; if that were true, John guessed her knowledge of the craft had deepened during her years as empress.

"I am in accord with the emperor on the guilty one," she said. "I have met the soothsayer and though I did not speak with him for long, he struck me as a vicious, unprincipled man, one who would not blink at murder."

John stared pointedly at a drop of grease shining at the corner of the empress' mouth. She licked away the tiny gobbet.

"A word of caution, Lord Chamberlain. Being too observant can be dangerous."

Chapter Thirty-seven

Peter dug his spoon into his bowl of lentils and gingerly tasted them. "Overcooked," he complained to the diner perched next to him on the splintery bench.

"Don't say that too loudly at the Inn of the Centaurs, especially not within hearing of the mistress of the house." His neighbor was mopping up the remains of his meal with a chunk of bread, making the table with its uneven legs wobble alarmingly. Peter had noticed the man's gaze drifting constantly around the room as he ate.

Was he a thief? Or being sought for a crime? A criminal avoiding arrest?

Peter had the feeling the man was dishonest but couldn't have said why. "The mistress here is outspoken, is she?"

"Yes, and possessing a temper making whips and scorpions seem like a child's playthings."

Peter looked dolefully around at the scattering of mismatched tables, the stained plaster walls, the noisy crowd of travelers and clerks. He was beginning to regret his decision to come here. He felt sorry now that he had made up the story about a sick friend to give him an excuse to be absent from his employer's house for a while.

But, he reminded himself, the master needed his assistance. Hadn't he overheard him telling Anatolius that he wished he could visit the inn secretly to investigate?

"This appears to be a fairly well-run establishment," Peter said doubtfully, pushing his bowl away with one hand and steadying the table with the other. "Did you come to the city to attend the celebrations?"

"That, and other business I had in hand. Lucky to find somewhere to stay too. Every room's taken, and noisy all night."

"I suppose there's no hope of lodgings?" He realized he was not as disappointed as he should have been at the possibility that he might not be able to spend the night in this uncouth place.

"Probably not in most places, but the owner here is the sort who would move cots into his cellar to get a few more coins in his pocket," the other replied, stuffing a last bit of bread into his mouth as he got up. "I wish you good fortune."

Peter's face fell. He had already begun to concoct a miraculous speedy recovery for his sick friend. But at least the thief, or criminal, or whoever he was had left.

The innkeeper's wife appeared from the kitchen, frowning, an untidy thundercloud wiping her hands on a grubby cloth.

"I wish to, er, compliment you on your cooking," Peter said, as she cleared plates from the table. "Do you have a room I could rent for a night?"

She glared at him. "We don't run that sort of establishment if you are contemplating bringing a lady friend here for an evening of carnal delight. What profession do you follow? We only cater to the best here, you know."

Peter flushed. "I am in the city to carry out commissions for a distributor of pottery ware," he told her, using the story he had invented on his way from John's house.

"Is that so? I notice you don't carry samples. Still, we can accommodate you in your friend's room."

"You mean the man I was dining with? He's a stranger."

"Well, then you won't feel inclined to stay up all night talking, will you? Of course, if you object—"

"No, no, it is an excellent arrangement," Peter murmured faintly.

Peter was relieved the shifty-eyed stranger was absent from the room he was shown. He eyed its few furnishings—straw mats, a chair, a couple of cots, a brazier—and wondered if he would be able to sleep at all.

Fortunately he had a job to do.

He tried to push aside his uneasiness. The Inn of the Centaurs could have been worse. Hadn't the spies Joshua sent into Jericho stayed at a house of prostitution? At least he did not have to visit Madam Isis' establishment to investigate.

But what was he to do? What could he find out?

He went upstairs and past closed doors, listening.

Unfortunately he didn't hear anyone declaring loudly that he had killed Leukos.

He climbed to the third story and moved quietly down its hall. One door hung open. Peering around it, he saw similar furnishings as those downstairs. If they knew anything about Leukos' murderer they remained mute.

Closed doors and empty rooms were not very enlightening.

Peter knew the Lord Chamberlain had been particularly interested in two other guests here, an old soothsayer and the knight Thomas. Then too, members of the bull-leaping team were also staying here. Not that Peter had eavesdropped, but an attentive servant could not help overhearing as he went about his duties.

Perhaps he could find out what rooms they were all staying in.

A woman's cry interrupted his musings.

By the time he'd scampered in the sound's direction it became obvious that it had not been a sign of distress. He crept past the door, from behind which there emerged coarse giggling and grunting, and went back downstairs.

Several intoxicated patrons were engaged in a dissonant rendition of a military marching song. He took a seat beside a young man dressed in the distinctive garb of a charioteer. Only after he had settled himself did he notice to his chagrin that the stranger with whom he was to share a room lounged on the other side of the charioteer.

A cup of wine crashed down in front of him. "Here's the drink you ordered," said the innkeeper's wife. "I'll add it to your bill."

Before Peter could protest, the charioteer slapped him on the back. "Come on, old fellow. Wet your throat and join in. Do you know the song?"

Peter considered fleeing. But, no, he had to play the role of a traveler. He was a spy for the master after all. He took a gulp of wine and began to sing. He knew the song well from his days in the military.

Before it ended he began to feel dizzy. He wasn't used to strong wine. Or was it the heat in the room?

"He's got a good voice, hasn't he?" the charioteer asked Peter's roommate. Did the young man know that shady character? "I can tell by the look of you, you're an old soldier."

Peter proudly admitted he had been with the military, without mentioning that he had been a slave cook at the time.

"What's you name?"

"Er…Joshua…"

"You must know a lot of marching songs, Joshua."

"Well, yes." Peter felt suddenly emboldened. "Enough to cross the whole length of Isauria without repeating one!"

With the charioteer's encouragement he taught the group a bawdier song than the one they'd been singing. Then another.

At some point his cup must have been refilled, and he must have emptied it, more than once. He amazed himself with the lyrics he recalled. He'd had no idea they were still in his mind but the notes of the songs pulled the words straight out of the darkness of his memory. Words he hadn't had any use for since he'd put away his soldier's boots.

The charioteer was laughing and slurring his words. "I've never met a man with such a wealth of obscene lyrics!"

Peter wondered if he had gone too far, not to mention drinking too much wine. "Perhaps we should try a hymn. I know one written by the emperor."

He squeezed his eyes shut and opened them again, trying to bring the room into clearer focus. He was certain he recited the pious lyrics correctly, until the rowdy patrons began singing. Surely the hymn didn't mention Theodora and the apostles?

He decided to temporarily retreat to his room to clear his head. He had hoped Thomas or the soothsayer might appear but they hadn't, and if any of the singers belonged to the bull-leaping troupe he was unable to tell.

As he got to his feet and started unsteadily toward the stairs he could see into the kitchen, where the innkeeper sat at a table counting coins. His wife appeared to be chastising him, but the uproar in the room where Peter stood drowned her words.

He moved closer to the door. As he did so, he felt the sting of a boot applied to his backside and stumbled forward. Turning, he saw his assailant looking startled.

"You're not the person I thought you were," the man said. "You look like him from the back."

"Do you usually greet your friends that way?"

"It was meant in jest."

The bulk of the innkeeper's wife loomed beside them. "You must be looking for the other old man who's staying here, that ancient scoundrel of a soothsayer."

"That's right. I was hoping to see him on a matter of business."

"If you find him, remind him his bill here's due," snapped the innkeeper's wife.

Might this acquaintance of the soothsayer possess useful information? Peter tried to fix the man's face in his mind but all he could register through the fog that had settled around his thoughts was that he was bigger and younger than Peter, which included practically everyone these days.

Then, abruptly, the man was gone. Peter hadn't noticed him leave. He shook his head. It felt as if filled with bees.

By now the other guests had decided to take turns kicking each other's behinds to the rhythm of a song Peter had never heard. Its thunderous refrain of "Theodora said to him, to him Theodora said..." was followed by many stanzas declaring what it was the empress had said to the emperor and what the emperor subsequently did to the empress.

It was not the sort of scene that would end peacefully.

Peter wobbled upstairs and collapsed onto a cot. He would rest a little while and wait for the tumult reverberating up through the floorboards die down.

The next thing he knew he was in Jericho. Why he was sure it was Jericho was hard to say, because all he could see of his surroundings was a long corridor whose walls were painted with rows of scantily clad women marching through rugged mountain terrain, singing.

No, they weren't singing, that was the sound of trumpets he heard.

Which meant something but he couldn't remember what, exactly.

Then the walls began to shake, cracks appeared, and the marching women disintegrated into multi-colored dust.

Seeking to escape he flung open a door and found himself in a tiny cubicle containing a bed occupied by the innkeeper's wife who was clothed in only—

He came awake in a panic.

Heavy footsteps thumped down the hallway.

Struggling to his feet and lurching to the door he opened it a crack and saw an exceedingly old man clothed in a worn brown tunic, carrying a satchel.

Was it the soothsayer John had mentioned? If so, he appeared to be in trouble because he vanished down the stairs escorted by a group of armed men.

Chapter Thirty-eight

The sun had not yet risen above the rooftops when John left his house on the way to the Inn of the Centaurs, scattering raucous seabirds scavenging in the deserted square. He wanted to speak to Ahasuerus again. He was determined to find Leukos' murderer no matter what Justinian ordered.

Theodora's slyly menacing words still rankled. Had they been meant to impress upon him that, as she had said, observing too closely could be dangerous? If so, he was going to put himself in very great danger because he intended not only to observe but also to actively investigate.

A Mithran or any man knew his duty and the fact that a duty had suddenly became more onerous did not alter the necessity of fulfilling it.

He was also relieved to be out of the house. Though he had arrived home late from the banquet, he had slept poorly, confused thoughts of Leukos, Cornelia and Europa, Justinian and Theodora, Berta, running imperceptibly into nightmares of which he awoke with no memory aside from the last trembling echoes of some overwhelming horror.

The presence of the two women in the house he shared with Peter seemed palpable. More than once he thought he heard voices or footsteps but when he came fully awake he had realized it was only the sounds buildings make at night or the wind. He feared for the safety of the women. Should he have asked for a guard to be posted?

A cat raced past him as if all the demons of hell were after it. Startled, John paused and looked around for whatever was chasing it. A stray mongrel seemed the most likely culprit, but nothing appeared. So perhaps the cat was the pursuer and not the pursued. It was often hard to distinguish in Constantinople.

John heard the shriek as he came to the archway leading to the inn.

His first thought was someone was being murdered. He raced across the courtyard, into the inn, and following the continued shrieking, sprinted upstairs.

There was a crash and a rusty brazier rolled out of a doorway at the end of the hall.

Entering the room he saw a distraught Kaloethes standing, a fleshy Mount Athos of despair, while his wife screamed and stamped around.

"He's disappeared in the night!" she bellowed. "The cheating old fraud! If I catch him, I'll tell his fortune with his own gizzard, and it won't be a pleasant fortune either, nor a long one!"

"What happened here?" John asked quietly.

His sudden entrance didn't detour Mistress Kaloethes from her anger. "The miserable old vulture has gone without paying me a single coin! And with all the rich folk who came up to listen to his lies, he must have made a fortune! Money up their arses, they have!"

"How do you know he's not returning?"

"He's taken all his possessions, such as they were," put in Kaloethes. "Just a few things. Tools of his trade."

"Tools!" his wife spat out. "Some colored rocks and his fancy chicken-splitters. You call those tools?"

John's gaze scoured the room. "I wanted to speak with him. When did you see him last?"

"At the evening meal yesterday, when else? Christ himself couldn't have broken enough loaves!" The woman took an enraged step toward the window, perhaps intending to see if the missing man might still somehow be lurking in the courtyard below. She winced as her bare foot came down on something. She picked the object up. John recognized the round, green stone as one of the charms Ahasuerus gave to his clients. A brief search garnered several similar stones. Why hadn't he gathered them up before leaving? Could he have been in such a hurry?

"You have no idea where he might have gone?" John asked.

"No," spat Mistress Kaloethes. "To hell I hope."

"It's just the opposite," came a voice from the doorway.

To his amazement John saw Peter, hair tousled, clothes disheveled.

"I saw the soothsayer taken away under armed guard last night," Peter continued. "I followed them. They escorted him to the palace of the patriarch."

Chapter Thirty-nine

John's first thought as he stepped into the nave of the Church of the Holy Wisdom was that Justinian was unknowingly erecting a tribute to Mithra, Lord of Light.

The overwhelming impression was one of light. The enormous dome overhead curved upwards gradually, as if the sky itself had been pulled earthwards and brought close enough for its true immensity to be grasped. The dome was pierced with numerous, blindingly bright openings through which sunlight flooded, filling the vast space beneath with the other-worldly radiance that presages a violent storm.

John's second thought was that the events of the past few days, the deaths of his friend and of Berta, the reappearance of his old love, must have upset his humors, rendering him dangerously susceptible to his emotions.

He became aware of the smell of wet plaster and the echoing of hammers. He lowered his gaze from the dome and scanned the interior for the patriarch. John was determined Epiphanios would explain why he had sent guards for Ahasuerus.

The patriarch found John first. "Lord Chamberlain! You have finally graced my church with your presence!"

John turned toward the querulous voice. Scaffolding clustered on all sides. Laborers were ill-defined shadows flickering against the brilliant openings in the dome. Dust filled the air.

The patriarch was a bent figure dressed in simple white robes.

"It is as magnificent as everyone claims," John replied.

"High praise indeed." The voice was forced and thin, a whisper from a sickbed. "It is nearing completion. The mobs who burned the old church merely cleared the ground for a more glorious tribute to the Lord."

"I noticed that you have the building well guarded."

The patriarch shrugged bent shoulders. "There are forty thousand pounds of silver decorating the sanctuary alone. Each seat will have silver revetments."

"An impressive tribute to one who lived among beggars."

"It is a measure of our Lord's power, is it not, that man must spend a fortune in silver and gold to achieve merely the palest imitation of the glory found in the poorest part of His creation?"

The patriarch looked at John with red and watering eyes. Perhaps it was the dust. John ignored the question.

"Let me show you my church, Lord Chamberlain. Over there, we are already installing the reliquaries." The skin of the bony hand that gestured toward the shadows at the base of the wall behind the columns and scaffolding was ancient parchment through which John could see the faded writing of veins. "The fragment of the True Cross will be displayed in that spot, for example. One day many of the most holy relics of the city will be gathered in this magnificent place, and we are in the process of obtaining even more, both minor and major."

John, who believed a saint's bones to be indistinguishable from the bones of any other man, changed the subject. "The effect of the light is remarkable." The quality of the light, insubstantial as it might be, struck him more forcibly than any physical manifestations of the patriarch's religion.

"Wait until the lamps are lit, Lord Chamberlain. There will be hundreds, suspended from the dome, fastened to the columns, set in wall sconces. The architects were instructed to leave not a single shadowed place. The whole of the interior must be illuminated."

"Surely a man passing by a lamp will cast a shadow?"

The patriarch allowed himself a weak chuckle that turned into a rasping cough. "You are a theologian. But then, in Constantinople, who is not?"

They walked out into the center of the nave. Beams of sunlight, given tangible shape by the dust clouds filling the air, appeared from this vantage point more substantial than the dust-obscured pillars along the aisles.

"You attended the funeral of the Keeper of the Plate?" asked the patriarch suddenly.

"Yes."

"What was it like?"

"A simple ceremony. It might well have been in the countryside. Birds were singing."

"It was a dignified burial then?"

"Very much so."

"Excellent. I had opportunity to deal with Leukos frequently. He looked after some of our reliquaries, ceremonial goblets, and the like. After the last fire, much of what would usually be stored in the church treasury was placed temporarily in his care. He was a good Christian."

John followed the old man until he came to a halt near a partially disassembled scaffold leaning against a pillar. The patriarch looked up at the dome.

"It may surprise you, but I am as puzzled as the poorest peasant by the ways of our Lord."

John, in fact, was not surprised, but remained silent.

The patriarch continued, "Just a few days ago, a young laborer, a country boy, was gravely injured. He fell and landed right where I am standing. I am given to understand that part of the scaffolding gave way. And so he fell through that glorious light down to these beautifully laid tiles. But at least he was serving in the house of the Lord. And when I heard about it I thought of Leukos, dying in the darkness of a filthy alley."

John wasn't certain what point the patriarch intended to make. "About your guards. You sent several for an old soothsayer. They dragged him from an inn and took him to your residence."

John expected a denial. The patriarch's response surprised him.

"You are well informed. I ordered the arrest of the self-styled fortune-teller, the man Ahasuerus. A murderer."

Was that why Justinian had ordered John to cease his investigation? Had it been decided by the time of the banquet the patriarch would have Ahasuerus arrested?

But why then was the patriarch involved?

"Why was he escorted to your residence?"

"I presume they wanted to question him at the guard station there."

"He is still in custody?"

"Alas, no. He escaped."

"Escaped?"

"A little way at least, Lord Chamberlain. They found the scoundrel at the docks, seeking transport no doubt. He is drowned. He flung himself into the sea to avoid recapture."

John felt disappointment settle with the dust in the back of his throat. "This is certain?"

"I am told the undertow pulled him down immediately. The body has not yet come to light, but there is no doubt as to the location of his black soul. You seem distressed?"

For an instant giddiness washed over John. The golden air, pierced by shafts of light, took on an underwater aspect.

"I sympathize," the patriarch continued. "Drowning cannot be a pleasant death. The mouth opening for air, finding only brine. A fall from a scaffold would be preferable. On the other hand, drowning can be no worse than a knife in the ribs. Or am I wrong? I have no experience of these things."

"You referred to him as a murderer. What reasons do you have to think so?"

"One receives information. What does it matter why he was suspected since his guilt has now been proved?"

"By the fact he threw himself into the sea?"

"More than that. In his panic the soothsayer dropped the satchel he was carrying. It contained numerous implements of his blasphemous trade, including two ceremonial, elaborately decorated daggers, an exact match for the dagger with which Leukos was murdered."

Chapter Forty

"So it's over?" Anatolius said.

He sat talking with John in John's garden. He had come to the house hoping for a glimpse of Europa but aside from a hint of exotic perfume, possibly imagined, as he crossed the entrance hall lit by a single lamp there was no evidence of her.

"As far as Justinian and the patriarch are concerned it is over."

"And as for you?"

John's lips tightened. "I instructed the prefect to inform me of any bodies recovered from the sea."

"For what purpose?"

"For one thing, he might have had something on his person that would offer a clue to why Leukos was murdered."

Anatolius was almost sorry he had asked John about his investigation. He had listened with one ear while staying alert for the sound of light footsteps on the garden path.

A few rays of dying sunlight straggled over the house roof to coruscate off a pool fed by a soothing trickle from the mouth of some unidentifiable, time-worn creature. John sat on a bench and Anatolius perched on the smooth edge of the fountain basin.

"You say Justinian instructed you not to pursue the matter further, even before those incriminating daggers were found in Ahasuerus' possession?" Anatolius continued. "Doesn't that suggest he knew then that Ahasuerus was about to be arrested for the crime?"

"It might have been nothing more than one of his whims," John said. "There also remains unexplained the disappearance of Xiphias, who worked with Leukos."

Anatolius shrugged. "From what you've told me about Xiphias, John, there's no mystery there. He was a cruel and vengeful man. Had he been in your position, seeing an opportunity to exact revenge on an old tormentor, he would have leaped on the chance gleefully. Men like that always believe the hearts of others are as black as their own."

"I've been Lord Chamberlain for a long time. Had I wanted to relegate Xiphias to the dungeons or deprive him of his head, I could have done so at any time, and for no reason at all."

"Reasonable men make the mistake of thinking everyone else is reasonable."

John directed his gaze toward the eroded creature in the middle of the fountain. "Look at that poor beast," he mused. "The elements are sending him back to the lump of stone from which the sculptor coaxed him."

"Are you unwell, John?"

"Tired. My mind wanders when I'm tired."

"Mine just lies down and sleeps." Anatolius' attempt at levity was apparently lost on John. His friend, who always had the look of an ascetic, appeared even more drawn and hollow-eyed than usual. It was not surprising. Being reunited with a lost love might not be a joyful experience, considering the circumstances.

"Anatolius, you remember I mentioned I had visited a stylite a couple of evenings ago? I haven't had the opportunity to tell you much about that."

"It must have been harrowing to be out in that terrible storm."

"Worse yet trying to climb up an exceedingly narrow and slippery ladder in order to converse with a taciturn holy man ringed in his own filth and not in the best of tempers. Especially with the wind plucking at my cloak and plunging cold fingers into my tunic."

"Reminds me of some wild actresses of my acquaintance," Anatolius remarked, still hoping to elicit some sign of good humor from his friend.

John frowned. "This young religion has acquired some strange encrustations. I wonder what the patriarch thinks about having this pious beggar sitting up there in his crow's nest, communing with the Lord, not a stone's throw from that great church filled with gold and silver?"

"The stylite might not be looking at the church. Perhaps he watches the chariot races."

John smiled at last, if wearily.

"I've only seen the fellow from the ground. What was he like?" asked Anatolius.

John wrinkled his nose at the recollection. "It would be difficult to guess his age. He is bearded and dressed in rags. At least he isn't the sort who stands there semi-naked, wearing just chains."

"You make him sound like someone who's managed to get on the bad side of the empress. Or perhaps the good side."

John shook his head in mock disapproval. "You must watch your tongue, my friend."

Anatolius made an even more scurrilous joke.

"You shock me," John was stern-faced but faint lines of amusement were blossoming around his mouth and eyes. "I hope you will not be a bad influence on Europa." The admonition went home.

"No, of course not."

"Do you think I haven't noticed you sitting there with your head cocked to one side, only half hearing what I'm saying, glancing around every time a bird rustles a branch? Or guessed why?"

Anatolius looked at his feet. "You are observant, John. You must surely have learned something from the stylite."

"I learned that Constantinople is a small city full of twisting alleys. We live here in such close proximity, each to all. Leukos' murder was the sort of tragedy that happens in the poorer byways of the city all the time, but they are practically as close to the palace as to the tenements."

"You've lived here long enough to know that."

John ignored the comment. "And as for you, my friend, you judged Ahasuerus to be an honorable man."

Anatolius looked uneasy. "It seems I am a poor judge. We know Leukos met the soothsayer. He had that green pebble in his pouch, just like the one that Ahasuerus gave me." A look of alarm crossed Anatolius' face. "It occurs to me that I'm fortunate the old villain didn't follow me into an alley instead."

"You've changed your opinion of him?"

"When he's found to have had daggers matching the murder weapon in his possession, what choice do I have? I suppose I trusted his prediction for me because I wanted Europa to believe it also," Anatolius concluded.

"Do you mean because a young lady is not likely to accept the word of a murderer that her admirer will be lucky in love?"

Anatolius flushed but remained silent.

"Do you think the soothsayer followed Leukos and stabbed him to death?" John asked.

"I don't know if he followed him. Perhaps they arranged to meet later for some reason. A longer reading, for example. Or Leukos might have been talking too freely about the valuable imperial plate in his charge, and Ahasuerus got the notion he was carrying a lot of money. Perhaps he just happened to see Leukos on his way to somewhere else." Anatolius was becoming exasperated. Although he knew it was unfair, he was angry at John for dampening his own good spirits.

"Why did Leukos seem so distracted at the Hippodrome?"

"He did, didn't he? I suppose he was anticipating his visit to the soothsayer. It wasn't the kind of thing he did every day."

"And what about Berta's death? Do you suppose that was unrelated? The alley where Leukos was murdered runs behind Isis' house. Berta was at the same palace celebration Ahasuerus attended. Now I fear Europa and Cornelia are in danger. After all, they were at the same accursed gathering."

"You think too much, John. It's just coincidence. And after all, in Berta's line of work, such things happen. As for Leukos, he visited the soothsayer. A few hours later the old man's dagger is in Leukos' ribs. Even a theologian would have to agree his murderer was the soothsayer. Ahasuerus was drowned when he tried to flee, pulled to the bottom of the sea. What better vengeance could you want? As I've already said, it is over."

"You're right, Anatolius. I do want revenge. I admit it. But drowning, no, I wouldn't wish that."

John fell silent. The setting sun had disappeared behind the roof. "It isn't reason that leads me to believe the soothsayer wasn't the murderer," he finally said. "It is a feeling. If Leukos' murderer were dead, it would be gone. If he were really avenged, this black creature inside me would have taken wing. But it has not, and I feel that if I don't bring his murderer to justice, it will gnaw at me for the rest of my life."

"But John, what has happened has happened. Leukos' death was unfair. But even if Ahasuerus were not the murderer, and I can't see who else could be, would finding the murderer make it any fairer?"

John did not answer the question. He looked grim. There were times when, even though he was a personal friend, Anatolius almost feared the Lord Chamberlain.

"I can't help feeling Cornelia and Europa may in some way be involved," John said. "and that makes it imperative that this mystery is unraveled. Until it is I am convinced their lives are in danger, and we can't guess which direction the danger will be coming from."

Anatolius was silent. In the gathering darkness the scent of the garden's spring flowers seemed stronger. He wondered what went on in his maimed friend's mind when he lay alone at night. What other demons that could never be exorcised raged inside John? What agonies that dared not be remembered hammered at the flimsy door of suppression?

And it occurred to Anatolius, perhaps because he was of a poetic turn of mind, that John's controlled and rational exterior might be no more than a thin varnish over madness and despair.

Chapter Forty-one

While one friend continued to seek vengeance for Leukos' death, two sought to make sense of Berta's. Felix and Thomas arrived separately at Isis' private rooms to offer their condolences but their expressions of sorrow soon turned to anger.

"Berta might have been popular, Isis, as you say, but what about the misbegotten bastard who strangled her?" Felix tossed down another mouthful of wine.

Isis studied the two callers seated opposite. The big, bearded men were alike so many ways they might have been a peculiar pair of brothers. The one was shaggy and dark, the other red haired. Felix was bulkier, built like a great bear. Thomas had the broad shoulders of the gladiators depicted in ancient sculptures. Tears streamed down Felix's face and his mouth trembled. Thomas' expression was rigid, his cold gaze a contrast to his fiery hair.

"We've never had such a thing happen before," Isis said. "And what I can't understand is who it could have been. So far as I know, only our regular guests were here." Her dark eyes were somber. "Is no one to be trusted these days? I do believe I shall have some wine myself. Thomas?"

The knight shook his head. Felix banged down his goblet. Isis scowled. In her house, displays of anger led to a swift and oft-times undignified exit aided by the brawny Darius. Murder was—or had been—unthinkable. For the first time in the years since she had arrived from Alexandria alone and afraid, she felt unsafe.

Shuddering, she poured more wine.

"She had a fine funeral, my Berta," Felix said. "I am paying for it myself." Despite the wine he had imbibed, his words were carefully formed and clearly spoken, but shaped by that terrible frozen grief of the newly and suddenly bereaved.

Isis dabbed at her eyes. "Poor Berta. Only a few days ago, dancing at the palace, and now the only people she will be dancing for are the dead, and that after her heart is balanced on the scales against the feather of truth."

"I spit upon your feathers!" Felix snarled.

Thomas, who had been largely silent since arriving to find the morose Felix with Isis, inquired about the feather, less from real interest than to calm a situation which might turn ugly.

"Oh, yes," Isis replied, "yes, when we die, our hearts are weighed against the feather of truth. It is an ostrich feather, such as is worn by our goddess Maat. She represents truth and justice, you know. If the scales of judgment balance evenly, then the departed are judged worthy. If not, they are destroyed."

Felix rose ponderously from the couch. "That may well be, Isis. But Mithra will surely aid me, and a veritable tribunal of judges of the dead, a whole milling herd of ostriches, none of these things will hide the truth of it, for I shall find out who did this thing, and I shall…." He paused, wiping tears from his face. "Let me repeat this, as Mithra is my lord, I shall personally ensure that justice is meted out. I shall take great pleasure in squeezing the miserable dregs of life out of the bastard who took my Berta away from me. But slowly, very slowly, you understand? I want his agony to be long, and when he dies, the only prayer over his body will be mine, that Mithra will continue his agony in the next life for all of eternity." His words were the more terrible for being spoken in a gently conversational tone of voice. "And now, I must go."

Neither Thomas nor Isis spoke for a while after the bereaved man staggered out. Finally, Thomas broke the heavy silence by wondering if Felix would ever find the man he sought.

"I wouldn't lay a wager on it. Felix has made a lot of bad wagers."

"Perhaps Felix would like a memento of Berta," mused Thomas. "Didn't she have some jewelry? I recollect some barbaric bracelets. I would be happy to deliver them to him if you would trust me."

"That's kind of you, Thomas. As it happens, I already gave him some of her small pieces as remembrances. If I didn't know that my girls' all have hiding places for their valuables I would never have found them."

Thomas nodded. "Excellent, excellent. She was very fond of green, wasn't she?" He sounded wistful.

Isis stared at him with surprise. She heard genuine emotion in his voice. "You were fond of her?"

He blushed. "Yes."

Isis knew that men could quickly form attachments if they met a girl at the right time. It was the source of no small amount of trouble in her business. "You only saw Berta once, as I recall?"

"That's true but she had something about her…I think she took a liking to me too, although I wouldn't say so to Felix. She was fascinated by my travels."

Isis did not point out that being fascinated by clients was part of Berta's job. What an innocent the man was. But then what could you expect of someone from the far edge of the empire? "I've done some traveling myself, Thomas. Have you been to Alexandria? That's where I'm from."

"There are few places I have not been."

"The Lord Chamberlain lived there for a while." A soft smile briefly illuminated her plump face. "You know, he is a good man. He has suffered much, and yet remains kind."

"No higher praise can any man, or woman for that matter, have bestowed upon them. I would be proud to have that said of me."

"I think, Thomas, that your heart is true and you need not fear the weighing of it when the time comes. What a strange and terrible city this is! I shall be glad to return home eventually. I daresay you feel the same way? Do you think it will be a long time before you return home?"

He shrugged. "It's been too long since I've walked under the gray skies of Bretania, yet I can't say when I'll feel its kindly rain on my face again."

"You are quite the poet, Thomas!"

"All men wax poetical about that which they love."

"And there is no doubt that Felix loved Berta." Isis, having drunk too much, had put aside her goblet and was peeling an apple. "If only we knew who murdered her. Here is an apple for knowledge, as the Christians say. Perhaps it will work for you."

Thomas chewed the proffered fruit thoughtfully. "In the northern part of Bretania where I was born, apple-cores are called gowks. Yet you could put apples in huge piles and ask a man from the south to find the gowks, and he would look forever. They would be there, in plain view right in front of him, yet hidden, so he would not find them. Well, not unless he asked someone from the north, I suppose!"

"It seems that the moral of your tale is that with good will and many eyes the hidden cannot remain so forever." In her current state of inebriation it struck Isis as a profound insight.

Thomas nodded solemnly. "Let us hope so, for I fear Felix is going to be a dangerous man until he exacts his revenge for Berta."

Chapter Forty-two

It was not wise to seek out the emperor in his private residence in the middle of the night.

The thought flashed through John's mind as a shadowy figure bulled into him.

As the shock of the assault faded he realized there could be no connection with his intended visit. He was crossing the gardens and had not even reached the Octagon. The emperor's eyes seemed to be everywhere and his reach had no limits, yet he was not omniscient.

"…what about her? What about her?" his attacker roared. "They killed her too!" The words were slurred by wine.

Hands fastened claw-like on John, intent on dragging him to the ground.

As John staggered backwards, his attacker began to emit gasping, inarticulate noises. John recognized first that the man was sobbing, and second, that it was his friend Felix.

"Captain!"

The man's grip loosened. "Berta," he mumbled as his legs buckled and he fell forward. John helped him to a nearby bench.

"In your condition it's fortunate you ran into me rather than one of your own men or some administrative troublemaker."

"Berta's dead."

"I know, Felix."

"But you've been looking for Leukos' murderer. And even though the old soothsayer's dead, the bastard, you're still looking."

"Who told you that? Anatolius? Have you waylaid him tonight also?"

The burly captain let his head drop against John's shoulder and continued to sob. John hoped his friend was intoxicated enough so as not to remember much in the morning. Of those three things that relieve men of their senses and dignity—wine, religion, and women—wine, John thought, offers the least recompense.

Intoxicated or not, Felix was right. Berta was dead too. John must not forget there were two murders to avenge.

"Best get you home. Can you stand?"

Felix grunted and clambered unsteadily to his feet.

John steered him deeper into the garden. Who at court hadn't taken too much wine on some occasion or other? Yet there was no misstep so slight that it would not be noted and used at an opportune time.

Distracted by his efforts to keep Felix upright, John left the path. Felix lurched into shrubbery, dragging John with him.

There was a muffled oath, movement in the dark, a transitory gleam of naked flesh, rounded, a knee, or breast.

"Zeus take you!" came a hoarse male voice. "Find your own spot, you two!"

Summoning all his strength John pulled Felix back to the path. Muted giggles, faint as a memory, pursued him out of the thicket. The night closed in like dark water.

When he had dragged Felix back to the captain's house, he tried to prop Felix up with his back to the wall but his friend's legs were so wobbly he slid down until he was sitting.

John rapped at the house door to alert a servant to their arrival.

It swung open.

Had Felix been drinking before leaving the house and forgotten to secure the door? Had his servants failed to notice? It seemed unlikely.

John slipped the captain's sword from its scabbard.

He stepped quietly into the house. From somewhere, perhaps the colonnade surrounding the garden, enough torchlight filtered in to reveal the rough outline of the holding basin in the center of the atrium. John took a few steps toward the gray rectangle of a doorway just visible across it.

Felix's sword was far heavier than any John would have chosen. He paused, listening. A cricket trilled nearby.

Did he hear breathing? He had the distinct sense the darkness enclosed something more solid than the cricket's repetitive song.

He heard movement behind him and when he turned he could see a dim patch of light on the tiles, escaping from a partially covered lantern, giving enough illumination to avoid stumbling but not reaching beyond its owner's feet.

"Home at last, captain?" The voice was muffled. John could discern no more than the outline of the speaker. Felix's visitor must not have been able to distinguish so much as that to mistake John for Felix.

"I hope Fortuna has treated you more kindly tonight than it did when last we spoke," the voice continued. "Although I'm not sure it is Fortuna's fault if you insist on backing the Greens every time she gives victory to the Blues or if you will call four fingers when she ordains five. Don't worry. I have been authorized to offer you the usual arrangement. But we must know by tomorrow at the second hour. By the way, you should have wagered against your marriage. I put ten nomismata against it and made a killing!"

The words must have been loud enough to reach outside and penetrate Felix's befuddled haze.

"No! I'll take no more of your dirty money!" Felix's slurred shout echoed around the atrium. Somehow he had got to his feet and his form filled the doorway. "Tell your master to find someone else!"

The captain lurched forward, lost his precarious balance, and fell.

In the instant John's attention was drawn away from the intruder the man flung the covered lantern.

It came at him like a fireball.

John knocked it aside with his sword. By the time he had blinked away the effect of sparks and flame, Felix' visitor had vanished.

Chapter Forty-three

John was deep in thought as, having handed over his dagger to the doorkeeper, he made his way through one guarded doorway after another on his way into the heart of Justinian's private quarters. Passing near the emperor's residence on his way home from Felix's house he had impulsively decided to try to persuade Justinian to allow him to continue his investigation of Leukos' death. He knew Justinian worked in solitary late into the night and under such circumstances was often more agreeable to suggestions. A familiar visitor at all hours, his demand to speak to the emperor on urgent business admitted him.

As he walked, he kept turning the episode at Felix's house over, as if his memory of the vague, dark shape of the intruder might on yet reveal a detail he had missed.

Could it have been Gregorius? The man mentioned racing and playing micatio. However, Felix had surely gambled at micatio with any number of others. John could not say whether the voice was familiar. He had only spoken to Gregorius briefly and in the atrium the words had a sepulchral ring.

A door opened, sending a wave of heat and musky perfume into the brightly lit hallway and revealing a purple-hung room beyond.

A petite woman dressed in layers of silk stepped between the excubitors flanking its entrance.

"Lord Chamberlain."

"Highness," John responded, a dark curse at his ill fortune in meeting her tonight of all nights trembling on his lips as he knelt before the woman as protocol demanded.

"You are late seeking your master tonight," Theodora observed, extending her shoe to be kissed as she always demanded. No, John saw, she was barefoot. Her toenails were painted gold. "But then imperial affairs brook no delays. What is your business?"

"I wish to consult him on the matter of the Keeper of the Plate, Highness," John replied. It was dangerous enough to speak the truth to Theodora, let alone lie to her.

She gestured him to stand. "You have been instructed to end that investigation." Her words had an knife-like edge. "Do you intend to refuse a direct order from the emperor? I advise you to think carefully before proceeding on a course you will come to regret."

John remained silent. He did intend to continue his investigation even if he couldn't persuade Justinian to allow it.

The empress' eyes with their unnaturally large pupils might have been drawing the thoughts from his mind. "You don't believe that wretched soothsayer committed the murder?"

"I do not."

"Despite the evidence?"

"The distinctive daggers he was carrying? I do not see it as certain proof that he thrust one into Leukos."

"Do you suppose the old man was not capable? He was. Oh, he certainly was." Theodora smiled. "He told my fortune privately, using a chicken. Oh, yes. He knew how to use those blades of his."

"A man isn't a domestic fowl, Highness."

"To an empress they are." Theodora giggled. "The soothsayer must have come straight to my banquet with Leukos' blood still on his hands. How delicious to contemplate."

John felt a chill run down his back, even as his face prickled with the heat issuing from the doorway, heat that was no doubt the result of several braziers yet seemed to radiate from the empress herself. Through the doorway he could see a haze of incense.

"Can we be certain the soothsayer is the murderer when the torturers never had a chance to question him?"

Theodora's kohl-outlined eyes narrowed. "There is that. I do regret he was able to escape into the sea. I would have had him tell my fortune with his own entrails."

John noticed the men flanking the doorway stood frozen like statuary, while their gaze flickered to the empress' bare feet and over her voluminous but near transparent silks. Their faces had turned pale, but yet they could not draw their gaze away.

John offered a silent prayer to Mithra.

Did Theodora's scarlet lips quirk into a fleeting smile? Had she sensed his entreaty to a pagan god?

"Highness, consider this. The soothsayer could well have had an accomplice who will go unpunished if the investigation ends."

"No wonder the emperor finds you persuasive, Lord Chamberlain. Much too persuasive in my opinion. Yet if you find the supposed accomplice will you fillet him yourself, for my pleasure?"

Her musk was suddenly choking. "Highness." He forced out a rasping reply. "I am not skilled enough to offer you the pleasure the torturers can."

"I disagree. You and the torturers together might offer me exquisite entertainment one day. Particularly if you flaunt your emperor's commands."

If John continued his efforts to avenge Leukos he would be risking not only death but a terrible death once word of his efforts reached Justinian, as they surely would sooner or later. John was, nevertheless, determined to persevere so, he realized, those efforts had better be successful.

Theodora leaned forward, as if to speak confidentially. "You may be willing to risk your own life, Lord Chamberlain, knowing that the emperor is a merciful man and may not see fit to have your ears and tongue removed. However, I am told you no longer live alone. If you suffer, you will not suffer alone."

John's stomach lurched. He could have broken her delicate white neck with its golden chains in an instant, before the guards could react. It would almost have been worth his own death. But then, others would die as well.

He struggled to keep his face impassive, seeing from the amusement that played over Theodora's features that he was not entirely successful. "I shall keep your advice in mind when I speak to the emperor."

"You will not be speaking to the emperor. He is not in his study. It is not theology with which he is wrestling tonight, Lord Chamberlain."

She smiled at him, stepped back into the hot, smoky room, and shut the door.

Chapter Forty-four

Kaloethes' fears pounded in his head like a creditor at the door. He had awakened in a panic to familiar thoughts. All his bills were falling due at once. Debts, taxes, fees.

It was an impossible situation.

The innkeeper crept out of the suffocating room he shared with his wife, half expecting the woman to awake and thunder after him, demanding to know what he was doing. He escaped down the stairs and into the courtyard safely, but his accounts did not add up there either.

Half asleep, tatters of nightmare still clinging to his mind, his eye was drawn by the glimmer of the water in the fountain, the only hint of light in the courtyard. He contemplated throwing himself into it but then realized even that dramatic gesture would be doomed to failure for the basin was too shallow.

He was saved from whatever more practical solution might have occurred to him by the sound of a footstep.

"Who is it?" he demanded.

The figure that solidified from the darkness was the big red-head, Thomas. He should have guessed.

"Ah, innkeeper. Taking in some of the night breezes too, I see? I find the city most pleasant just before dawn."

Kaloethes was fully awake now but his black mood remained. "You would know. I suppose this mysterious wandering in and out at odd hours is what you Britons call a quest?"

"I hope I haven't disturbed anyone. I wasn't trying to run off without paying my bill, by the way. As I told your wife…"

"Yes, she keeps pointing out to me how fortunate we are to enjoy your good credit. If only my own creditors could enjoy it as well."

"If there's been some misunderstanding, I'll pay on the instant."

This was a chance the innkeeper could not let pass, whatever the hour. Cautioning Thomas to tread quietly, he led him through the kitchen and into a cramped cell of an office, striking a light to the clay lamp he kept beside the door.

"There," he said, tapping a meaty finger on the figures in the codex under Thomas' account. "You're in arrears to a sum of almost, well, see for yourself."

"I'm afraid I must leave that task to you. But my purse is open."

Kaloethes opinion of Thomas soared as coins fell into his hand. Perhaps he had been too sharp-tongued with the man.

"Look, come and share some of our excellent wine. I can't sell the stuff anyway, so we might as well enjoy it."

They sat at the kitchen table. The trembling lamplight struck sparks of gold in Thomas' beard and accentuated the concavities around the innkeeper's eyes.

"I am sorry if I gave the impression I mistrusted you, my friend," Kaloethes said. "But you have been in this damnable city long enough now to know its ways. A nomisma to take a drink, two to take a breath."

Thomas nodded silently.

"I am besieged by an army of officials demanding a ransom an honest man could never raise."

"It's a bad situation." agreed Thomas. "Although besiegers usually carry swords."

"Swords? What can a sword do but rip out your guts? A pen, now, applied to the right scrap of official parchment can rend you to your very soul! I tell you, I'd rather they came at me with swords, the bastards."

"They say a man with a sword is no match for a pen. That hasn't been my experience."

Kaloethes studied Thomas' apparently open, somewhat stupid, face, wondering how many more coins the so-called knight carried and how he had come by them. Kaloethes always wondered how people came by what they possessed.

"You've made no secret about this quest of yours. Perhaps I could help? I do have business contacts, including some at the palace."

"Mine is a dangerous quest."

Kaloethes drew his bulk up straighter, causing the wooden bench to creak loudly. "I am familiar with danger myself."

Thomas coughed, releasing a spray of wine. "I don't doubt it, having met your wife."

Kaloethes grinned and poured Thomas more wine. You couldn't hold against a man what he said when his tongue was loosened by drink. He'd seen babes in arms who could hold their wine better than Thomas. "My wife has large ambitions, Thomas."

"Indeed, everything about her is large."

Kaloethes felt the need for more wine himself. "Can you believe that when I met her she was a wood nymph?"

"As easily as I could believe the girls at Madam's were once husky charioteers."

"Well, it is true. And now? I can see that beautiful young girl in my memory but there's nothing else left of her." Kaloethes felt his eyes stinging. "She is gone, Thomas. Dead. That young girl I once loved is dead."

Kaloethes noticed Thomas' face darkened suddenly and his features tightened into a grim frown. Obviously the knight sympathized with his plight.

"You know people at the palace?" Thomas asked. "How about whoever's replaced the unfortunate Keeper of the Plate? It might be useful if an interview could be arranged."

"Now, that might not be out of the question although gold would almost certainly have to change hands. But I thought it was some sort of relic you sought, not palace treasures?"

"Yes, but—"

"Come with me," Kaloethes said suddenly. Taking the lamp, he lifted a trapdoor in a corner of the kitchen. The men descended a rickety ladder into a musty catacomb.

"We keep our stores down here," the innkeeper explained.

He could see Thomas' eyes widen as he looked around at the crates and boxes piled to the ceiling. Several were open and close enough to make out clothing, cheap pottery, and domestic bric-a-brac. Balanced precariously on and among the boxes were chairs, ornate tables, and decorated chests.

Thomas stooped to pick up a scrap of shredded fabric. "Your vermin at least live well with nests of silk. I know I am not alone in taking comfort at Madam's." He smiled. "If you have a favorite there, I'm sure she would appreciate some of these things."

"Most of them belong to my wife. She'd notice if anything was missing."

Thomas raised his eyebrows. He took an unsteady step and leaned against a pile of crates.

The thought occurred to Kaloethes that he was alone with an apparently inebriated man who was carrying a large amount of money. It was immediately replaced by the thought that the inebriated man was armed with a sword.

Kaloethes reached into a long, wooden box and drew out a yellowish bone. "Look, this is what I've brought you to see. An authentic relic of Saint Prokopios. Not just a knuckle or a finger. The entire thigh bone that bore his blessed weight."

He turned the bone around in the feeble lamp light.

"Martyred by being thrown into a pit of rats and devoured by all appearances," Thomas observed.

"It is somewhat distressed, I agree, but that is no doubt why it was offered to me for a very reasonable price."

"No, my friend, this is not the type of relic I am seeking."

Kaloethes tossed the bone back into the box. Perhaps Thomas held his wine better than it seemed. "I was assured it was authentic and I have no reason to distrust the rag seller's nephew," he grumbled.

They climbed back up the ladder, Kaloethes breathing hard with exertion and frustrated by his inability to persuade Thomas to part with some of his remaining coins. His opportunity was slipping through his fingers.

"I know you are on a quest, Thomas, but even one on a quest has to pay the bills. You strike me as a man who would dare much. I might be able to offer you some tasks which could benefit both of us financially."

"I fear not, friend. The task I have undertaken is enough for now."

Through the window Kaloethes saw gray light creeping into the courtyard, as dawn arrived to reanimate his besieging army of creditors.

"Think about my offer, Thomas," he whispered as they crept up the stairs. "At least think about it."

Chapter Forty-five

John suppressed a yawn while the elderly Quaestor worked his way through the legal preliminaries to reading Leukos' will with the patient determination, but none of the artistry, of a spider spinning its web.

It had been another late night.

Felix had had to be assisted to bed. He kept blubbering Berta's name. John found it distressing because the memory would humiliate Felix, if he were to recall it.

Then there had been the encounter with Theodora. That was definitely an occurrence best forgotten. As were his hopes of negotiating approval of his investigation from Justinian.

John stifled another yawn, tensing his jaw painfully. The reading had been scheduled for a cramped hearing room near the law courts. There were no windows. Apparently the reality of the outside world was considered an unwanted intrusion.

John had brought with him the pouch Leukos had been carrying when he died. The few trinkets it contained were worth little. But it was part of Leukos' estate, and John was hoping that someone from Leukos' family would be there to claim it.

The Lord Chamberlain glanced around at the handful of people seated in the stuffy room. There was no one he recognized. A few men who appeared to be minor officials, professional acquaintances of Leukos, perhaps. Several others might have been hangers-on, present just in case they were mentioned in the will. It had been foolish of him to hope that some relative might attend, someone who could shed some light on Leukos' past, perhaps even on the recent past, and on what may have caused his death.

There were more yawns. A fly explored the wall behind the droning Quaestor, and in the end, those assembled learned that Leukos, Keeper of the Plate, had granted manumission to his slaves and placed the bulk of his estate in the hands of John, Lord Chamberlain, to dispose of as he saw fit. John signed and swore out the required documents before the Quaestor.

When he was done, John returned to Leukos' house. Perhaps he had missed some pointer to the truth during his recent visit. Certainly a person's home should reveal something about its inhabitant, but Leukos' residence was barren of the man's personality. How—why—was this so?

The house had the air of a building to which no one would return. The water clock remained dry. The kitchen walls retained the odor of meats that had been boiled there. In the hall the suggestion of recently consumed meals mingled with the cloying perfume used in preparing Leukos for burial.

Someone, presumably the servant Euphemia, had thrown open cupboards and chests prior to packing their contents into the crates strewn about the tiled floor. John examined several plates, an ornamental lamp, a set of candlesticks. Compared to the treasures with which he had dealt, Leukos' possessions were simple.

John found Euphemia in Leukos' bedroom, carefully removing clothes from the chest at the foot of the bed and smoothing out their wrinkles one last time.

"I'm happy to see you're still here," John told the girl. "I wish to ask a few more questions."

Euphemia turned her gaze to the robe draped over one arm. Her finger traced the gold embroidery along the hem.

"If it's about my master's visitors or his doings, I can't tell you any more, sir. I've thought about it since we talked, but I've told you all I know."

"And the other servants?"

"I asked them. They know less than I do."

It was hard for John to imagine that Leukos would have intentionally involved himself in any questionable activities. Could he have unintentionally done so? There were the mysterious night time visitors. And Leukos had worked closely with Xiphias, a man who was capable of anything.

"Did Leukos ever mention a man named Xiphias who worked with him?"

Euphemia shook her head. "He never spoke of his work to me." She placed the gold-embroidered robe on the pile of other clothing on the bed.

"These men who brought things to the house from time to time, none of them were named Xiphias?"

"I don't know their names, sir."

"Do you recall a middle-aged, stooping man?" Knowing that he had described half the clerks at the palace, John searched for a more exact portrait of Xiphias. "A man with a hard face. A scowl. Tight-lipped."

Euphemia looked at him blankly.

John was describing how he saw Xiphias. The man's viciousness overrode in his memory any objective description. Then again he was a nondescript man, or was that also John's perception?

Euphemia glanced down at the linen undergarment she'd removed from the chest, reddened, and placed it quickly with the other clothes.

John took Leukos' pouch from his belt. There had been no one at the reading of the will to claim it. He emptied its familiar contents onto the bed.

"Do you recognize any of these things?"

Euphemia looked puzzled. "No, but the necklace is lovely."

John picked it up. "For a new love, or a remembrance of an old one?"

"Truly, sir, I've never seen it before."

"Did you take care of his personal belongings, look after his jewelry?"

"Yes, though the master didn't have much jewelry. Just a few rings. He must have purchased the necklace very recently."

John looked thoughtful. "So you are returning to the countryside where the mice are friendlier?"

The girl was startled. "Did I mention how much I hate the mice here, sir? I shall not miss them."

John smiled, convinced he was missing something very important.

Chapter Forty-six

It was mid-afternoon by the time John reached Leukos' grave, carrying a basket holding small cakes, the traditional meal for the dead. It was not, Peter had warned him, the proper day for kollyba, but then added that he imagined his God would nevertheless respect the gesture made on behalf of a man who had no family to perform the ritual.

Leukos had wished to be buried in a simple manner. His tomb was marked by what appeared to be the top of a vault but was only a thin layer of plaster over a mound of dirt. A lamp stood on a low pedestal beside the grave and, unlike most of the other lamps in the cemetery, it still burned.

John set the basket on the grass and removed a cake. He felt more awkward than he ever had in directing court ceremonies.

"Will it help or hurt you, my friend, to have a pagan eat kollyba before a god he doesn't believe in?"

His voice sounded much louder in the open air than it did when he spoke to the mosaic girl in his study. Was Leukos now, like Zoe, no more than a vision in his imagination?

Christians believed in the immortality of the soul just as Mithrans did. But was it huddled amongst Leukos' bones in the earth, waiting for his Lord's return, or had it, as John believed, already escaped its crumbling body and begun its ascent of the heavenly ladder? And if it had, how would Leukos, good man, good Christian, pass by the fierce guardians along the way? Leukos had not had the benefit of learning the mysteries in which John was initiated.

"I am sorry I didn't share meals with you more often in life." John addressed the earthen mound. As he raised the cake to his lips there was a pitiful mewl, and glancing toward a nearby stele he saw the black cat he had glimpsed after Leukos' funeral. He broke off a piece of the kollyba and threw it to the animal. The cat pounced instantly.

After the long night and the long walk up the Mese to the cemetery, John felt sleepy. Lulled by the peaceful surroundings, he didn't notice he had company until he felt the tip of a sword prodding his side.

He turned slowly, knowing a sudden move would only mean death. He was surprised to find himself staring into a face as gaunt as many buried around him.

The skeletal man laughed with a wheezing sound, as if some of his breath were escaping through the rents in the loose tunic flapping on his thin frame. "You've picked the right grave, you have. The Keeper of the Plate himself. Some fine things he must have carried down with him. But you've not been careful enough. So I've got you at last."

"You're mistaken. I'm not a grave-robber. I've come to pay tribute to my friend." John displayed the piece of kollyba he held. "I am from the palace."

"Ah, so you're a liar as well as a grave-robber."

"Can't you see?" John indicated his expensive robes.

Another death-bed laugh issued from the man's thin, color-less lips. The sword point bit more deeply and John felt a warm trickle of blood. He saw that his captor's eyes were milky.

The man was half blind.

"You've sported with me for months. Now it's my turn." The gaunt man took a long, jerky stride forward, forcing John back a step. "Plenty of room for the likes of you around here," he added. And John, looking carefully in the direction the man indicated, saw that they were standing not far from one of many fresh graves.

John remembered the kollyba in his hand and the scavenging cat. Praying to Mithra that the animal was still lurking nearby, he dropped the cake.

As John had hoped, a black shape erupted from the long grass and pounced onto the cake like a demon springing at a damned soul.

John's captor, confronted unexpectedly by what must have appeared to him only as a terrible black specter, gasped, tottering backwards on thin legs. Then he was lying on his back, John's knee digging into his ribs, the sword hovering over his throat.

The cat stood nearby, eyes alert for danger or more largesse, refusing to retreat as it desperately attempted to swallow the remains of the kollyba in a single gulp.

"Fortunately for you," John told the cemetery guardian, "I really am from the palace. I am Lord Chamberlain to the emperor. Were I a common grave-robber, you'd be dead." He let the man up.

"Spare me, excellency." The man cringed, hunching over in terror until his head was almost level with John's knees. "We have had trouble here. Sacrilege."

"They aren't simply stealing grave goods?"

Realizing he was to be spared, the cemetery guardian straightened up. "Oh no. Not just jewelry. The skull of John the Baptist. Leg bones of martyrs, saints' knuckles."

"You make it make appear all the apostles and fathers of the church were buried here."

"You'd think so, seeing what's been dug up and put on display." The man lowered his voice. "Years ago, I was digging a grave and, God forgive me, I came too close to someone who'd already been here a while. I accidentally sliced into his side. He was just rotten cloth and bone by then. No complaint there.

"But not long afterwards, I was in a church, I won't say which one, but what do you think was there, displayed in a reliquary? It was our poor Lord's rib, the very one they say was damaged when his side was pierced by the centurion's spear. Well, excellency, I could see better in those days, and so I can assure you that the only problem with that relic was that the nick in the rib was identical to the outline of the edge of my spade."

John could well believe it. "This place is large and you are but one man. How did you come to notice me?"

"I heard you talking. My ears are better than my eyes. And then I saw a shape coming out of the field right where the aqueduct cuts through."

"But I came from the road."

The guardian frowned. He turned his head to one side, then the other. "I thought there was something. Yes. Listen."

John could discern only insects heralding the approaching night.

"A spade. I hear a spade!"

The guardian bolted away. John followed. Although nearly blind the man dodged around grave markers and mounds as if he had ingrained the topography of the place in his mind.

The intruder, no doubt alerted by the noise of their approach, had vanished by the time the two reached where he had been digging.

"Grave robbing in broad daylight!" cried the guardian, flailing his sword around. "How could anyone dare it!"

John thought it might not have required much daring, considering that the cemetery's guardian was more or less blind and the grave in question was in a nondescript corner, partially concealed by shrubbery.

A pile of dirt lay on one edge of a hole that reached down to the tile-lined crypt where a partially exhumed body lay.

John knelt by the graveside. As his eyes grew accustomed to the darkness of the pit he made out green silk robes and blond hair.

It was Berta.

Chapter Forty-seven

"The body hasn't been disturbed." John shuddered as he brushed dirt off his clothes. Despite the warm sunlight it had felt cold in the shadows beside Felix's intended wife. "We must have frightened the robbers off before they finished their job."

"Whatever their job was." The cemetery guardian had returned after going to send an assistant to fetch the urban watch.

It was time for John to leave. He did not want to be detained by the prefect's men.

He was rounding a grove of pines when the sound of hooves made him think he had left the cemetery too late.

However, it was not the urban watch. A group of mounted men came into view, among them Gregorius.

The young charioteer glanced at the sky as if trying to avoid John's gaze, but when it became apparent the two men had seen each other, he hailed John. "Lord Chamberlain. What brings you out here?"

"I have been paying my respects to one of the departed."

"So have I. You're not planning on walking all the way back to the palace, are you? Take my apprentice's horse. The boy's young. A little exercise will do him good." His tone suggested he was hoping John would not take him up on the offer, but John disappointed him by accepting it.

The youngster dismounted, casting sullen sideways glances at John and his master, and then slouched off down the road as if he were hauling a block of granite on his back.

John pulled himself up into the saddle and Gregorius waved his companions away.

"You're looking at me suspiciously, Lord Chamberlain. We have been visiting a teammate, killed during practice a couple days ago. Some bastard sawed the axle of his chariot practically all the way through and it was so cunningly done it wasn't noticed. I could have been driving that chariot, and then I'd be the one beneath the mound back there."

"Do you think someone's trying to kill you?"

"Not me in particular, but the Blue teams have been having too much success lately. Certain people are losing wagers too often, and heavy gamblers don't like losing money. Some are not averse to bribing team members not to try too hard to win, though when it comes to arranging accidents...."

"Chariot racing has many dangers. Have you considered finding a safer way to make a living?"

Gregorius laughed without humor. "Something illicit, you mean? There's certainly dangerous. And so is a man in your position walking around by himself."

"I enjoy my own company after working with courtiers and high officials all day. I don't have to worry about ruffling my own feathers."

"I understand a Master of the Soldiers is worth a ransom of 10,000 nomismata. What might a Lord Chamberlain be worth?"

"That would depend on Justinian's mood the day I was abducted."

They rode past the Church of Holy Apostles, the dilapidated timber roof of the church contrasting with the glittering brass and gold dome of Constantine's mausoleum beside it.

At the Forum Theodosius they parted ways. Gregorius said he would instruct his apprentice to retrieve John's horse from the imperial stables. "Despite the intrigues I'll be sorry to leave here," Gregorius went on. "No other city can match Constantinople.

Not Antioch, or Thessalonika, or Alexandria. Whenever I depart, no matter where I'm going to race next, I'm on my way to the hinterlands compared to this city."

John rode back toward the palace. He felt like a mosaicist who kept gathering more and more pieces of colored glass. Something about the colors suggested the picture that might be assembled from the tesserae but as yet he couldn't discern what it looked like.

He stopped at Felix's house. He wanted to question Felix about the events of the preceding night. The captain had professed not to recognize the intruder, but had been intoxicated and almost incoherent at the time. Apparently he had recovered from his excess quickly because his servant reported he had left hours earlier.

When John reached home he was relieved he had not been able to spend time questioning Felix since much to his displeasure he found Thomas visiting Europa.

Peter clucked angrily as he followed John upstairs. "The so-called knight has been bending her ear for hours, master. I can't get rid of him. They're in your study."

"Don't worry, Peter. I'll attend to Thomas."

The big redhead leapt up from his seat when John strode in. "Lord Chamberlain! We were beginning to worry!"

"What are you doing here, Thomas?"

"Oh, I've just been telling Europa I'm looking...."

"I mean here in my study?"

Europa began to explain. "As I told Thomas, I was informed by Peter that in Constantinople men are not allowed to visit women in their rooms. So I suggested that we talk here. The mosaic is beautiful."

"I would have preferred something less elaborate."

"I don't agree. I think it's wonderful. Except for that little girl." Europa's large eyes glanced at the even larger, darker eyes of the portrait of Zoe. "She frightens me. Watching all the time. And listening. She could tell you everything she's heard."

Did Europa dart a glance at Thomas? Was that a raised eyebrow, a flash of a smile?

Thomas cleared his throat. "She would only have heard about my travels and the wonders of my country." He tugged at his ginger mustache. "No wonder her eyes are glazed."

"Really, Thomas, you're too modest," Europa told him. "I could listen to your tales all day."

"According to Peter, you very nearly have," pointed out John. He felt uneasy, uncertain of his role. This young woman was, after all, his daughter. But how could he be a father to someone he had never known as a child? He felt an irrational anger at Thomas. Was it fatherly concern or jealousy over this almost stranger who reminded him so much of a young Cornelia? "Where is your mother, Europa?"

"She had some business with the troupe."

"I warned you both to stay at the house!"

"We aren't your underlings, Lord Chamberlain."

"I think you'd better leave us now, Europa." He found that the words came with difficulty. Strange that a man used to commanding high officials should find it hard to give orders to his own daughter.

Europa stood. She was graceful even rising from a chair. "As you wish...."

For an instant John thought she was going to add "father," but she did not.

She paused in front of Thomas and gazed up into his ruddy face. "You'll come back another time and finish your wonderful tales for me?"

Thomas grew even redder. He appeared to be struck dumb.

Then Europa stamped out of the study as John watched in dismay.

So this was what it meant to be a father.

When she had gone he turned his attention back to Thomas. "What are you really here for, Thomas?"

"As I said, we were talking."

"I seem to be running into you with remarkable frequency."

"Not surprising when I'm visiting a guest in your household, John."

"But on the street and in the palace gardens in the middle of the night?"

"Constantinople is small."

"To a traveler such as yourself perhaps."

"Something's upset you, my friend?"

"Some beast dug up poor Berta's grave."

"But this isn't wild country."

"I don't mean an animal," snapped John. "I meant some two-legged beast."

Thomas looked stricken. "That is unmanly."

John felt a softening toward the big redhead. Thomas had understood John's horror. They were both soldiers and soldiers were most solicitous of the dead.

"Why, John?"

"Grave robbing is common enough."

"Not in my country."

"Is this truly a surprise to you, Thomas? Are you really so horrified?"

The other looked up, his eyes glistening. "I did know Berta. Only briefly, I admit, but in a fashion better—" He stopped abruptly and apologized.

"Yes, you knew her much better than I could." John sat down. His eyes burned. "Leave now, Thomas. I would advise you not to beguile my daughter with your tall tales."

He slumped wearily as his unwanted visitor went out.

Almost immediately there came a knocking at the house door and Peter appeared to announce another caller waited downstairs.

The youngster at the door was out of breath, as if he had been running. "The prefect sent me, sir. A body's been found at the docks."

Chapter Forty-eight

John made his way to the harbor where the body had been discovered. The sun was setting as he crossed the great square called the Strategion. Merchants were packing their carts in preparation for departure.

The high sea wall cast its shadow out past the end of the docks, over the nearby ships. With a pang, John noticed one of them was the *Anubis*.

But he had left Europa safely at home and Cornelia had gone to see members of her troupe.

As he reached the steep covered stairs, he barely registered the four men gathered around a dark heap below.

Would the soothsayer's corpse speak as the entrails of the old man's chickens had—or as he claimed they had? Would his body offer a clue to the identity of Leukos' real murderer?

Or was it some other poor unfortunate who had fallen or leapt to his death? Emerging from the stairwell John found himself facing the *Anubis*. He heart gave a lurch.

He loped over to where three of the urban watch stood.

And forced his gaze to the body sprawled on the stones.

It was not Ahasuerus.

The figure was smaller. The pallid face, although marred by crabs, was one he had known for years.

It was Xiphias.

John worked to steady his breathing. The dock felt as if it was turning under his feet. One of the men was saying something about gold candlesticks.

"...had them tied to his belt. Meant to drown himself. Expensive weights."

John grunted an acknowledgment.

"There are no wounds. He must have thrown himself in," the prefect's man said.

"Or someone else helped," one of the others put in.

"Someone else would have used stones and kept the candlesticks."

Something prodded at John's memory. "Where's your colleague?" he asked.

"There are only the three of us."

"I saw someone else."

"Oh, a passerby, that's all. Looking for excitement. Wouldn't find death so thrilling if he had to see it every day."

"Where did he go?"

The man pointed down the docks. In the distance John could make out a dark shape. He started to run.

A line of warehouses sat along the seawall. John kept in the deepest shadows in front of the stolid, brick structures. He ran lightly and almost silently, steadily closing distance on the man ahead who strode along unaware of the pursuit.

John had nearly caught up with him when a dog exploded out of a dark doorway, snarling and snapping as it lunged at him. John knocked the beast away, sacrificing part of a sleeve.

The other man looked back over his shoulder and then broke into a run. His legs were less tired than John's but he was bulkier and slower. There was nowhere to hide with the sea on one side and the warehouses on the other. Ahead, however, loomed a dark break between buildings which, John knew, led to another stairway.

They were well beyond the wide space of the Strategion. If his prey made it up the stairs he would vanish like magick into a confusion of streets, alleys, and tenements.

John forced his legs to keep moving. His chest was on fire and there was a coppery taste in his mouth.

His quarry turned into the gap and John reached him as he started up the stairs. John lunged, caught hold of fabric, and yanked the man backwards.

The heavy body fell, tried to scramble up, but John kept the fellow's tunic in a vice-like grip. Then John's dagger was pointed at the man's throat.

"I'm tired of running into you constantly, my friend. It's time for you to explain your business here, unless you want to take the secret to the grave with you."

The tavern was what one would expect to find near the docks, a dismal cave crowded with Egyptians, Persians, Greeks, and Goths spewing oaths in a babble of accents and languages. The place smelled as if recently vacated by a family of bears.

John gulped wine.

Thomas' gaze wavered from John's face to the filthy floor. "I'm ashamed to admit I haven't been entirely honest with you, Lord Chamberlain, although I suppose I could argue that my duty to my king is greater than my duty to the truth."

"So you have been following me?"

"No, not you. The old soothsayer. I thought it would be him on the dock. Well, I should have made better inquiries. I met the messenger as I left your house, you see, and he told me that a body had been found."

"You weren't simply interested in Ahasuerus, you were actually following him?"

"Yes, I chased him to Constantinople after nearly catching him in Antioch."

"Explain."

Thomas smiled weakly. "As I told you, I'm an emissary from the court of Arthur, High King of Bretania."

"That was the truth?"

"Yes. And my quest for the Grail, that too is the truth. The king, and the kingdom itself, they are both in need of the Grail's healing power."

"Continue," John said, tiredly.

"I set off last year. Superstition pointed me to the east. I started searching in Jerusalem. From there certain stories directed me to Antioch. It was in the Kerateion, the Jewish quarter near the southern gate, that I heard of the soothsayer known as Ahasuerus. You are aware of the story of the crucified god, Jesus?"

John pointed out that he did, after all, serve in a Christian court.

"Of course, as do I. Well, as you know, Jesus was forced to drag the instrument of his death through the streets to his execution."

"That is so. A barbaric thing. Romans do not crucify criminals any longer. Not even pagans such as ourselves."

Thomas shook his head sorrowfully. "A terrible spectacle that must have been. Yet there were those who, seeing it, laughed and mocked him. One in particular urged him to hurry, following the condemned man through those dusty streets, shouting at him to make more haste toward his death. At last Jesus could tolerate this brutality no longer, for even though he was the son of God, he was also a man."

"Much blood has been spilled over that question," John remarked.

Thomas smiled ruefully. "I forgot even the laborers here are theologians. And so Jesus finally spoke. This was one who had performed miracles, raised the dead. Now he struck out with a terrible curse. The torments of flesh scourged and beaten had driven even him to despair."

John nodded wordlessly.

Thomas continued. "Thus it was that he foretold that the man who had so mocked him must wander the earth until the end of the world. And then he staggered on to his terrible death. And as for the man. His name was Ahasuerus."

The flame in the lamp on the round table where the men sat leapt and sizzled, guttering in a draft.

"That was five centuries ago, Thomas. Surely you don't believe the soothsayer Ahasuerus is the man you just mentioned?"

"I do. And what is more, if the stories I've heard are true, he is the keeper of the Grail. That also was part of his fate."

"Well, by all reports, the soothsayer has drowned."

"You believe that?"

"The patriarch does."

Thomas took a deep draft of wine, then shook his head. "He cannot drown, John. He is doomed to live until the end of the world. But is he now beyond my reach, along with this precious Grail? Yes, that, alas, is certainly possible."

"You say you followed him to Constantinople?"

"Yes. As I said, I almost caught him in Antioch. He had done readings there, and become well-known. I learned of his whereabouts from a barber who regularly trimmed the beard of a night watchman. This watchman reported he had seen the man I sought pass through the city gates before dawn that very morning, sitting in the back of a rag seller's cart. On this chance information, I purchased a horse and set off, expecting to catch up by nightfall. But just outside Antioch the road passes through a swampy region along the river. I don't believe that road could have been constructed by Romans, the stones were so badly laid, but I whipped the horse on, Mithra forgive me."

He stared sorrowfully into his cup for a time before resuming. "The poor beast caught a hoof in a hole and its leg snapped like a dry stick. I was thrown and ended up in the river. Nearly drowned, I did, and broke my own leg besides. I recuperated for weeks in a nearby hostel, nursed with lepers and dying flagellants and others of a religious nature. As you see, I still have a limp."

"How were you able to follow his trail here after all that time?"

"I was informed that the rag seller whose cart he had ridden off on was actually smuggling silks. The head of the hostel was a customer. He told me the rag seller had gone to Constantinople.

Again, I took a chance, hoping that I would find the soothsayer had come here too."

The two men fell silent. The racket in the tavern washed over them. Sailors from every corner of the empire were quarreling and trading boasts, but were any telling a tale as wild as Thomas' account?

"A fantastic story, Thomas. It has the sound of some poet's concoction."

"I wouldn't know. I am not a learned man."

"Which is not to say you lack imagination. What do you know of this Grail?"

"It is the most powerful of all relics."

"Here in Constantinople we have several fragments of that very cross that Jesus dragged through the streets, the pillar to which he was tied while scourged, and his crown of thorns, to name but a few. Not to mention several heads of John the Baptist. We also set great store in the Virgin's girdle. These holy relics are said to protect Constantinople. I would prefer to face a Persian with a sword rather than a relic but then, as you know, I am not a Christian. And neither are you. So why seek this Grail? Could you not serve your king in other ways?"

"The world has seen many religions and many miracles. What one person might attribute to one god, another might credit to some different deity. It is all a mystery to us mortals. But if the edge of my sword draws blood when the need arises, does it matter what forge it came from?"

"True enough. What does this Grail look like?"

Thomas admitted he was not certain.

"That complicates the finding of it, then."

"Oh, there are many tales. Some say it is a cup, others insist it takes the form of a plate. Still others believe it is a magickal stone."

"A stone?"

"Yes. It isn't the form that's important. Jesus manifested himself in human flesh, after all."

John took Leukos' pouch from his belt. He had been carrying it since the reading of the will at the Quaestor's office that morning. Opening it, he pushed aside the piece of linen, and drew from amidst the necklace and coins, the green stone.

"Could it look like this? It belonged to Leukos."

Thomas' eyes widened.

"The soothsayer was in the habit of giving them to all of his clients," John explained. "But they can't all be Grails. Anatolius has one, too. May I remind you there was also a monk who reportedly sold fifteen hands of Saint Prokopios?"

"Yes, you're right, they couldn't all be what I seek, but don't you think it shows...?"

The knight's hand twitched and John wondered if he was thinking of reaching for the stone. Thomas watched intently as it was returned to the pouch.

Thomas looked distressed. "Berta's pendant had a stone just like that. It was the talisman she tried to use on my leg. If someone mistook it for the Grail, could that be why she was murdered, and her grave violated?"

"Is there anyone else searching for this Grail? Tell me, were you at Isis' house the night Berta died?"

"You accuse me? A fellow Mithran?"

"Are you a Mithran, or is that a ruse to make me trust you? Who told you about the mithraeum?"

"A man at the inn dropped a hint about another man who mentioned off-hand someone else...we gave the appropriate signs...you understand how it works."

John nodded. "I shall return home now, Thomas. I trust I will not run into you again this evening."

Chapter Forty-nine

Old habits die slowly, and John, a veteran of many military encampments, still retained his ability to sleep lightly no matter how strenuous his day. It was a practice that was useful in Constantinople, where a court official camped as near to his enemies as did any soldier on the Persian border.

In sleep, John remained almost consciously alert for sounds of danger. Thus, while the downpour which dowsed the roofs of the city and their many crosses was merely a soothing background noise, a faint rustle in the hall screamed out that someone was making a stealthy approach.

John woke and, moving more silently than the intruder, was positioned behind the door by the time it swung open. His visitor paused. The lamp in the hall had gone out or been extinguished, for the opened door admitted no light into John's room.

Lightning flickered briefly as the intruder stepped forward, to be greeted with a choke hold.

A choke hold that was quickly released as John felt a woman's soft hip pressed against his thigh.

"Do you usually welcome ladies in this fashion?" Cornelia gasped, rubbing her throat. She turned to face him, but did not step away.

"Ladies who arrive unannounced at this hour are usually not ladies, and more often than not visit with evil intent."

"I couldn't sleep after all the excitement. I thought you might be awake too. I was hoping we might talk."

She was wearing only a thin sleeping tunic, and John was aware of her breasts brushing his chest. "Of course."

Cornelia closed the door and sat down uninvited on John's bed. The ropes holding its cotton-filled mattress creaked under her slight weight. He lit the lamp on the chest by the window and sat down next to her as she looked around.

"Well, John, it seems that despite all your fine gold-embroidered robes and silver goblets and late nights feasting at the palace table, your true tastes remain as simple as ever."

She laid a delicate hand along his thin face, and looked into his eyes. Her touch made him catch his breath, as it had on the *Anubis*. "Time works swiftly," she said softly, running her fingers down John's sunburnt cheek and along the line of his jaw. "You still look much as you did when I first knew you. Remarkably so."

"So your wish to talk has brought you here at this hour?" John asked, needlessly. He remembered Cornelia had difficulty sleeping and that when sleep refused to come, she liked to talk. He felt inexplicably awkward, a boy from the country again.

Cornelia lowered her voice. "There are too many people within earshot during the day."

John was aware of the clean smell of her hair. It was achingly familiar.

Cornelia, seeming not to notice the longing look on his face, rushed on. "I see you have a few scars you did not have before." She touched his chest. "Here, and here. And on your back. Was it as unspeakable as they suggest?" She hesitated. "I am aware of your grievous wound. It is common knowledge. That men should be treated so! May the goddess punish the bastards for what they did!" Her small fist smacked on the coverlet, her voice quavering with rage and distress.

The Lord Chamberlain face grew hot. He realized he was wearing only the loincloth he slept in. Was Cornelia wondering about the other scars that it hid? "There's no point in looking back, Cornelia. We go on or we die."

"And good Mithran that you are, you endured. Did you think of me at all, John, through those long years?"

"Often, Cornelia, especially on rainy nights like this." It was the truth. But he did not reveal how he had tried not to remember, and how he had cursed his inability to forget.

"On rainy nights, I thought of you, too, and prayed to the goddess that you were safe and would come home to us soon. Mark you, sometimes I called down demons on your miserable head. But I did not know...I would never have wished this on you, John. On us..." Her voice was almost drowned by the rain splashing hard against the window panes.

"Europa was talking with Thomas," John said abruptly, wishing to change the course of the conversation.

Cornelia laughed quietly. "He is harmless enough. Nothing will come of it. We move around, Europa and I. One day, there may be someone who will keep her from traveling. Not yet, I think."

"I would not keep you here, Cornelia. I am not who I was."

"Nor I."

"To look at you, though..." The lamplight was kind to the few wrinkles at the corners of her eyes and the threads of gray in her hair. "Why are you really here, Cornelia?"

"Because it is a rainy night and I wanted to be with you."

John's hands moved to her hair. "Silk. It's just like silk." He was vaguely aware how foolish and trite he sounded.

"They say the empress sleeps between silk sheets."

"Between silk vendors, or so it is has been whispered!"

They both laughed.

"And I see," Cornelia observed, "you no longer sleep naked."

"Not now."

"My poor lover." There was a catch in her voice.

John grasped her hands in his. He felt a sudden need to protect her, although he realized she was no longer the girl he had known but a woman who had made her way in life, with a daughter to shield from harm. "Don't feel sorry for me, Cornelia. How many die before they ever reach manhood? How many more are ill treated or starved of affection by those they desire? You gave me all the pleasure the gods will allow a man."

The ropes strung across the old wooden bed-frame had allowed the mattress to sag, bringing their hips together. The rising wind lashed rain against the dark diamond panes of the window and sent drafts through cracks around its frame. In the gathering chill, John could feel the warmth radiating from her body.

"I have some wine here," he said, taking the clay cup from the chest and placing it in her hands.

She took a sip and coughed. "Your taste in wine is still terrible."

"You sweetened it for me once, remember?"

"I still can."

She moved closer and John again tasted the sweet heat of her mouth. He sank into it, thin hands tracing the still familiar contours of her warmth and softness.

He pulled away. "It is just the same as in my memory at least." He was afraid she was about to cry. "Do you remember that cup?" She was still holding it. "I don't suppose you would recognize it. A plain clay cup. Peter has wondered aloud on more than occasion why, with that crack in it, I insist on using it when I'm alone. I wonder what he would think if he knew that I had had it made specially?"

Cornelia looked puzzled.

"It is because it is identical to the one we had when we were with the troupe," John explained. "Because your lips had touched its twin when I first knew you."

Cornelia smiled. "I do remember, John. And now I think on it, I also remember how you almost broke it when you knocked it off the table that time when…"

"As I recall, it was you."

Cornelia reached down abruptly and pulled her tunic over her head. She was naked.

"Cornelia, I can't."

"I know. I just wanted you to see me, John. Just look at me, lover. Or am I hurting you?"

John shook his head.

The rain beating on the window was washing away the sorrows of all the years, leaving only Cornelia. Cornelia of the silken hair, Cornelia of the small, firm breasts.

She looked at the cloth around his hips.

"No," he said. "I cannot...."

She rose and put out the lamp. The acrid smell of smoke mixed with her scent. "There, John. I won't look or touch. I just want us to be together."

He reached down, hesitant even in the darkness, and undid the garment.

She pulled him down on to the mattress and they lay together, joined at thigh, hip, chest, and mouth, intersections of warmth in the chilly room.

He tasted her mouth again. She moved against his lean frame, her body forgetting what her mind knew.

Suddenly she rolled to one side, apologizing.

He leaned over her. "Why should you be sorry? It always gave me the most pleasure, knowing you wanted me. But I'm afraid nature makes young men much too impetuous. I loved you then as a boy might, for myself. Now, I can love you as a man."

He kissed her deeply again. His slim fingers found that the language of his lover's body had not changed. Rain sheeted rhythmically at the window. His mouth finally left hers and moved downward.

By the time Cornelia awoke, the sun had long since risen over the newly-washed city. John was gone, having left her a single lily, the royal flower of Crete. It was balanced precariously in the cracked cup on the chest by the window.

Chapter Fifty

John sensed that time was running out.

As he sat in his study in the harsh light of morning, pondering what to do next, he felt that he could actually see the water steadily descending in the bowl of the water clock.

The identity of Leukos' murderer remained elusive.

John decided to start over at the beginning.

The alley where he had stumbled on Leukos' body.

Sunlight glinted sullenly off puddles left by the storm. Remembering the rainy night, he thought of Cornelia, even in this sordid place while on such a grim task.

John followed his shadow down the alley. The buildings rising on either side seemed to sag inwards. Overhead only a crack of sky showed. He stopped and scanned his surroundings.

A puddle gleamed where Leukos had lain. It turned John's thoughts to that night and he remembered the cobbles under Leukos' body had been dry.

If Leukos had been stabbed there and left to die, there should have been more blood. But if Leukos had not died there, then where had he been murdered?

A sound from above caught his attention. John looked up. Two stories up was the shuttered tenement window which had opened briefly the night he had found Leukos dead.

◇◇◇

Maera had pulled the shutters closed abruptly. Her heart leapt. It wasn't possible to get a breath of morning air any longer. What kind of place had Sabas brought her to, this filthy city where you couldn't even open your own window without some awful shock?

At least it wasn't a corpse this time. But for what good reason would a gentleman—and surely he was a gentleman, judging by his expensive robes and boots, even a country girl could tell that—for what good reason would such a person linger in an alley examining the ground under Maera's window? Right where she emptied the chamber pot.

Her husband Sabas, lying sprawled on a pallet by the wall, erupted in a series of gasping snores. There was barely room for him to stretch out. His eyelids fluttered but did not open.

Maera heard a footstep in the hallway and her heart thudded harder.

"No," she pleaded, "No." But even as she began to pray there came an imperative knock on the door. What to do? There was no escape. Again there was a knock. The door had no lock anyway.

Maera pulled it open a crack. She was trembling. It was the man from the alley. Closer, he looked even more elegant, tall and smooth-skinned. Not one who worked with his hands.

A hundred thoughts ran through Maera's mind. She had never had so many thoughts before she came to this place. Perhaps he was coming to help Sabas, perhaps he was coming to take him away. Or perhaps they were to be thrown out for not paying their rent.

"May I come in?"

The request was surprising. The voice was less imposing, gentler, than its master.

She looked around, unsure of what to say. Sabas' pallet occupied most of the floor space. The close room smelled of sickness. The gentleman stepped inside anyway.

She remembered she was clothed only in the thin, stained tunic in which she had slept.

"I'm sorry to disturb you. I am John, Lord Chamberlain to Justinian."

Lord Chamberlain? To the emperor? In this place? Surely the city had driven her mad. Yet why should she doubt him? His robes were hemmed in gold. He could have been Justinian himself or the patriarch. Maera instinctively shrunk away.

"I want to ask you a few questions," John continued quietly. "Your window overlooks the spot where a body was discovered."

Had he come to accuse her? "I don't know anything about it," she stammered.

"This has nothing to do with you or your husband. What is your name?"

"Maera." It stuck in her throat like a stringy scrap of meat.

"And your husband?"

"Sabas."

"Maera, did you see anything strange on the night of the festivities?"

Maera's expression must have given her away, because John's eyes narrowed. "You did see something, didn't you?"

Maera bit her lip.

"You looked out and saw something in the alley. What did you see?"

"Oh, sir, it was just as you said. I was going to empty the… But there was a dead man. Looking right up at me."

Sabas groaned and one arm slapped bonelessly at John's leg. Maera felt faint, but the gentleman seemed not to notice.

"Did you look out again?"

Maera shook her head.

"And before? Did you open the window at any time before you saw the dead man?"

Maera nodded. The Lord Chamberlain was looking at her, his face stern. She forced herself to speak. "It was dark in the alley. At first I thought it must be demons lurching along, stumbling and falling against the walls. Then I saw it was just two men, intoxicated, holding each other up. Quiet though, not like most who have drunk too much. And then I wondered again if they were really men or if I'd been right the first time and they were demons."

"What made you think of demons, Maera?"

"They were masked. Terrible bird-headed things. They must have been masks, don't you think? Or else they must have been demons."

"There's nothing uncommon about masked drunkards wandering the street during celebrations," John reassured her. "I saw quite a few myself that night. Was your window open during the day?"

"I usually keep it open but I don't look out much. There's nothing I care to see, sir. Just men using the side door of that house. And sometimes beasts that can't be bothered to get inside first."

"Did you know a girl was killed there recently?"

Maera paled. "It does not surprise me that someone working at such a trade would come to grief, God rest her soul. I shall pray for her."

"You have seen nothing unusual these past few days?"

"No."

"And you are certain you didn't see a well-dressed man pass by on the night of the celebrations? Completely bald, pale, older?" John made a final attempt to refresh the woman's memory.

Maera tried to remember.

A voice startled her."I saw such a man."

Sabas.

He had not spoken since his fellow workmen carried him back to her.

She knelt down beside him, taking his hand in hers. "Sabas!" For the first time she felt hope. He would live.

"Where did you see him?" John bent down to inquire softly.

"The Church of the Holy Wisdom." The words came in a hoarse whisper.

"My husband is a laborer," explained the woman. "He fell from the scaffolding. They thought he was as good as dead. It was a miracle he survived."

"Did this man come to see the church?" John bent closer to catch the mumbled answer.

"No. No. I would never have noticed, there's so many people there. But sometimes I work late or very early. I usually work high up in the dome. You can look out the openings where the light comes in and see as far as the city walls, and down into the patriarch's garden, into the guarded way that leads to the private entrance of his palace. It is always kept well lit. A bald man used to go in that way at strange hours."

"To the patriarch's private quarters? Was he alone?"

But Sabas' eyes closed again and he lapsed back into unconsciousness.

Maera's lips trembled. "Sabas! Sabas!" She turned tear-filled eyes to the Lord Chamberlain and saw compassion for her husband's terrible injuries. "We'll go back to the country when he's healed." she cried wildly. "I'd prefer he laid up stone walls than churches, if this is how God rewards poor workmen."

"He is alive, Maera. That is the important thing. No matter his injuries, he is alive."

Maera saw two gold coins in the Lord Chamberlain's palm. She had never seen even one such coin before.

"Here. There is a physician across from the palace gate. His name is Gaius."

"We are poor people," she protested.

"You are less poor now. Gaius will take one of these and heal your husband. Don't pay more. If he is intoxicated, go back when he's himself again."

Maera was transfixed by the coins. How could she take them? Weren't they part of the city which had so hurt her husband? She shook her head.

"Take them, Maera," John said gently. "I have many more. More than I can possibly spend in ten lifetimes."

"I can't. I can't take them from you."

"They are not from me. Consider that they came from heaven."

Maera took the coins in trembling hands. When the Lord Chamberlain had departed, she saw that indeed, though they bore the likeness of Justinian on one side, on their reverse they bore a cross.

Chapter Fifty-one

The establishment of Madam Isis was but a few steps from the entrance to the tenement where Maera and Sabas lived. As John entered Isis' house, he saw Darius, the doorkeeper, had not yet been liberated from the incongruous role of an enormous Eros. Darius shrugged in response to John's look of inquiry, making the tiny wings attached to his broad shoulders flutter.

"Fortunately, we won't be a Temple of Venus much longer. After Berta was murdered, Madam decided we'd have to change."

"To a motif that will suit you better, I trust."

Darius shrugged again. "I doubt it. It won't be a military encampment. I've suggested that more than once."

"I'm afraid I've come to ask more questions, Darius. They concern the evening of the celebrations."

Darius grimaced. "Most of the city was making merry but here we never worked harder. But as I told you already, I didn't see or hear anything out of the ordinary."

"And what about the night Berta was murdered?"

Darius shrugged again, flapping his stiff little wings. "No one. We had a few travelers—pilgrims by the look of them though they claimed to be traders. Except for them, it was just regular clients. You were here that night yourself, with Felix as I recall."

"What about Thomas?"

"The redhead who claims to be a knight? I don't think he's been here since you first brought him. But I don't stand guard every hour of the day and night. Madam can give you the names of the other guards and perhaps they will remember something useful."

"There's just the one door into the alley?"

"Yes. Some of our more discreet guests use it. Often those of high rank." Darius raised an eyebrow, creating an alarming effect for an oversized Eros.

John asked to be shown the door in question. Darius summoned an assistant to take his place, then led the Lord Chamberlain through a beaded curtain, along a wide door-lined corridor, and down a windowless hall lit by torches at each end.

The plain wooden door Darius halted before was a stark contrast to the elaborately carved main entrance.

"At our establishment, unlike the palace, the beggars enter in grand style while it is the powerful who often make their way inside in humble fashion." Darius grinned and gave the door a rap with his enormous fist.

John had been examining the walls and floorboards.

"Something has occurred to me," said Darius abruptly. "You asked about whether a completely bald man was in here the night of the celebrations. I didn't see anyone like that. But then again, more than a few who visited that evening were wearing fantastic headdresses or masks. A ridiculous-looking bunch."

"Ridiculous, indeed," agreed John. "And by the way, your left wing is crooked. Madam wouldn't appreciate that. Could I trouble you to stand aside, Darius?"

The big man stood back as requested. John bent closer to the doorframe. After a short time he straightened.

"This doorway appears to have been cleaned but in the crack down here, I can see what looks like dried blood. I shall have to speak to Isis."

When John entered her chambers the usually cheerful Isis was in a disagreeable humor. "If I say your friend Leukos did not set foot in this place that night, then he did not."

"He might have used an assumed name."

Isis laughed. "Who doesn't? Believe me, if the Keeper of the Plate was here, I'd know about it."

"A bald-headed man?" John persisted.

"Or a man with a birthmark on his bottom shaped like a bust of Caesar. We had such a guest last week, in fact."

"Did Leukos ever come here?"

"No, John. If your friend had been here, I would know. Why are you asking?"

"One of his servants told me he sometimes went out at night at odd hours and never said where he was going. He was a single man."

"Mine is only the best house in the city, not the only one," Isis pointed out.

"And something else. I have just looked at your door, the one opening into the alley."

"What about it?"

"When I examined it, I found traces of dried blood near the bottom of the frame. I'm hoping you'll be able to explain how it got there."

Gregorius shifted his heavy sack to his other hand and peered nervously up and down the street. The usual assortment of pedestrians strolled along by the towering wall of the Hippodrome. No one looked suspicious. He had half-expected to catch someone ducking into one of its entrances or stepping quickly into a shop. If anyone had in fact done so they had been too quick for him.

As soon as he emerged from the Hippodrome on his errand he sensed he was being followed. Perhaps it was his imagination. He had been on edge ever since his teammate was killed by the sabotaged chariot.

Such attacks weren't uncommon. Whoever had tampered with the chariot must have intended for the axle to snap during a race. The fool might have wanted to insure he won a bet against the Blues and hadn't given any thought to, or cared about, what happened to drivers whose chariots crashed.

Gregorius continued to study the street, hoping someone might peek out from a hiding place, but no one did.

There was always bad blood between the Blue and Green factions. Well, Gregorius would be out of the Constantinople soon enough.

This would be his final delivery.

And he'd be glad to leave too, with the Lord Chamberlain taking so much interest in his activities.

He continued on, the sack over his shoulder.

Immediately he felt the gaze on the back of his neck again.

Detouring into the Hippodrome, he went up and down several ramps connecting the upper and lower levels, zig-zagged through stables and storage rooms, and exited by a delivery gate which opened onto a tangle of alleys. By the time he reached the tenement that was his destination he felt certain he had lost his pursuer.

He trudged up creaking wooden stairs. The smell of boiled fish hung in the air. On the fourth floor he rapped at a door which was opened by a gaunt woman. He stepped inside and dropped his sack on the floor.

Three small girls leapt on it but their mother, who might have been beautiful if able to eat regularly, shooed them away. Then her eyes narrowed as she stared over Gregorius' shoulder. "You have brought a friend."

Gregorius looked around.

The Lord Chamberlain stood in the doorway.

John smiled faintly. "You led me on a good chase, Gregorius. When I happened to see you coming out of the Hippodrome, I wondered where you were going with that sack."

"Well, Lord Chamberlain, now you know."

"I know very little. What is in the sack?"

Gregorius bent down and opened it to reveal a jumble of loaves, onions, cheese, and other edibles. "Food for this poor woman and her family. What did you expect?"

"The Blues have been helping us since my husband died," the woman explained. "We found ourselves in the same position as Theodora's family many years ago and now we are being aided as they were. My husband died a few days ago. Like Theodora's father, he was a bear trainer who entertained at the Hippodrome."

Chapter Fifty-two

John sat in his quiet study with a jug of wine, trying to make sense of what he had learned. The trace of blood he had found on the door of Isis' establishment had come to nothing. According to Isis the bloody corpse of the bear trainer mauled to death in front of her house had been carried in that way to avoid soiling the entrance.

The lack of blood beneath Leukos' body where it lay in the alley was not so easily explained. Nor was it clear why Leukos would have visited the patriarch, if in fact the bald man observed by Sabas had been Leukos. Could John trust what the injured, feverish laborer claimed to have seen?

John's gaze fell upon Zoe. He began to ask her opinion but stopped himself. What sort of man was it who could talk to a mosaic girl more easily than to his own daughter? Who understood glass but not flesh and blood? But then glass could not grow and change and a mosaic girl could not speak, although it sometimes seemed she did. John averted his eyes.

Wasn't the Inn of the Centaurs the cynosure of it all? When he confronted Gregorius at the home of the deceased bear trainer's family he immediately recalled how he had first seen the young man, soaking wet after an immersion in the fountain. The charioteer was staying at the inn, as was Thomas. The soothsayer had been living there. Leukos had visited the soothsayer at the inn.

Gregorius' mission to the bear trainer's family had been innocent enough, which was not say that he did not supplement his
racing earnings with a little smuggling as he traveled around.

Xiphias may have been involved in some sort of illicit trade
as well. Was he so terrified by John's investigations that he had
killed himself?

Or was it apparently killed himself?

And had Thomas and Xiphias spoken or not? Thomas
admitted he was pursuing Ahasuerus for a relic he believed was
in the soothsayer's possession. Why then had he spoken with
the Keeper of the Plate? Did he suspect Ahasuerus had already
disposed of the Grail to Leukos, that it was in the palace, and
Xiphias might be bribed to help it disappear?

And what about Berta? She had entertained Thomas and the
soothsayer in different ways. Had those chance meetings entangled
her in the same web in which Leukos had become entangled?

What web was that?

The sky looked threatening. It seemed that the spring rains
would never stop. Dark clouds loomed low, and there was that
eerie hush that signaled yet another storm would be upon the
city within the hour. Gusts of heralding winds swirled about
the house. Several large seabirds strutted on the cobbles below,
shrilly squawking. Their ghastly cries suggested the screeching
of the Harpies tormenting their prey. John shuddered.

Zoe stared at him with eyes blacker than night.

John examined the facts he had gathered, each one akin to
a glistening bit of glass. He shuffled them around. He could
almost see the pattern. Place this piece next to that and then this
other over here and soon they would form a lifelike picture. As
lifelike as Zoe and then, like Zoe, they would speak to him and
whisper the name of Leukos' murderer.

John poured wine and pondered. Without realizing it, he
dozed.

A figure in a dripping hooded cloak stood before him. An
emaciated hand pushed back the hood to reveal the time-worn
face of Ahasuerus.

"I thought you had embarked on your journey across the Styx," John heard himself say.

The old man chuckled hoarsely. "That is a journey that I will not take for a long time. However, I am off on another sort of journey. Did you ever hear that the mantis warns travelers of danger, pointing the way to go to avoid it? Well, I've been hiding. For a while I was over there in the stables debating whether to stay." He gestured vaguely in the direction of the barracks. "When I awoke today what did I see but a mantis. It was pointing toward the sea. Even a soothsayer need not cast pebbles to know that it was urging me to depart."

"You look exhausted. Should I ask Peter to bring something?"

"Thank you, but I am not hungry. Tell me, Lord Chamberlain, where do you think I have been?"

"As I told you, I feared you were dead."

A gust of wind rattled at the window, underlining the old man's words. "I will tell you where I have been. I was summoned from the inn to see Patriarch Epiphanios. I cast the pebbles for him. Later, as I stood on the docks intending to take ship, something struck me squarely in the shoulder blades and I fell into the water. And, Lord Chamberlain, I cannot swim."

In the grip of nightmare John felt as if it were he who had plunged into the water.

"But as I told you, it is not time for me to take that journey into darkness. I survived. I hid. Now I have come on this rainy night to cast the pebbles for you."

John awoke in the gray light before dawn. The memory of his dream returned slowly. On the floor of the study several glistening patches of moisture marked where the wind had blown rain through cracks around the window frame.

Chapter Fifty-three

In the enclosed garden of the patriarchal palace pale morning light cast time's faint shadow across the face of a sundial.

Nearby, Patriarch Epiphanios bent over, examining a flower bed. At John's approach, he straightened up with obvious difficulty. He looked frailer than he at their last meeting.

"The dial reveals the hour, the flowers reveal the season," the patriarch commented. His skin showed the translucence of old age, as if the body were giving up its corporeal qualities. "What do you wish to speak to me about, Lord Chamberlain?"

"I don't know that this is the place."

"A delicate subject? Don't worry. We will not be overheard here. I prefer to be out in the garden today. The walls of my rooms feel much too close."

"Leukos, the Keeper of the Plate, was your frequent visitor."

"That is so."

Sorrow in the patriarch's expression confirmed what John had suspected. "Leukos was your son."

The patriarch smiled faintly. "Very few know that. How did you?"

"He was seen visiting at odd hours, using your private entrance. I was always been puzzled by his lack of a family, or any hint of family history. Most people will mention their relatives even if they are far away or long deceased. And when

I spoke to you in the Great Church you seemed inordinately interested in his funeral."

Patriarch Epiphanios shook his head. "How is it that God should choose a man to serve him in the highest capacity, and yet allow such a servant to remain enslaved by the same appetites as bedevil any man?"

"You may wish to keep this." John held out the silver necklace he had found in Leukos' pouch. The patriarch took it in a shaking hand, and brought it closer to his tired eyes to examine the entwined fish.

"Thank you, Lord Chamberlain. I gave it to Leukos as a keepsake. It was his mother's. She is dead. She was married."

"You took good care of your son, even if you could not acknowledge him publicly. It was you who asked the emperor to stop me from investigating further?"

"I was afraid you would discover the truth."

"I would not have sought to use the knowledge against you. My only interest was in seeing my friend—your son—avenged."

"He is avenged. The soothsayer is dead."

"Ahasuerus wasn't the murderer. The murderer is still free."

"But the soothsayer stabbed Leukos. His dagger was in Leukos when you found him, wasn't it? As I told you before, two matching daggers were found in the satchel he left behind when he threw himself into the sea."

"You also told me that your guards had gone to the inn to arrest Ahasuerus for the murder and brought him to the guard house at your residence even before those daggers were found."

The patriarch put a trembling hand to his forehead. "Did I? Yes, of course. Pardon an old man's faulty memory. My guards had received information pointing to Ahasuerus. The daggers confirmed what they were told."

"I regret I find your story hard to believe."

The patriarch's lips tightened and his hand moved to his side, fingers whitening as they pressed into his ribs. He made no sound. Then the spasm had passed—or else, John thought, he had given himself enough time to formulate a response.

Epiphanios gave a dry, bitter laugh. "Trying to hide anything from you is like trying to hide it from heaven. Look there. Do you know what I had planted?" He indicated the plot he had been examining when John arrived.

"I've never been skilled at identifying plants."

"It is monkshood. I hope to see it reach its full growth one more time. My physician has been giving me a concoction of it for the pain. It makes me feel very cold. I think it numbs the soul as well as the body. The Greeks say the plant springs from the spittle of Cerberus. Were I a pagan I would expect to be seeing the beast soon. As it is..." The weak voice trailed off.

"As it is?" John prompted.

"I am afraid when my angel leads me up to heaven, the demon toll keepers on the way will charge me heavily for my sins. You are quite right, Lord Chamberlain. It was not the soothsayer who murdered my only son. It was I."

It was obvious the patriarch was near death. Had he lost his mind as well? Or was it the effect of the medicine he was taking? John asked for an explanation.

"I murdered Leukos," the patriarch repeated. "It was that vile soothsayer who wielded the dagger—who else? But it was I who placed Leukos in his path. I asked him to consult Ahasuerus on my behalf, to inquire about the Grail. What greater relic could I have acquired for my—for Justinian's—new church?"

John recalled what the servant Euphemia had said about strangers bringing things to Leukos' house late at night. "It wasn't the first time Leukos had rendered such services, was it?"

"He blessed the city with more than one sacred relic. Sellers of costly goods sometimes acquire other sorts of treasures and Leukos was in a position to know when such valuables became available."

"How did you know the soothsayer purported to possess such a relic?"

"Rumors he had it in his possession reached me. There was also an adventurer in pursuit of the Grail."

"Is that why you had Ahasuerus escorted away from the Inn of the Centaurs in the middle of the night? You were afraid the adventurer, or let us name him, Thomas, would purchase the relic before you could?"

"The soothsayer and I negotiated a fair price. Then he left."

"And went straight for the docks to take ship. He didn't have to be prescient to realize you might not want to risk anyone finding out you had purchased this supposed holy relic from a fortune-teller."

The patriarch rubbed his eyes. "It was a misunderstanding. My guards were instructed to see he was sent safely out of the city. It appears he panicked and threw himself into the sea."

John supposed there was no way he would know whether that was the truth or not. He noted Epiphanios had not explained who had told him the soothsayer owned daggers identical to the one found in Leukos' body.

The patriarch stared down at the sundial. "Did you know this relic is said to be a heal-all?"

"So I have heard."

The patriarch's eyes looked glassy in the thin light filtering out of the cloudy sky. John could not tell whether it was the sheen of tears or the effect of physicians' concoctions.

"My son died because I was so afraid of death that I grasped at a chance to preserve my own life." A quaver had entered the patriarch's voice. He smiled wanly. "You realize I am only telling you this because I am a dead man, Lord Chamberlain?"

"And the Grail?"

The patriarch reached inside his robe and produced a jewel-encrusted box.

"Come closer, Lord Chamberlain."

John stepped forward.

The patriarch's hands trembled as he opened the lid of the box. "The Grail," he breathed. "It cost me dearly but now the most holy relic in Christendom will reside for all eternity in the empire's greatest church. Perhaps now I will be forgiven for all my sins."

John stared down into the box.

Inside lay a round stone, green, flecked with red, perhaps three times the size of the stones Ahasuerus had given his clients, but otherwise identical.

Chapter Fifty-four

Peter disliked sharing his kitchen so he was doubly distressed to have both Felix and Anatolius crowding him as he cooked. Thankfully, Felix did not seem inclined to stay long.

"I had hoped to find John home," he was saying. "I wanted to thank him for his assistance the other night."

"You look grim enough to be on your way to the wars, Felix," observed Anatolius.

Felix grunted. "I've had a lot on my mind and some hard decisions to make. And what about you? Since when does a scribe arm himself?" He indicated the scabbard at Anatolius' hip.

"Since I achieved the rank of Soldier."

"Well, it might impress the ladies more than your poetry. It's a pity you can't say anything about it!"

"It is hardly an affectation, Felix. There seems to be more then the usual amount of danger about recently."

Peter noisily stirred the pot on the brazier. He was of the opinion that in Anatolius' unskilled hands the sword would be about as useful as Peter's iron spoon.

Anatolius inquired about the bundle Felix carried.

"Isis gave me some mementos of Berta. Jewelry. I did keep a bracelet I'd given her, but the rest, who knows where or who they came from? I don't want to think about it. I know a merchant who deals in such things, who'll give me a good price. Enough to cover the cost of Berta's funeral."

"Then you know a merchant I don't. Could I take a look?"

Felix undid his bundle and laid out its contents on the table. Peter frowned, wishing the two would leave. Nevertheless he glanced over his shoulder at the jewelry.

"Your Berta favored green," Anatolius said. "I know a lady these could adorn, and I wager I can give you a much better price than your merchant."

"All right. I'll leave the jewelry for you to look over. Now I need to be off to attend to other business."

"Of an official nature?"

Felix stamped out without answering.

"Am I the only one in my right senses?" Anatolius exclaimed. "John's looking for a murderer already dead. And there's Thomas with his foolish quest."

Peter muttered under his breath. Anatolius had been in his way for an hour while supposedly waiting for John. In reality, Peter guessed, the young man was hoping Europa would emerge from her bedroom.

"What do you think of the so-called knight, Peter?"

The servant stirred the boiling mixture in the pot hard enough to slop a few drops over its side. They hissed on the charcoal in the brazier. "It isn't for a servant to comment on his master's associates."

"You don't trust Thomas, do you?"

Peter had disliked Thomas at first sight, although he couldn't have said why. "The master is a better judge of character than I am," was all he said.

"Sometimes John's too intelligent for his own good. He can't see what's right in front of his face." Anatolius tapped his fingers on the table. "Why can't he see through the man? Thomas has been behaving suspiciously ever since he showed up. Now, consider this, Peter. He's staying at the Inn of the Centaurs, which is also where Leukos, like me, visited the soothsayer. The soothsayer's dagger was used to murder Leukos. But couldn't

Thomas have stolen it, followed Leukos to the alley, and then killed him?"

"I admit I don't like the man Thomas, but I do not see him as a murderer," Peter responded. He did not add that he thought Anatolius' opinion was colored by the attention Thomas was paying to Europa.

Anatolius banged his fist on the table. "I must confront him! If John won't, then I must. In fact, I shall go around to the inn right now and demand to see Thomas immediately."

He leapt from his chair and bolted from the kitchen, leaving the jewelry on the table. Peter shook his head at the impetuosity of youth. As he added boiled fish to the sauce, he wondered if Thomas would even be at the inn. For Anatolius' sake, he hoped not. Putting the thought aside, he turned his mind to matters of more immediate concern, and tasted the sauced fish. It might be possible to make a passable dinner after all. If John ever returned and if the women ever emerged from their rooms. A little more oregano, perhaps?

There was a loud rapping at the house door. "The devil take you, whoever you are," Peter muttered.

The old servant did not recognize the caller but the man's rough tunic and breeches did not speak of the palace.

The stranger held out a folded sheet of parchment and spoke without preamble.

"Thomas asked me to bring this urgent note."

Anatolius strode into the courtyard of the Inn of the Centaurs.

The heavy scabbard rubbed painfully against his leg and he kept his hand on the sword hilt, less to be ready for action than to attempt to keep the scabbard from swinging in such an irritating fashion. He was greeted by the imposing, albeit unarmed, Mistress Kaloethes.

"I must speak with the innkeeper at once," Anatolius demanded. "It concerns one of your guests."

"My husband isn't here," she snapped. "What's your business?"

"I am investigating a murder."

Mistress Kaloethes glared at him. "You're the second inquisitive visitor I've had today. You won't be wanting to rummage through my clothes too, will you?"

Anatolius was given no time to respond to this unexpected question because Mistress Kaloethes, bristling with rage, swept on, her shrill voice rising. "He went through everything! He even examined the marks on my silver plates and tossed my personal belongings about. And can you imagine the gall, he stole one of my best table linens!"

"I assure you, I am not here with any such intent. I wish to speak to Thomas."

"Him?" Mistress Kaloethes gave a sudden laugh. "What would an emissary from the court of the king of Bretania have to do with such a foppish youngster as you?"

"I am secretary to Justinian, madam."

"So you're from the palace?" The woman gave an appraising look at Anatolius. "Still, scribblers aren't paid much, are they?"

"Is Thomas here?" Anatolius persisted.

"I am here, Anatolius."

Thomas had just entered the courtyard. He moved to the fountain. "Mistress Kaloethes," he addressed the woman, bowing slightly. "If you would leave us alone."

"Certainly, sir. Let me know if you need anything," she simpered, and retired into the inn.

"What do you want of me?" Thomas demanded, his voice going cold. "It must be important since you've armed yourself. Is it about Europa?"

"No, it's—"

"She is a very attractive young lady. But like myself, she must travel from country to country. Soon we will all go our separate ways, she and I included. Did you think you would be able to convince her to stay here with you?"

"That is none of your business," Anatolius responded hotly. He grasped the hilt of his sword more tightly. His heart was pounding.

"I did not come to your city to have romances with young ladies, my friend. I came on a much greater quest, a quest that requires many sacrifices. Indeed, for it a knight must sacrifice even love."

"And will a knight kill to further his quest?"

"If it should become necessary. Do you propose to test me?"

"You killed Leukos, didn't you?" Anatolius was mortified his voice quavered as he forced the accusation out.

A smile flickered underneath Thomas fiery mustache. "People entertain many strange beliefs in this city."

Anatolius reached for his sword. Before it was even free of the scabbard, Thomas' sword was resting against the young man's chest.

Ice closed around Anatolius' heart. In the wink of an eye, he would be covered with blood. Not the blood of a sacrificial bull this time, but his own.

Instead of driving the sword home, Thomas spoke. "You are fortunate that I am beyond feeling the sting of your petty insults, lad. I have just met a traveler from Bretania. He told me the High King is dead. There is no need for me to continue the quest."

Thomas lowered his weapon.

As he did so, John burst into the courtyard. "Peter said I'd find you here, Anatolius," he called out. "Both of you, hurry! Cornelia and Europa have been abducted!"

"What?" Anatolius was at a loss for words.

"When I returned home," John explained rapidly, "Peter told me that a note from Thomas had been delivered for Cornelia and Europa. Despite her mother counseling caution, Europa rushed off and Cornelia naturally followed. They're on their way to the Cistern of Hermes."

Thomas blurted out an obscene oath.

Anatolius looked toward John in confusion, then back at Thomas.

The knight snorted impatiently. "Of course the note wasn't from me, you hotheaded young fool. I can't write!"

Chapter Fifty-five

The dying sun cast a confusion of shadows through the discarded statues crowded in front of the abandoned imperial records office under whose eroded portico lay the entrance to the Cistern of Hermes.

Emperors, philosophers, and generals, the statues might have been a congregation of the dead waiting to pass through the portals of the underworld.

John, Anatolius, and Thomas stood amid the frozen figures, nearly indistinguishable from them in the gathering shadows, but alive for the moment.

Anatolius peered around anxiously. "Why didn't you send for the excubitors, John? With just the three of us we might not be a match for whoever's waiting in there. It's not likely there's only a single person holding two women hostage."

"No doubt there's a gang. The same gang that's been trafficking in imperial goods, forged relics dug up in cemeteries, and probably any other crime you can think of. There are only the three of us here because as soon as the rogues spotted excubitors they'd murder the women and flee. They've probably had a ransom note delivered to my house by now, but their aim isn't ransom, it's to kill me. They must have realized I now know who murdered Leukos."

"Then what are we waiting for, John?" Thomas demanded.

The sun was vanishing, leaving a glorious orange and gold streak low on the horizon. Raven-like black clouds scudded across the livid gash of the sunset. As the men reached the portico, sunlight flashed off what remained of the flaking gilt on the statue of Hermes set above its entrance.

"Mithra blesses our attempt," John murmured.

The building's atrium smelled of smoke, damp, and unwashed bodies. Voices echoed in its cavernous space, barely illuminated by small fires around which ill-clad beggars gathered for warmth.

John threw his cloak to the floor. His white tunic seemed to glow in the dimness. "A soldier fights unencumbered," he told Anatolius. Thomas had discarded his travel-worn cloak. As soon as the men stepped away, shadowy figures fell on the abandoned clothing in the manner of rats swarming over a discarded bone.

Out of the darkness came a wheezing laugh. "Does our young hero seek to free more captives?"

John, aghast at their early discovery, turned quickly toward the source of the taunting question.

It was only an old woman huddled beside a pile of wicker cages.

"I purchased some birds from her not long ago." Anatolius' voice shook with relief.

The crone's cackling accompanied them on their way.

Access to the cistern was through an opening little more than a rectangular gap in the wall. Beyond, worn stone steps disappeared downwards.

John's stomach lurched as he led the way. He was not afraid of battle and bore the scars to prove it. But to descend into the depths of his private Hades, into that dark, water-filled space, was the stuff of his wildest nightmares. "Mithra help us," he muttered.

As the three descended, the air grew colder. Light from the fires upstairs filtered through chinks in the floor and down the stairwell. As his eyes adjusted, John could see the interior of the cistern chamber. The water's surface threw wavering reflections onto concrete walls and up the regular rows of pillars soaring up from its depths to vanish into deeper shadows beneath a vaulted brick ceiling.

He heard the magnified dripping of water and an almost imperceptible liquid murmur.

"Did you hear that?" Thomas whispered. "They are on the opposite side."

Only a narrow ledge of stone skirted the cistern. John forced himself to move along it. Glancing down in the semi-darkness he saw the menacing glimmer of the water a few hands-breadths away. His boot slipped on moisture and he tottered, pressing himself back at the last instant against the rough wall behind him.

How deep was the water?

He continued to slide sideways, back pressed to the wall. The water was a monstrous entity waiting to pull him down and devour him.

He heard what sounded like a faint cry. Cornelia? He signaled to Thomas and Anatolius to stop. All three listened intently.

Again there came a whispering echo. Clearer this time, it was a woman's sobbing. John tapped Thomas' elbow lightly, attracting his attention. The knight touched his ear and nodded.

The wraith of sound sighed again across the water. John felt an exultant surge of joy. They were here and alive!

At this realization, the scorching heat of mingled exultation and rage welled up in his chest. In the semi-darkness of his watery Hades, John began to resemble a demon himself, his thin lips drawn back in a feral snarl. Abandoning his crab-like shuffle, he broke into a lope, one elbow scraping the wall as he maintained his balance.

At the cistern's far end the ledge ended at a wide platform, its margins fading into shadow. John could distinguish two dark shapes huddled at the base of a pillar rising from the platform.

The women had been bound to the pillar. As John stepped forward, intent on cutting their bonds, Europa's head jerked upwards. He had only an instant to register the startled expression on her pale face as she gazed past him, then a low voice— Thomas' voice—growled, "Stay where you are!"

John turned. Seeing the knight's raised sword, he had a sensation of falling, though he could feel his feet still firmly planted on the concrete. Had he miscalculated the man so badly?

"I thought I saw movement in the shadows," Thomas said, lowering his weapon. "I think it is safe for now."

John cut the women loose. Cornelia was unconscious, her face bruised. As he lowered her into a reclining position she felt as heavy as the dead, as heavy as old sorrows.

"Cowards!" cursed Anatolius. "They'll pay for this, Europa, I promise you!"

John shook his head. "We must get the women to safety."

"The stairway they brought us down is over there." Before John could protest, Europa ran in the direction she had indicated. She was brought up short by a booming voice.

"Lord Chamberlain! You of all men should know it is impolite to enter without being announced. However, since you are here, you are welcome to our hospitality!"

Two men emerged from the darkness in front of the girl. One was a tall, muscular man whom John did not recognize. The other, as John expected, was the innkeeper, Master Kaloethes.

"We have them outnumbered," growled Thomas.

Even as he spoke Anatolius bellowed. "Europa, watch out!" He charged toward the men, swinging his sword clumsily, unbalancing himself. The innkeeper grabbed him by the shoulders as he stumbled and threw him against the wall. He fell to the floor and lay motionless.

Two more men appeared out of the shadows, cutting Europa off from her would-be rescuers. One of the new arrivals stepped toward the girl.

The innkeeper chuckled. "It appears we have recaptured at least one hostage. I expect when it comes to such goods, the price for one differs little from the price for the pair. You know what the price is, Lord Chamberlain. Please drop your sword and walk forward slowly."

For an instant John and Thomas stood still. It was Europa who suddenly moved. She took a single step forward. Then she had catapulted herself into the air. The innkeeper's accomplice stabbed upwards, too late. The girl's hands barely touched his shoulder as she vaulted over his blade, just as she had vaulted over the equally deadly horns of so many bulls. She sprawled safely at Thomas' feet.

Thomas bounded over her. It was a less graceful leap than Europa's, but one which brought him face to face with one of the newcomers, who drew a single gasping breath before the knight's blade pierced his throat. Shoving his corpse aside, Thomas engaged the second man. The swordplay was brief.

"Now," remarked Thomas with a grin, "now, my friends, we are even."

John and Thomas instinctively became a fighting unit, moving forward in concert. John's lips curled back in a wolfish grin. Rage iced his veins. The siren song of combat, so long absent from his ears, sang in his blood. He was prepared to kill and to enjoy the killing.

The innkeeper, displaying unexpected skill, brandished his sword as he moved slightly to the right. At the same time, the man at his side stepped left, drawing Thomas away from John's side.

An unholy shriek rebounded around the subterranean chamber. Before its rolling echoes had died John, from whose throat the animal sound had burst, was upon the innkeeper, slapping the weapon out of his hand with the flat of his own sword. Kaloethes grabbed for the thin-bladed knife at his waist.

John had dropped his sword and was ready, dagger drawn. A sword, he well knew, was too clumsy for hand to hand fighting. The men moved toward each other, jabbing and slashing. Then the innkeeper backed up as John pressed his attack.

In his rage, John became careless. Kaloethes slashed John across his cheek, opening a welling furrow from eye to mouth. But it brought him too close to John, who seized the opportunity to get under the other's guard, his blade biting into a meaty shoulder.

The innkeeper shrieked with surprise and pain. John yanked out the blade. The quick movement threw him off-balance, and the innkeeper, automatically using a maneuver that had won him victory in more than one street brawl, brought his knee up into John's groin.

The maneuver did not have its usual devastating effect.

John merely grunted with pain and staggered backwards, then leapt forward, to drive his dagger deep into the innkeeper's neck. Kaloethes sank screaming to his knees, but, keeping his wits about him, jabbed upwards toward John's stomach.

John kicked the weapon out of his opponent's hand. The unarmed innkeeper tried to crawl away. John was only dimly aware of Thomas trading sword thrusts with the remaining kidnapper. Now nothing could distract John from indulging his lust to inflict as much pain as possible on the man groveling at his feet—until he slipped in the growing pool of the innkeeper's blood.

John went down on one knee at the edge of the cistern, catching a nightmare glimpse of his reflection springing up at him. For an instant, all he could think about was avoiding the horror of that waiting water.

It was enough. With a shout of rage, Kaloethes leapt up and forward, closing his huge hands around John's throat, thumbs sinking into the flesh. John tore at the innkeeper's death-grip as the pressure was steadily increased. A reddish tint was creeping into what little vision he had. He began to feel faint, gasping for air. His lungs were bursting, the pain shooting hot rivulets of fire across his laboring chest. Blood from his face flowed like scalding tears.

The fog shrouding John's mind suddenly cleared. He realized he was going to die in this echoing underground chamber. At least it would be an honorable death. And yet what would become of Cornelia and Europa? He knew they could expect no mercy. He began to lose consciousness, his fading thoughts of Cornelia and their daughter, the daughter he had cherished so briefly.

A bellow cut through the roaring red darkness engulfing him.

The grip on his throat loosened.

Above him, swimming into his blurred sight, was the face of Felix. Felix grinning broadly, both hands fastened on Kaloethes' throat.

The innkeeper's head snapped back and his hands clawed at the stranglehold Felix had on him.

"Kaloethes," Felix addressed him, his voice eerily calm. "I've just come from the inn. Your widow said I would find you here. She thought I'd come to assist you as in the old days when you paid me well not to notice things I should have reported. 'Hurry up, they're at the Cistern of Hermes', she told me. Oh, she was beside herself. It had all gone wrong. You'd been found out, she said. It was all your fault. And you never got the object you were seeking either, despite desecrating that little whore's grave."

Felix paused. A frown passed across his face, and then he continued, speaking louder to drown the noises the innkeeper was making. "She was angry at Berta, you see, because she wouldn't give the accursed pendant to you. So you killed my beautiful Berta, didn't you, you murdering bastard?"

The innkeeper pawed ineffectually at the iron grasp on his throat. John, on his hands and knees, gagged, as the world darkened again.

He heard another voice, more shouting, and peered into the gloom. Thomas' sword had gone. Surely it was not possible that such a man had been vanquished by a mere criminal? John knew he must stand and go to the aid of his comrade in arms but his legs refused to cooperate.

Now Thomas' assailant was grinning, raising his sword to dispatch him.

As if he had simply decided against killing the knight, he paused. A strange expression crossed his face. Then he pitched forward, pulling with him Anatolius, still gripping the sword he had thrust into the man's back.

And now there was only one man left, and he was coming to his end. John, Anatolius, and Thomas looked around at Felix. He was straddling the innkeeper's back, pinning down his flailing arms with his knees, and began to sing loudly as he held Kaloethes' head under the water.

John gagged again.

Felix, still singing merrily, pulled the innkeeper's dripping head out of the water. Kaloethes gasped for air, begging for his life. Felix spat in his face, screamed, "Did Berta beg?" and pushed the innkeeper's head underwater again.

John recognized what Felix was singing. It was an obscene marching song.

Thomas staggered over to John and helped him to his feet. "It isn't a soldierly way to take a life," he muttered. "And yet who can blame him?"

Felix's singing reverberated louder in the vaulting overhead. There was a frenzied thrashing in the churning water. Reflections leapt madly against walls and pillars.

Anatolius was on his feet, trembling. Thomas clasped his shoulders briefly. "Thank you, my friend. You saved my life."

Anatolius began to sob. "I stabbed him in the back! All I did was creep up behind him and stab him in the back!"

"And he is dead and we are not," Thomas said gently. "That is the difference between life and poetry. But now you are a true Soldier of Mithra."

Cornelia had revived and John helped her to her feet, glad she had not witnessed his madness.

They thankfully left the hellish place. As they climbed back toward the cool night air, they were accompanied by echoes from the semi-darkness below.

The echoes of the exultant singing of a man slaking his blood-lust, slowly drowning the man who had murdered his beloved Berta.

Epilogue

"Now that Leukos is avenged, the black creature that was gnawing inside of me has flown," John said, lifting his wine cup to his lips.

The day after the fight in the cistern, John and Anatolius sat in the Forum Bovis opposite the great bronze bull head Europa had admired. John explained how he had identified Kaloethes as the murderer of both Leukos and Berta.

"When Thomas and I visited Isis we saw Kaloethes arrive, and his greeting to Berta indicated he had visited her before. Isis told me that Berta had been boasting about an valuable pendant she had been given worth more than all the wealth in the city, or so she claimed. Kaloethes no doubt heard about this piece of jewelry from Berta, and tried to make her give it to him. And indeed Mistress Kaloethes told Felix her husband killed Berta because she would not do so."

"But to attempt to rob her grave…!"

"Many do far worse things than that for far less reason."

Earlier in the day, Anatolius had accompanied Cornelia and Europa to the docks. John exchanged private farewells with his family and then, standing at his study window, watched them leave. Although he was a master of elaborate court ceremony, the simpler, unwritten rituals of everyday life such as leave-takings made the Lord Chamberlain uneasy.

Anatolius' gaze moved around the forum coming to rest, it appeared to John, on two patrolling members of the urban watch.

"I heard from an impeccable source today that four men were found dead this morning in a cistern," Anatolius said. "The authorities suspect robbery and aren't inquiring too closely."

"Just as well."

"Why did Kaloethes want to murder you, John?"

"He must have feared that I suspected he was the murderer, that my coming to the inn to speak to Ahasuerus was only a pretext. If so, he overestimated me. I wasn't certain until yesterday when I went back to search his establishment."

"Of course! You were the inquisitive visitor Mistress Kaloethes complained about!"

"Yes. When I noticed she had a set of table linens matching the one found in Leukos' pouch, that is to say with the imperial mark, I was convinced she and her husband had had a hand in his death, not least because I also found imperial plate in their cellar. Leukos had to be silenced."

He paused. "I suspect that was the reason for Xiphias' flight. Who else could have sold them stolen palace plate? He must have decided drowning was preferable to Justinian's torturers."

Anatolius shook his head. "Imagine the odds on the Keeper of the Plate going to an inn where, among other things, stolen imperial goods are in use!"

"He would have recognized them at once. I assume he wanted to take some proof away. A piece of linen is easier to conceal than a platter or goblet."

"And Kaloethes saw him take the linen?"

"If he had, he would never have left it with the body. No, I am supposing Leukos insisted on searching for more imperial goods and Kaloethes caught him examining the plate."

Anatolius frowned. "But what caught your attention about that piece of linen in Leukos' pouch? How did you know it didn't belong to Leukos?"

"He didn't have it earlier that day at the Hippodrome because I recalled him wiping his face with his hand."

Anatolius remarked with admiration that only John would have noticed, let alone remembered, such a small detail.

"Small details are essential in court ceremony, are they not, and I have had to cultivate a keen eye."

Anatolius grew quiet, his face darkening. "Stolen imperial plate. Imagine the punishment! Mutilation would be the least of it!"

He took a long drink of wine as if to fortify himself against the thought. "No wonder Kaloethes panicked. I'm surprised he let poor Leukos get as far as the alley before stabbing him."

"He didn't. He drowned Leukos in the fountain at the inn. Held his head underwater, as if he were reviving an intoxicated reveler like the charioteer I saw him bringing to his senses."

John closed his eyes, trying to control his emotions, and then continued. "I should have realized at once when I saw Leukos' blue lips. I'd seen it before, when my brother in arms died in that icy stream in Bretania. Perhaps I didn't want to be reminded."

"But how did Kaloethes get the body to the alley without being noticed?"

"It isn't far from the Inn of the Centaurs to Isis' house. I was reminded of how small Constantinople is the night I climbed the stylite's column. During the celebrations the streets were full of reeling drunkards, many of them in costume. Kaloethes donned a mask, tied one on Leukos, and staggered through the streets dragging Leukos along with him. They would have looked like just another pair of revelers. However, I also found a young woman who saw them from a tenement window, although she mistook them for demons."

"And why wasn't the body found earlier?"

"Kaloethes must have hidden it in the inn until the streets were crowded and it was less likely anyone would pay attention to him."

"But the soothsayer's dagger—what about that?" protested Anatolius.

"Stolen from his room easily enough," John replied. "I suspect it was Kaloethes who pointed suspicion in Ahasuerus' direction.

After all, the old man was a foreigner and a soothsayer to boot, and there was no one to speak for him. Once Leukos' alleged murderer had been caught, no further investigation would be made."

"Kaloethes was extremely busy."

"Yes. It seemed likely to me the night I helped Felix home the man who appeared at the house was one of the innkeeper's accomplices, there to coerce him into assisting them with their schemes. He might very well have been the biggest of those rogues we fought in the cistern. Felix refused but in doing so revealed he had had dealings with the intruder in the past, most likely to pay off gambling debts. Felix confirmed the connection by what he shouted at Kaloethes."

"You told me there was an intruder on the *Anubis* when you visited Europa. Could that have been Kaloethes?"

"Possibly. Cornelia has told me she and Europa went to the inn and they might have aroused Kaloethes' interest. He could have followed them back to the *Anubis* and then returned after dark the next night, or sent an accomplice, to see if there was anything of value to be found. Whoever it was, it was one more reason for them to come to my house."

Anatolius fell silent but could not contain his natural curiosity for long. "What do you think of this Grail business?" he blurted out. "I hear the patriarch has acquired some holy relic more remarkable than any in Constantinople. It's being talked about all over the palace. Do you suppose......?"

John laughed softly. "When I visited the patriarch he showed me a stone. He believes it is a artifact of great value, at least judging from the amount he said he paid for it. He purchased it from Ahasuerus."

Anatolius looked amazed. "You mean that scoundrel did have the Grail and it was not a cup or a platter but rather a stone?"

John looked down into his wine. In the bright sunlight, he could see the wisps of cloud in the sky reflected its surface. "Tell me truthfully, did you ever desire something because someone else wanted it?"

A puzzled look crossed Anatolius' face.

"Did it ever occur to you," John continued, "that our friend Thomas talked a great deal? I gather he attempted to get audiences with every person of importance at the palace. Would you go about a quest like that?"

"I've never thought about going on a quest. Are you saying that Thomas was trying to persuade people to take an interest in the Grail, the better to raise its price?"

"What better place than Constantinople to sell a priceless relic or, for that matter, a counterfeit? Especially now, with Justinian completing his Great Church and the patriarch so ill…dying and grasping at straws. No doubt the patriarch believes that the stone he purchased is the Grail. In any event, with this great project, he and the emperor spurred the greedy and unscrupulous to take advantage in any way they could."

"Is it possible Ahasuerus and Thomas were working together?"

John shrugged. "Thomas may really have been a questing knight. Ahasuerus may indeed be the keeper of the Grail. And perhaps he must live until the end of the world."

Anatolius shook his head wearily. "I don't know what to believe, John, except that by all accounts Ahasuerus drowned. Nobody seems to have seen him since that night"

"Strange then that hours after his reported demise the soothsayer visited and cast the pebbles for me," John said. "Perhaps it was in a dream. He told me I would find my treasure underground."

"An accurate prediction."

John agreed with a slight smile. "Thomas told me Berta's pendant had a stone like the one Leukos was carrying, the type of pebble the soothsayer gave his clients. You have one yourself. Leukos' was somewhat smaller but otherwise identical to the stone the patriarch purchased from the soothsayer and believes to be the Grail. But what if Ahasuerus did indeed possess the Grail and rather than selling the real one to the patriarch, he gave the pendant containing it to Berta for safekeeping, planning to retrieve it to sell it later?"

"The pendant with the green stone? But John, I purchased that with one or two other items of jewelry from Felix! I gave them to Europa and Cornelia. So if you're right they now possess the Grail!"

"I am afraid not," John said, thoughtfully swirling the clouds and sky in the bottom of his cup. "Before she left, Cornelia gave the pendant to me and asked that it be returned to Berta."

He could not help wondering about the pendant he had had buried with Berta. Could such a Grail truly exist?

For an instant, as he mused over his lover and his daughter— lost, found, and now lost again—regret breached the barricade of John's self-control and he allowed himself to think what he would never have spoken.

Mithra forgive him, but did there live in Constantinople any man who had more need of such a mighty heal-all than John?

Afterword

One for Sorrow was inspired in part by evidence for the existence of a historical King Arthur who defended Britain against invaders around the time of Justinian I. The well-known legend of Camelot and the Knights of the Round Table solidified during the Middle Ages. Although the Holy Grail is generally considered to be the cup from which Christ drank at the Last Supper (Robert de Boron in his verse romance *Joseph d'Arimathie*, late twelfth/early thirteenth century) it has also been envisioned as something very different: a platter (Chretien de Troyes, *Perceval or Le Conte du Graal*, circa 1190), a cauldron (Celtic legend), and even a water-filled glass ball (Lady Flavia Anderson, *The Ancient Secret*, 1987). In Parzival (ca. 1210) Wolfram von Eschenbach presented an interpretation of the Grail as a stone from heaven.

Glossary

All dates are CE unless otherwise noted

ARISTOMENES
See PINDAR.

ATRIUM
Located in the central part of a Roman house, an atrium featured a square or rectangular opening in the roof over a decorative pool whose purpose was to catch rain water for household use. The opening also permitted more light to enter the building.

BATHS OF ZEUXIPPOS
Considered the most luxurious of Contantinople's public baths, and famous for their large number of classical statues.

BELISARIUS (505-565)
General whose exploits included retaking northern Africa and successful campaigns against the Vandals and the Persians. He is said to have relied heavily upon advice from his wife Antonina.

BLUES
See FACTIONS.

CARIA
Province in western Asia Minor.

CHAMBERLAIN
The Lord (or Grand) Chamberlain, typically a EUNUCH, was the chief attendant to the emperor. His duties included supervising those serving in

the palace and he also took a large role in court ceremonial. His real power arose from his close contact with the emperor, which allowed him to wield great influence.

CHURCH OF THE HOLY WISDOM
The Hagia Sophia, still standing in Constantinople.

CONCRETE
Roman concrete, whose ingredients included lime, volcanic ash, and gravel, was used in a wide range of structures from humble cisterns to the Pantheon in Rome, which has survived for two thousand years.

CURSE OF THE 318 FATHERS
Invoked to prevent the theft of documents and used in documents of sale, the practice is said to have been derived from anathemas issued at the First Ecumenical Council held at Nicaea in 325, which was attended by 318 bishops.

CYRENAICA
Roman province in North Africa.

DALMATIC
Wide-sleeved over garment.

EUNUCH
Eunuchs played an important part in the military, church, and civil administration of the Byzantine Empire. Many high offices in the palace were typically held by eunuchs.

EUTERPE
In classical mythology, the muse of music and lyric poetry.

FACTIONS
Supporters of either the BLUES or the GREENS, taking their names from the racing colors of the chariot team they supported. Brawls between the factions were not uncommon and occasionally escalated into city-wide riots.

FUNERARY PORTRAITS
Paintings on wooden panels from the Egyptian city now known as Faiyum.

GREAT CHURCH
Commonly used to refer to the CHURCH OF THE HOLY WISDOM.

GREAT PALACE

Located between the HIPPODROME and the sea walls of Constantinople, the Great Palace was not one building but many, set amid trees and gardens. The palace grounds included barracks for the EXCUBITORS, ceremonial rooms, meeting halls, the imperial family's living quarters, sports grounds, churches, and housing for court officials, ambassadors, and various dignitaries.

GREENS

See FACTIONS.

HECATE

Greek goddess associated with the underworld, magick, night, the shades of the departed, and crossroads.

HIPPODROME

U-shaped race track. It had tiered seating, and could accommodate up to one hundred thousand spectators. The dividing barrier, or spina, down the middle of the track included statues and obelisks. The Hippodrome was also used for public celebrations and other civic events.

ISAURIA

Largely mountainous country in Asia Minor. Its natives were notorious rebels.

JUSTINIAN I (c 482-565)

Reigning from 527-565, Justinian's ambition was to restore the Roman Empire to its former glory. He regained North Africa, Italy, and southeastern Spain. He codified Roman law and after severe riots in 532 rebuilt the CHURCH OF THE HOLY WISDOM as well as many other buildings in Constantinople. He was married to THEODORA.

KEEPER OF THE PLATE

In addition to ceremonial items, imperial plate in the Keeper's care included platters, ewers, goblets, and other tableware.

KOLLYBA

Small cakes made of wheat, nuts, honey, and raisins, eaten at a graveside or during services commemorating the departed.

KNUCKLEBONES

Game similar to today's jacks. The knucklebones used were usually those of a sheep.

MASTER OF THE OFFICES
Head of the imperial civil administration.

MESE
Main thoroughfare of Constantinople. Its entire length was rich with columns, arches and statuary (including secular, military, imperial, and religious subjects), fountains, churches, workshops, monuments, public baths, and private dwellings, making it a perfect mirror of the heavily populated and densely built city it traversed.

MITHRAISM
Of Persian origin, Mithraism was the worship of the sun god Mithra. It was spread throughout the Roman Empire via adherents in various branches of the military, becoming one of the most popular religions before it was superseded by Christianity. Adherents were required to practice chastity, obedience, and loyalty and advanced through seven degrees, Corax (Raven), Nymphus (Bridegroom), Miles (Soldier), Leo (Lion), Persus (Persian), Heliodromus (Runner of the Sun), and Pater (Father). Parallels have been drawn between Mithraism and Christianity, because of shared practices such as baptism and a belief in resurrection.

MITHRAEUM
Underground or otherwise hidden temple used by adherents to MITHRAISM.

NARSES (c480-c574)
Armenian who served JUSTINIAN I with distinction both as CHAMBERLAIN and general.

PINDAR (518 BC-c438 BC)
Greek poet, particularly noted for commemorating athletic champions such as the wrestler ARISTOMENES.

PREFECT
Urban official whose main duty was to maintain public order.

QUAESTOR
Official who administered financial matters.

SAINT PROKOPIOS
Martyred in 303 during the persecution of Christians by Emperor Diocletian (245-313).

SYRINX
Pan pipes.

TAUROBOLIUM
Bull sacrifice. A ritual in MITHRAISM.

THEODORA (c497-548)
Wife of JUSTINIAN I, on whom she exercised great influence. Before her marriage she was an actress and allegedly worked as a prostitute. Her father was a bear keeper for the GREENS.

ZURVAN
Persian god of time and destiny.